CW01574689

Omega Amy

Bella Donna

OMEGA AMY

First edition. March 2025.

Written by Bella Donna.

ISBN: 9798307810705

This book has been typeset in Garamond.

Trigger Warnings

Blood

Swear words

Bodily fluids

Sex (with graphic details)

Death

Sexual abuse (not in the pack)

Harassment

Violence (not in the pack)

Injury

Kidnapping

Nudity

Physical assault

Rape (not in the pack)

Screaming

Stabbing

Torture

Weapons

Chapter 1

Moonlight sliced through the blinds as my alarm clock jolted me awake. Its numbers glowed green in the darkness, blinding me as I struggled to make out the time. Almost midnight.

Shit. I bolted upright and my hand instinctively reached for the suppressant bottle on my nightstand. One pill left. Just one between me and a life sentence as an Omega.

The air was musty, tinged with the lingering scent of desperation and fear. "Fuck," I muttered, tipping the tablet onto my trembling palm. The familiar bitterness coated my tongue as I swallowed it dry, chasing it with lukewarm water from last night's glass.

Dragging myself out of bed, the weight of another day crushed down on me. As I pulled on my Beta clothing; practical gray pants, and a nondescript gray sweater, I caught my reflection in the cracked mirror. Striking green eyes stared back at me, a fire burning behind them that even the Omega Taskforce couldn't extinguish, and my best feature, if I didn't say so myself. I may have had to cover every other part of me, but my eyes told the tale of a life worth living.

Eyes are the windows to the soul, my mother used to say. My heart wrenched at the thought of her. Taking a deep breath, I stood tall, tied my long blond waves into a tight ponytail, and plastered on a fake smile, grabbing my coat and keys. "Just another day in paradise!"

As I reached for the door of my downstairs apartment, a wave of dizziness hit me. Shit. The tablets hardly had any effect anymore. I steadied myself against the wall, willing my body to cooperate. With one last deep breath, I stepped out into the world, ready to face whatever fresh hell the evening had in store for me.

The silent streets of the city assaulted my senses. The air was thick with the biting, acrid stench of industrial smog, clinging to my throat with every breath. Even at this ungodly hour, there was still a sea of gray uniforms and downcast eyes. They moved somberly, as if bound by an unspoken agreement not to acknowledge the world around them.

I kept my head down, muscles tense, ready to bolt at the first sign of danger. An Alpha in a crisp black uniform with the caged raven crest shoved past me, and I held my breath, praying my scent didn't give me away. They were a pretty nasty pack, and not one to be messed with. We wore the crowned wolf, a crest that dates back centuries, or so I was told. My dads were pretty proud of it.

"Watch it, Beta," he snarled.

I bit back a retort, forcing myself to look appropriately cowed. "Sorry, sir," I mumbled, picking up my pace.

My mind raced as I weaved through the throng. How long before the suppressants failed? How many more days could I keep up this charade?

The pitch-black sky stretched above as I sprinted through the narrow alleyways, my heart pounding in time with my footsteps. The midnight run had become a ritual, the only reliable method to steer clear of the patrols that prowled the streets. Shadows clung to the walls, and I kept close to them, my breath visible in the crisp night air. I needed suppressants, not just for myself, but also the girls at the Safehouse—a refuge I'd built for the Omegas in hiding. Each batch of suppressants I secured was a lifeline, a promise of hope in a world that hunted us.

Gillian's clinic was the drop site and the haven that kept my wild side at bay. My Omega was like a drug, a hard and fast sex-craving drug. She would hump every Alpha that came near her if she had the chance. Let alone all that, she'd bend over backwards to do anything for them. That girl wasn't me.

After my dad's pack forcefully took my mom at eighteen, birthing me and four Alpha asshole brothers determined to drive me insane, I vowed to suppress my wild side and show the world my new Beta side instead. I liked Beta Amy. She was in control. She was tall, muscular, and could hold her own in a fight. I didn't need any Alphas to take care of me or force themselves on me, locking me away like my dads did to my mom before she gave in.

I stood in front of the clinic and wiped my sweaty palms on my ragged jeans. The neon tube light saying 'Free Clinic' flashed on and off above me. Taking a deep breath, I walked in. The antiseptic smell was a welcome change from the stink of the streets.

Doctor Gillian Holmes was seeing another customer, bandaging some guy's leg over the other end. "Ah, Amy! You're late!" she shouted. "Grab an apron and help me out girl!"

I groaned, picking up the nearest grubby apron and fastening it around my waist.

As I walked closer to the guy, he smelled all kinds of wrong. Like burnt corpse wrong. Which, yes, I know, it's not a scent I should know at eighteen. But well, my family was pretty dark! I shook my head, remembering Ted Landery, the first Alpha that tried to scent me. He was the burnt corpse. Burgers. That's what he smelled like, burgers. But not the nice, mouth-watering burgers, with cheese, sauce, and a splash of side salad. No. He smelled like a rock solid burnt crispy charcoal burger, completely different to my scent of maple syrup, which I'd always believed was because my mom craved the stuff while she was pregnant with me.

"You alright?" Gillian whispered to me, away from the patient. Her eyes narrowed.

I pursed my lips and feigned a smile. I still couldn't fake getting past vile scents like his. "Yeah, just tired."

"Hand me that tape, will you?"

I grabbed the micropore tape and walked over to the patient, passing it to her. As I moved closer to the Alpha, his nostrils flared, and he grabbed my hand. I froze, my heart hammering against my ribs. Shit. Shit. Shit.

His eyes locked onto mine, a predatory gleam that made my skin prickle.

"You smell... different," he murmured, leaning in closer.

I forced a laugh, focusing on cleaning his wound. "Must be the new soap I'm using. Eau de Disinfectant is very trendy these days." I said, pulling my hand out of his grasp. Gillian tried to gain his attention by telling him care advice about his wound, but he didn't listen.

His eyes narrowed. "No, it's something else. Something... familiar."

I felt sweat beading on my forehead. Think, Amy, think!

"Well, I had garlic bread for lunch," I quipped. "Maybe that's what you're picking up on. Though I gotta say, if that's what's getting your attention, you need to rethink your priorities."

He chuckled, but I could see the suspicion hadn't left his eyes. "You're a feisty one, aren't you?"

I shrugged, "Someone's gotta keep you Alphas on your toes." Smiling at him, I walked away, disappearing into the back room to cool down.

When I was free, I closed the curtains behind me, peering back through. Gillian patted the Alpha on the back and said, "There. Now no getting into any more fights."

He laughed, a booming, hearty laugh that filled the room. "Sure thing, doc!" he said, then left.

The next thing I knew was being in Gillian's arms, as she soothed the shaking right out of my system. Besides my family and a few trusted friends, she's the only other person who knew I was an Omega. "It will be okay, Amy. You handled that well!"

I half-laughed, half-cried, wanting to hide-away. Instead, decided to agree..

"Come on, let's clean up and get you an injection." She pulled away and brought out a needle, syringe, and vial.

"Not the needle," I groaned. "Won't the tablets do?"

"No girl, you need coverage fast," she waved her hand in front of her nose. I laughed. "I'm surprised that guy didn't realize."

"Well, shit! I didn't know I was that bad."

"Yeah, it's because you've come of age. You're going to have to come see me more often now." I nodded. "Here," she patted the chair, and I sat down, pulling up my sleeve, and she fitted a tourniquet. I watched as she drew up the liquid into the syringe, changing the needle for a sharper one afterwards.

"Ready?" she asked. I gulped.

"As I'll ever be." Turning away just in time as she inserted the needle.

A deafening bang erupted from the front of the clinic. Glass shattered. Footsteps pounded on the floor and a smoke grenade billowed through the air. We both froze. The sound reverberated through the small room, setting my nerves on fire.

"What the hell was that?" I hissed, adrenaline surging through my veins.

Gillian's eyes were wide with alarm. "I don't—"

Another crash, followed by shouting. My heart was pounding so hard I could feel it in my throat.

"Shit," I breathed. "Please tell me that's not what I think it is."

The curtain pulled back.

"EVERYBODY HANDS WHERE I CAN SEE THEM!" a man in a black tactical uniform bellowed. His torch created a wall against the smoke, as he threatened to fire his weapon at us if we did not do as he instructed.

The syringe was still in my arm, with Gillian's hand still attached to it.

"DROP THE SYRINGE NOW!" he bellowed, as three team members shouted clearly as they entered each side room.

Gillian looked at me through the smoke. I could see her wide eyes, which must have matched my own. She pushed the plunger as quickly as she could, giving me the suppressant I so desperately needed. Because she knew, and I knew, why they were here... for me.

Chapter 2

They came at me in waves, hands reaching, trying to clamp down on me. I twisted away from one enforcer's grip, only to find myself up against another. His fingers brushed the fabric of my shirt before I darted aside just in time. My movements were honed and sharpened by years of relying on suppressants to keep my reflexes sharp and my instincts just a fraction quicker than theirs.

"Give it up, Omega. You're coming with us," one grunted, but I was already moving, my mind racing as fast as my heart.

"You're going to have to do better than that," I taunted, my voice dripping with sarcasm as I stood firmly, feet planted on the worn out wooden floor. The air crackled with tension, and my eyes locked onto my opponent's, challenging him with a defiant glare. This was more than just a fight. It was a declaration of both my spirit, and unyielding refusal to be caged.

I identified the bulky guy with the beard as the leader. I'd seen him on billboards, Warden Xavier Gray, and he was always standing beside Mr Calloway, the tyrant in charge of the Omega Taskforce.

Warden Gray's steely gaze tracked my every step, his eyes narrowing with a calculating intensity that sent a chill down my spine. It was as if his stare alone could weigh me down, brimming with an unspoken threat of vengeance. Yet for every advance they attempted, I had a counter, my movements honed through countless hours of sparring with my brothers in the dimly lit training hall. When an Alpha lunged at me with raw power, I twisted away, my movements smooth and strategic, embodying the finesse and cunning of an Omega who refused to be defined by her rank.

"Nice try, Omega," one of them sneered, his fingers finally catching hold of my wrist with an iron grip. The others swarmed, and like a pack descending on prey, they pinned me to the cold clinic floor.

"Get off me!" I spat, thrashing wildly beneath them. A knee pressed into my back, forcing the air from my lungs in a sharp exhale. My muscles screamed in protest, every fiber igniting with the primal need to escape. But as much as I twisted and turned, trying to leverage my training against their brute force, it was futile.

"Such spirit," Gray's voice dripped with disdain from somewhere above. "It will break beautifully at Stonehurst."

As if on cue, a sharp prick at the base of my neck signaled the end of this skirmish. The sedative coursed through my veins, a creeping numbness that dulled my senses and sapped my strength. My vision blurred, the edges of the room melting into shadows as my captors' faces turned into smudges of gray.

"Damn you," I managed, the words slurring, my mind waging war against the encroaching darkness. But even as the fight drained from my body, the fire within me refused to be extinguished. They could bind me, drug me, beat me, but they couldn't snuff out the spark that was Amy Anderson.

Waking up in the back of a van with a hood over my head was not how I'd envisioned spending my Monday morning. At least I think it was Monday. I pursed my lips in frustration. Through the faint glow filtering in from the bottom edge of the hood, I could tell that it was daytime, at least. I wriggled against the cold, unyielding metal of my cuffs and groaned. They wouldn't budge.

A gruff male voice laughed in front of me. "Having fun there?"

I narrowed my eyes and mentally stabbed him in the groin. "Where are you taking me?"

"You'll see, Omega." He stressed the word Omega. Well, I guess that cat was out of the bag then. I groaned again, letting my head fall back against the side of the van, banging it every time we hit a pothole.

"Where's the doc?"

"She helped to hide an Omega. Where do you think she is?"

"She's innocent!"

"That's what they all say," he said, chuckling.

"Asshole!"

He stopped laughing and shocked me as he grabbed my chin, his thick, dirty fingers feeling for my mouth under the hood. "Talk to me like that again and I'll cut your tongue out, Omega!"

He released his grip, and I gagged as the overpowering stench of rotting dog food invaded my nostrils. Yet, for the next ten minutes of the journey, I sat in tense silence, my mind racing with thoughts of escape.

My heart ached for Doctor Gillian. She was one of the good ones. She had been discreetly providing suppressants for the girls I sheltered at my Omega Safehouses. Gulping, I wiped my sweaty palms on my sweater. I knew what happened to traitors. I'd seen them every time I walked through the shopping district by the memorial wall. They'd be hanging there for everyone to see, reminding them that to harbor an undocumented Omega was a death sentence. I dug my nails into the flesh of my palms, the sharp pain a welcome distraction that forced my tears back. I refused to let them see me cry.

It was clear that the Alpha in the clinic had reported me. Likely calling the Omega Taskforce's tips line or something similar. Especially considering no Omega was allowed out on her own after dark unless accompanied by her Alpha pack. And for those that didn't have a pack, well, they were forcefully matched into one, whether or not they liked it. It was reminiscent of what happened to my mom all over again, and I'd be damned sure it wasn't happening to me!

The problem was that Omegas were practically an endangered species. We were rare. And rarity filled the pockets of the rich here. Especially given the breeding crisis that loomed over us like a dark cloud, we were the sole hope for birthing the next generation, or some shit like that. But me? I refused to be a pawn in this so-called sacred mission of spawning our future. I wasn't about to sacrifice myself, allowing men to ravage me, while my body betrayed me by craving more. Hell no. That's how it felt to me, and precisely what echoed in my mind when my mom recounted how she first met my dads. She endured.

Love shouldn't be a test of endurance. It should be about hogging the duvet and nestling your frozen toes between the hot thighs of a passionate lover. It's the small, cherished moments like finishing one another's sentences, savoring breakfast in bed and holding hands as you strolled through the park.

The van pulled to a stop.

Light flooded through the material of the hood as the back van doors opened. My guard said something to someone, then grabbed my arm and yanked me out. I stumbled and fell on a rough surface, feeling the dry dirt beneath my cuffed hands.

"Get up Omega!" The dog food guy yelled.

I did as he asked, still planning on running for it as soon as I knew where the hell I was.

But as soon as he removed the hood from my head, blinding light assaulted my eyes. I instinctively raised my arms to shield my eyes from the harsh glare. Without warning, he released me from my handcuffs. I frowned in confusion. My mind raced. Was he crazy?

As my vision returned, I scanned my surroundings; mountains to the left, dense forest to the right, and... shit! In the distance stood the gothic arches known to the one building I'd never wanted to step foot in: Stonehurst Academy.

I gulped. Stonehurst Academy was supposed to be where people were sent to disappear. It was a prison for Omegas like me, run by an ogre of a headmistress, metaphorically speaking of course! I'd heard stories of runaway Omegas entering these grounds, never to be seen again. It wasn't just the headmistress that I'd have to watch for. Heck no, it was the alphaholes that roamed these halls too. Fucked up packs that were deemed too dark for society. I'd be fresh meat in that place, and this suppressant wouldn't last forever! Biting my lower lip to stop it quivering, I stood tall. I wouldn't let them see me as a weak little thing. No. I was Amy Anderson, born Omega, turned Beta, and in control of my own future.

This was my chance to run.

"Going somewhere?" he asked, smirking as he watched me.

He pulled out a metallic choker, and grabbed me by my hair, forcefully pulling me towards him. I cried out in pain.

"What the hell!" I protested, but before I could finish my sentence, he placed the choker around my neck and secured it with a beep.

"There." He smiled. "Go on, continue with your escape plan."

I narrowed my eyes again. Why didn't he care if I escaped? So, I stepped toward the open gate, and back the way we'd came. But as soon as I'd crossed the threshold of the gate, my choker beeped rapidly, almost screeching at me.

"That's your warning," he taunted. "I suggest you come back."

Fuck that, I'll get this damn thing off when I'm long gone. I continued forward.

But, in the next moment, I was writhing in agony on the floor. My body was a battlefield of torment as every muscle in my body seized, every nerve igniting with electric energy as the collar unleashed wave after wave of electricity. Each jolt was an unyielding assault that tore through me, leaving me gasping and convulsing in an unending nightmare of excruciating pain.

The man cackled with delight. "It never gets old!" he howled with laughter.

"Fuck's sake Henry, the Warden will cut your knackers off if you break this one!" He walked towards me. "Help her back inside the gates!" A man's voice said.

He huffed and two sets of hands grabbed my agonizing body, carrying my feet and hands as I convulsed, vomiting all over myself.

Once I crossed the threshold, the collar stopped beeping, and the shocks stopped destroying every cell in my body.

The other man, burnt corpse guy, was wiping the sick from my mouth. "The headmistress is going to be pissed you've bought another one in like this."

"What! At least this one didn't piss herself."

I growled, or at least tried to, but it came out as more of a cry.

As they dragged me across the expanse toward the enormous, looming stone building, my senses dulled from exhaustion. The shock collar at my throat felt like an icy finger tracing the line of my jugular, a constant presence that threatened with silent promises of pain.

We entered through towering, dark wooden doors, finished with iron hinges that screeched their disapproval at being disturbed.

Inside was a grand foyer lined with black marble floors so polished I could see my distorted reflection etched with pain and humiliation. Ornate gold chandeliers hung above us, casting pools of light on classical portraits lining the walls, faces that stared down at me in silent judgment. In the center was the pot-bellied, gray-haired, stern-looking man who had first slapped the cuffs on me. Warden Xavier Gray.

"Welcome to your future, Omega," the Warden sneered as he rounded the corner to greet me. This was no future; it was a finely crafted end—a place where they hoped to snuff out the defiance smoldering within me.

I could barely stand when we arrived at what appeared to be an administrative office. Inside the room, rich, dark wood paneling that gleamed under the dim lighting, and shelves crammed full of leather-bound books, smelling like dust and authority. A stern-looking woman sat behind a large mahogany desk; its surface polished to a high shine. Her glare intensified under thin-rimmed glasses perched at the tip of her nose.

"Another feral one," she sighed deeply without lifting her eyes from the paperwork the Warden handed her.

"Always a pleasure Ms Stone," the Warden said. The headmistress nodded, and then he left.

Henry deposited me into an overstuffed chair opposite hers, then hovered by the door frame, waiting for some sort of distraction or escape that never came his way. Soon enough, he grunted resignedly before retreating outside, leaving only cold air trailing after him.

Headmistress Lucinda Stone finally raised those piercing eyes towards mine. Her thin-rimmed glasses perched on her hawk-like nose, eyes piercing through me, causing shivers down my spine. I raised my hand to my collar, pulling it away from my neck as it felt tighter under her gaze.

She studied me for a moment, her gaze piercing as I shifted in the chair.

"So, Amy. You're an Omega hiding as a Beta. Why?" Her voice was calm but probing.

I met her eyes and frowned, pursing my lips. No one had asked me why before. "I, er... well, it's a long story." I stammered, unsure of how much to reveal.

"They're not usually long stories Amy, just ones tangled in misinformation. So why don't you want to be an Omega?" she pressed.

"I need to be in control," I confessed, my voice barely above a whisper, but firm with conviction.

"What makes you think you won't be in control?"

I let out a half-laugh, a bitter sound, then quickly caught myself. "Have you seen the Omegas walking around, always surrounded by their packs? They're in their prim and proper dresses, perfect manners on display," I said, waving my hand as if to dismiss the image.

"And? What is the issue with dressing respectfully, Amy?" she asked, her tone measured and patient.

"Why should they have to be placed on a pedestal every waking hour?" I retorted, my frustration bubbling up. "Why should every Omega be at an Alpha's beck and call? What if I wanted to be a lawyer? A doctor? A teacher? Why should I be a homemaker, tending to children and cleaning up after the Alphas, spreading my legs whenever they want me to?" My voice grew stronger with each word, the fire behind my eyes unmistakable.

"That's where you are mistaken."

"What?"

"It is also whenever the Omega wants to, as well. The Omega controls their heat. Not the Alphas."

"But, well... I don't know. All I know is I like being a Beta. Why can't I just be left alone?"

She shifted in her chair and sat upright, her patience waning. "Because you were born with the rare gift to birth our next generation, Amy. It is a gift that should be celebrated."

"Well, I don't want it."

She growled under her breath. "You have no choice."

I crossed my arms.

"Here at Stonehurst Academy, you will learn to be an Omega. If you do not find a pack before you graduate, a pack will be chosen for you."

"So, I have no choice."

"No." She watched me for a moment. "And if you do not conform, you will be sent to the Birthing Grounds."

My eyes widened. Shit. I'd heard of them, but I'd always called bullshit whenever anyone tried to warn me. "They're real?"

"Of course. We need our future generation, Amy. If our Omegas will not conform willingly, then we will force them to do so."

"So, this is a prison?"

"We like to think of it as... a sanctuary."

I remained silent.

"Remember, obedience is your ticket here," said the Headmistress, mistaking my silence for compliance. I rolled my eyes so hard I almost saw my brain. Obedience was their game, but resistance was mine, and I played to win.

So let them have their shock collars and their cold, emotionless rooms. Let them think their gothic fortress could contain my spirit. Because, while Stonehurst Academy might be where they planned to clip my wings, it was also where I'd learn to fly.

Chapter 3

The Headmistress called for assistance on the intercom, and soon the door swung open to reveal an Omega who appeared to be about my age. Her bright ginger hair was neatly fastened back with a black bow, standing out against her pale complexion. She wore the academy's distinctive uniform: a deep blue pleated skirt that fell to mid-thigh, swishing softly with her movements, and a blue blazer adorned with four gold buttons. The blazer bore the academy's crest, a symbol of the cage I now lived within. Underneath, a tight-fitted white shirt threatened to pop open over her chest. Draped across her shoulder was a blue messenger bag, its gold piping accentuating the design and matching the gold elements of her attire. The bag displayed the school's Omega crest, embroidered with the head of a wolf, and above it, three symbols: an all-seeing eye, a gleaming sword, and a heart, each representing vision, strength, and compassion.

"Yes, Headmistress," the Omega said, curtsying as she entered the room. I rolled my eyes.

"Janine, can you take Amy to her room to shower and change before dinner, please?" Janine nodded, looking at the state of my sick-covered clothing. "Then show her around. She begins classes this afternoon."

Janine smiled sweetly. "Yes, Headmistress."

"Amy, please see the receptionist for your key and timetable. Your uniform and everything you need will be in your room."

"Ah yes. Because it's a sanctuary... right?" I asked, rolling my eyes again.

"Yes Amy, that's right." The headmistress continued to look at her paperwork and scowl.

I smirked, stood up from the chair, and followed Janine out as she made her way to speak to the receptionist.

"Jane, this is Amy. Do you have her timetable and key, please?"

"Why yes, of course, my darling!"

Jane, with her bright and bubbly smile, and one too many cake crumbs on her ample-sized Beta breasts, stood up and walked over to the printer to fetch the timetable. When she was gone, Janine turned to me.

"Right. You're near me. You will do what I tell you to and nothing more. Got that. I'm nearly out of this shit hole, so you'd better not fuck this up for me!"

My eyes widened. Damn, this girl had a mouth on her. I smirked. "Yes Ma'am," I said, grinning. Janine plastered on a smile as Jane came back.

"Oh my, look at you two chatting and all. You'll be the best of friends before you know it!"

Janine nodded and smiled as she took the timetable and key. "Thank you, Jane, you're so sweet! Come on Amy, it's this way," she said with a well-rehearsed smile. I almost wanted to give her a round of applause.

The walk to the Omega Complex was silent, the halls a blur of blue and white as I passed other Omegas caged by collars, their eyes downcast or fixed on distant points, anywhere but here.

As we left the main building, Janine's boots crunched along the gravel path, her stride purposeful and her back straight as if she were marching to the gallows with pride. I followed close behind, taking in the lush grass and the curated flower beds that lined our way; a stark contrast to the shadows of dread that clung to my mind like cobwebs.

We found ourselves on a path leading into the woods, illuminated by those shitty LED lamps that were no more use than an ornament. It didn't matter right now though, considering it approached lunchtime, but by nightfall, it wasn't somewhere I'd want to be when the wolves came out to play.

"Seems far away," I said to Janine.

"It's on the other side of the woods, thankfully far enough from the main building and Alpha Complex."

"The Alphas stay here too?" I asked. She nodded.

My brow furrowed. "How do they control them around the Omegas, though?"

"Most of the time, they don't give a shit. All they want is an Omega to get knocked up and find a pack. Then for her to do as she's told for the rest of her life."

"Sod that," I grumbled.

She smiled. "You may grow on me yet," I smirked. "So, where'd they catch you?"

"Mid shooting up in a clinic."

"Shit!" I nodded. "So, you're what... eighteen?" she asked as we continued walking through the woods.

"Yeah."

"Then you've got what, a few weeks on your suppressant before you can be scented?"

"I guess so." I chewed on my lower lip, thinking. "But I plan to get the hell out of here before then."

She laughed, and we turned a corner, leaving the woods behind us. In front was a gated complex with high walls, full of three-story buildings that appeared in dire need of repair.

"Don't you think I've tried to escape?" she finally said, breaking the silence. "We all have. You've got to watch yourself. If you end up on their radar, they'll discard you."

"What, to the Birthing Grounds?" I joked, then stopped when I saw the seriousness on her face. "Shit. Is that place real?"

She shrugged. "It must be, as the room you're going to be staying in was full last week." The chill of unease skittered down my spine. She sighed. "Her name was Scarlett. She was only sixteen when the Taskforce captured her. But with multiple escape attempts and violent outbursts... well, they made her disappear." She looked at me and stopped before we reached the gates. "Make it longer than she did."

I pursed my lips, inhaled, and nodded.

We stopped before the gates. "Welcome to the Omega Complex, a paradise within a prison," Janine said, her voice laced with sarcasm so thick it could cut through the tension hanging in the air like fog. A mockingbird's call echoed beyond the high walls, a reminder of the freedom we couldn't grasp.

Two guards stood watch at the gates, both female Betas with weapons. Janine put on her fake smile and swished her ginger hair as she walked up. "Hey girl, this is our new Omega, Amy Anderson."

The guard nodded. "Your apartment is 13F, Amy," the guard said.

"Thanks," I said and forced myself to smile, taking Janine's advice.

The other guard radioed in and the gate opened. Janine led the way. "Come on, you're in the apartment opposite me. So, no playing banging or causing any shit, alright."

I smirked, "Sure thing, boss!"

She snarled.

We walked across what felt like a prison compound with brick-built buildings that looked like dilapidated squares, sat on a grass pedestal. Janine informed me they housed two apartments per floor, each having the same facilities. The common room in the center of the complex appeared modernized. It housed a gym, pool, and sauna. Apparently, its attendant provided amazing massages. But was booked up weeks in advance, though.

Walking past two square buildings, we finally entered the third, tapping in the pin code 9999. I rolled my eyes at that one, then groaned when I learned my apartment was on the third floor, without an elevator.

I followed Janine inside. The air was stale, thick with the scent of fresh paint masking something older, something musty. It was like stepping into someone else's life—someone who didn't exist anymore.

The room was a box, clinical and cold. A single window offered a view of the complex, a reminder of the cage it was. The furniture was minimalist—a double bed with a flawlessly made blanket, a few scatter cushions to give the impression of luxury, a rickety old wardrobe, and a desk that had never known clutter. The Omega crest loomed from every corner, on every piece of fabric, branding my life from here on out.

"Cozy," I muttered, the word dripping with sarcasm.

"Right, you have fifteen minutes," Janine said as we entered. "Jump in the shower as you stink of sick, then chuck these on." She threw a uniform at me from the wooden wardrobe by the double bed.

I nodded, wondering how they knew my size before I'd even got here. The thought of it freaked me out.

The bathroom was just as whitewashed. Turning the lock, a sound more ominous than welcoming, as I stepped inside. I started the shower, allowing it to reach temperature while I undressed.

The water hit my skin like a thousand tiny accusations, hot and unrelenting. I reached for the collar, its presence a constant pressure against my neck.

Tugging at it, I choked back a panicked cry. My fingernails scraped against the locked clasp. My heart clenched, a mix of fury and fear knotting in my chest. The water turned from comforting warmth to a torrent of icy reality as I confronted the helplessness of my situation. I let out a ragged breath that morphed into a sob; the sound bouncing off the tiles mocking me.

It wasn't something I could stop. It wasn't something I usually did. I hadn't cried in years. But today, with everything that had happened, and the lack of sleep and pain from such a torturous entrance to the academy. I was exhausted. My knees gave way, and I sank to the shower floor, the stream now a backdrop to the silent scream building within.

Each droplet was a reminder—I was no longer just Amy Anderson; I was property, tagged and cataloged. An Omega viewed as nothing more than a walking womb, waiting to be filled and filed away.

Clambering to the corner of the shower, I cradled my legs, sobbing under the jet stream of the shower.

It didn't help that rage boiled beneath my skin, pure tense anger knotted my muscles, twisted my body and raveled me up in its inferno. I needed to scream, to burst free and beat down every living thing in this place. But I couldn't. Not with the threat of the Birthing Grounds. I couldn't. All I could do was let every salty tear caress my lips as I washed away the pain and said goodbye to the life I'd once known.

By the time I'd composed myself, dried, dressed and brushed my hair, I came out to find Janine sat looking dismal on my bed. "Are you okay?" she asked.

I took a deep breath. I couldn't, wouldn't show any more weakness, so I nodded.

"I remember my first day." She looked at me. "It gets easier." I looked at the floor, my hands clasped hard in front of me. She looked at them. "Come on, I'll show you around and we can get something to eat."

"Don't you have classes?"

She smiled. "Perks of bullshitting," she said, grinning. "As one of the Omega leaders, I get to show the newbies around, and if it takes all morning to do so, then we both get the morning off."

I smiled, following her out of my room. She locked up and handed me the key.

"Right, if you need any more uniform or general day or nightwear, then you place an order with Jane, the receptionist you met earlier."

"Okay, thanks."

"But first, I'm going to book you in for a massage in a few weeks. It will give you something to look forward to."

"But I don't have any money here."

She smiled. "You don't need any honey. That's one of the good things about being an Omega. We are sooo precious," she rolled her eyes. "They want to make sure we're physically and mentally well. Thus free massages."

I nodded, feeling a flicker of excitement at the prospect of a massage. It had been ages since I last indulged in one. In fact, it felt like an eternity! Ever since I'd presented, I'd been cautious, avoiding letting anyone get too close, fearing they might catch the subtle hint of what I truly was beneath the surface.

As we walked past the square buildings, Janine asked, "Do you have a family that will look for you?"

I shrugged. "My dads hated that I fought against being an Omega. They didn't talk to me after I started taking the suppressants. But my brothers, they will probably look for me."

"Are they Alphas?"

"Yes, all four of them. But they probably think I've gone on the run. I'm hoping they'll come and find me."

"Even if they do, with that collar, you're not getting out of here."

I gulped. "They'll break down every door to get me out if they have to."

She smiled. "I hope so, honey, for your sake."

We arrived outside a large complex with a glass front showing a swimming pool on one side, and gym equipment in a room on the other side. I followed Janine in and through to the back. She flicked through a book on the empty reception desk and signed my name. "There, two weeks on Thursday. You have the six o'clock massage." I smiled.

"Thanks!" She nodded, and we left.

"So, what about your family?"

"Let's head for food?"

I frowned. She'd skipped that question.

"Er, yeah sure."

Chapter 4

The moment I stepped into the library, the click of my boots on the polished black marble floors sounded like a gunshot in the oppressive silence. It was eerie, the way it echoed off of the towering bookshelves, whispering back at me, taunting me. I met the judgmental gaze of classical portraits hanging high on the walls, aristocrats, and scholars from ages past, their painted eyes following me, full of scorn.

"Great," I muttered under my breath, "not even dead guys can mind their own business."

"What's that?" Janine said.

"Nothing, just admiring the portraits."

"Creepy aren't they!"

I laughed, and then a woman shushed me from a table nearby. Janine smirked, took my arm and pulled me further into the library.

"I've got to drop off a book," she said. "Have a wander around, and meet me in the cafeteria for lunch."

I narrowed my eyes. "Err, where's that?"

She smirked and passed me a map, pointing it out. "See, just down the hall, and over to the right. You can't miss it. Everyone will head there."

I pursed my lips and looked at the enormous library before me. "Okay."

"I'll save you a space." She smiled and disappeared through the eaves.

I nodded, then pushed further into the heart of the room, my fingers trailing along the spines of ancient tomes that had likely never been cracked open by anyone who didn't use them as a prop to look smart. The further I walked in, the more the weight of all the gazes, both painted and real, bore down on me.

A gnawing sensation circled inside me, clawing at my insides. It was the kind of feeling that made you think you've forgotten something important, like the fact that I not supposed to be here, or that I'm one false move away from being outed for what I truly was.

For years, I'd masqueraded as a Beta, blending in with the nondescript crowd, but now? Now, there was no hiding the truth. With every step, I felt the absence of my Beta-self like a ghost limb; a part of me cut away, leaving raw, exposed flesh behind. The truth of my past dissipated like an open wound begging to be healed. I was an Omega now, and there's n't a damned thing I could do about it.

Being both an Omega and the new girl at school made me an easy target, and everyone was aware of it. Even if I'd wanted to, I couldn't conceal my reality; the glaring uniform broadcasts my status to every Alpha and Beta who noticed me. I'm a moving target for their stereotypes and their desire to dominate.

"Welcome to the cage, Amy," I whispered to myself, the sound almost devoured by the cavernous space around me. My voice reminded me that I'm still here, still fighting, even if it was only against library decorum and oppressive silences.

The silence shattered like glass as the library door slammed against the wall, an obvious violation of the sacred quiet that ruled this place. I didn't need to look up from the ancient text in my hands to know it was an uptight Alpha who had made his presence known. They were all the same. All uptight pricks with a stick up their ass.

The pungent scent of days-old caviar drifted through the air as the stocky Alpha paraded his way over to me like he owned the air we breathed. I looked up and his blue eyes locked on me with a chilling intent that made my skin crawl. My heart skipped a beat, not out of fear, but a surge of adrenaline as I braced for whatever came next.

"Enjoying the read, Omega?" His voice dripped sarcasm.

"Immensely," I shot back, my grip tightening on the book's spine. But before I could indulge in another barbed exchange, his hand lashed out, swift and precise. The book spiraled from my grasp, landing with a resounding slap against the marble floor. The sound echoed throughout the library and heads turned. Hushed whispers flowed as they watched our exchange.

"Oops," he smirked, tilting his head in mock apology.

It was difficult to decide between puking on his shoes from his rancid scent, or punching him in the bollocks for being an utter dickhead. But I felt neither would score me any brownie points on my first day.

I took a moment, schooling my features into an impassive mask. Bending down, I retrieved the book, my fingers brushing against the cool floor. I moved slowly and deliberately, allowing myself those few extra seconds to quell the raw impulse to wrap the tome around his smug face. It would have been satisfying, sure, but my mother didn't raise a fool. I knew better than to play into his hands.

"Clumsy me," I replied, straightening up with the book securely in my hold. My wavy blond hair tumbled over my shoulder, a silent witness to the little power play he seemed so fond of. "Should've known better than to expect manners from an Alpha."

"Careful, Omega," he warned, the word leaving his lips like a curse. "You should address me as Alpha Andrew Calloway," he demanded, as though his name should mean something to me. Personally, I didn't give a shit.

Gritting my teeth, I rose to my full height; the book clutched like a shield. The air between us crackled with tension, my every muscle coiled and ready for a fight I knew better than to start.

"Are you listening?" His voice shredded the silence of the library as he snapped his fingers inches from my face, the sound an unwanted punctuation to his question.

"Clearly," I huffed, my voice laced with disdain but kept low, a rumble of my escalating irritation. "Your ability to state the obvious is astounding." My head bobbed in a forced nod, acknowledging his demand for attention while my mind raced through an obstacle course of potential retaliations. Each more satisfying than the last, each more dangerous, too. I could imagine the swift satisfaction of planting my knee in his perfectly pressed slacks, watching that arrogant smirk dissolve into surprise.

Instead, I bit back the urge, digging my nails into my palms, trapping my anger deep within, frustration simmering just beneath the surface. He seemed amused by my restraint, the corner of his mouth twitching upward ever so slightly.

"Girl," he said, the word dripping with condescension like poison from a snake's fangs. "Keep that up, and we might get along after all."

"Or maybe," I countered, "you'll learn not to underestimate an Omega with a grudge."

The growl that erupted from his throat vibrated through the stale library air, a primal sound that seemed to rattle the dusty volumes on the shelves. His broad silhouette closed in on me. Before I could brace myself, he shoved me backwards, and the cold stone library wall met my back with a thud that knocked the breath from my lungs.

"Let me make something crystal clear," he sneered, his face so close I could count the flecks of ice in his blue eyes. "You are under my rule here, Omega. My father runs the

Taskforce, and one word from me, you'll find yourself tossed into the Birthing Grounds."

A smirk tugged at my lips, almost by reflex—was he for real? It was like listening to a child play dictator, only this child had the power to ruin lives. "Oh, is that so?" I managed, injecting mockery into my tone even as the wall chilled my skin.

"Compliance will make your life much more pleasant," he continued, undeterred by my reaction or perhaps spurred on by it. His voice oozed entitlement, each syllable laced with the arrogance of someone who'd never been told no.

"Thanks for the tip," I said, my words sharp enough to cut. "I'll be sure to lose sleep over it."

His eyes narrowed, but his smile didn't falter. It was the grin of a snake before it struck. However, I wasn't some helpless mouse. No, this Omega had fangs too.

His face boiled red, and his lip vibrated. He was losing it! Too late. He lunged forward and grabbed me by my neck, the pressure building like a vice as the edges of my vision danced with specks of darkness. I could feel tears betraying me, welling up not from fear but from the raw instinct to survive that scraped at your insides when air became a privilege.

"Got it, little Omega?" he hissed, spittle coating my face.

I focused on the rhythm of my heartbeat, pounding defiantly against the walls of my chest. Inhale. Exhale. Whatever breath I could muster was precious fuel, keeping the ember of rebellion alive within me. His hand tightened further, and for a moment, I wondered if he saw the irony. The more he tried to choke the fight out of me, the hotter it burned.

The survival training with my brother Kurt buzzed at the back of my mind, a silent chant reminding me that this was not how I went down. Biding my time, I let every shallow gasp serve as a reminder that I, Amy Anderson, was under no one's control.

"Listening... closely," I managed through gritted teeth, the words scraping out of my throat.

His fingers dug into my flesh, as a bitter laugh echoed in my skull. Oh, how he'd regret this. Every touch, every threat was just another log on the fire, and I was becoming an inferno in human skin.

The iron clamp of his fingers eased. Air rushed into my lungs, coarse and burning like sandpaper as it dragged through my trachea. I doubled over, hacking, the sound ugly, yet music to my ears all at once.

"Understand me, Omega?" His voice was a velvet-covered brick, soft on the surface but hard and unyielding underneath.

My response came out as nothing more than a ragged whisper, "Yes." It tasted like bile on my tongue, this feigned submission, but it served its purpose—a mask to hide behind while my mind sharpened its knives in the shadows. The word was a pebble thrown to distract a hound, and I could almost smirk at how easily he lapped it up.

The distance between us widened as he, satisfied with his display of power, turned and left. I gradually stood upright. The cold imprint of the wall lingered against my skin. The shaking I felt wasn't from fear; it was raw, unbridled defiance.

Alone again, with only the dusty books for company, I allowed myself a moment to feel the weight of what had transpired. The library, with its towering shelves and the scent of ancient leather, seemed to close in around me, a tomb of knowledge that now contained one more secret. My fingers grazed the bruise that I knew would bloom on my throat, a testament to Andrew's claim over my body, but not my will.

The Alphas may think they can control us, tame us, and make us their obedient little pets. I scoffed at the idea. Well, this Omega might play the part, but I wasn't about to roll over for belly rubs, especially not from the likes of him.

With each step toward the exit, my resolve hardened like the marble beneath my feet. Anger simmered in my chest, a potent brew of adrenaline and contempt. It fuelled me and carried me forward.

I pushed open the library doors, their groan echoing my impatience to break free from this gilded cage. Stonehurst Academy loomed around me, its oppressive presence a constant reminder of the battle ahead. But I damned well knew I wouldn't cower. I'd plot, I'd strategize and I would escape this hellhole if it was the last thing I ever did.

Chapter 5

The cafeteria appeared cold and dismal, a stark contrast to the rest of the buildings. It lived in my newfound prison's oldest area. Old moldy wallpaper from rising damp was a festering disease waiting to take flight. Arching high into the rooftop, painted walls gave way to peeling wallpaper due to a leak from one of the windows. This place was separate from the rest of the oh-so-glorious academy and dingy at best.

Janine had said the staff didn't come in here. They had their own brand-new canteen built in the main academy. Well, except the guards that patrolled the place. I looked at two guards stationed on what I could only call baby versions of guard towers, and smirked. It was a half-assed attempt at raising them above the rest of us, so they could keep watch. The guard at the other end stood yawning. He stretched, then answered something on the radio attached to hids hip.

I understood the need for the guards, but it puzzled me. They want to prevent Alphas from claiming Omegas without permission, right? Yet, isn't the whole idea to match an Omega with a pack? I shook my head in confusion and entered. Janine was seated at a rectangular table waiting for me.

I smiled and continued to look around as I headed to the table. Despite being trapped in this prison cafeteria, the windows managed to let in some light. Positioned high above, they were small and narrow, casting an ambient glow that illuminated the dust which cascaded through the space.

The incessant chatter of students, well prisoners, all droned into one, a monotone noise that spelt the thoughts of many.

As I walked through, I sparked silence around me, whispers between packs, sniveling scowls from what I could only presume was the bitchy Omegas table, and finally laughter and pointing. I rolled my eyes. The only way this would stop was if I, Amy Anderson, made a fucking point.

Stepping up onto the crusted bench of the bitchy girls' table, I kicked a tray out of the way and stood on the table.

"Hey! Watch it!" a girl yelled.

I raised my hands high, turned around real slow and said, "Yes, I'm Amy Anderson, the new girl, a prisoner just like you. So take a good fucking look!" The bitchy girls gasped when I swore and stared at the guard who was now walking over. "Because that's the last you'll get!"

"Get down! Quick," the bitchy girl below me said.

I narrowed my eyes at her, but the fright on her face told me another story. No matter how hard an image she portrayed, she was petrified of this place.

I jumped down and bowed.

The guard walked up. "You," he bellowed. "Don't step on the tables!"

"I apologize, officer. I'm new, I didn't realize," then I gave him the sweetest smile. Something Janine had taught me earlier.

"Oh, well... Well, no swearing! That's not allowed!"

"Oh, I'm so sorry officer, that was naughty of me. I'm trying to scrub out my old ways. It won't happen again."

He nodded and smiled. "Good. You will do well here, Miss Anderson."

I smiled sweetly, and he returned to his baby guard tower.

The bitchy girl finally breathed again, then smiled at me. "Clever," she said. "You might just make it here after all!"

I walked to the table where Janine was still sitting, mouth agape, staring at me in awe. Smirking, I moved past the whispered "Newbie," and "Prisoner" while Alphas sniffed, testing if I was their scent match. Like fuck I was. Even if I was, it'd still be my choice. I didn't care what this damned academy pushed upon us. It had to be my choice. It was my body. I would choose who I would live with. I belonged to no one.

That was the brutal reality of this world. Omegas were reduced to mere objects, possessions to be claimed, cherished, and maintained... if fortune smiled upon them. But if not, they're condemned to a frigid cell, imprisoned and shackled, exploited and mistreated, dragged out only to serve as playthings for others' gratification. Those packs, devoid of compassion, didn't even bother to support their Omega during the torment of heat. As I said, mere property, and nothing more.

Neither option seemed very appealing, and I felt sorry for the latter. Several Omegas here saw the world through rose-tinted glasses. Their eyes would light up whenever an Alpha walked by, swooning over his body or the way he spoke. If he gave them even a little attention, they would giggle, laugh, and be at his beck and call. What kind of existence was that? Didn't these girls have minds of their own? Didn't they want more out of life? Why were they programmed to be so naïve and childish, or was it the way the Academy taught us? We were instructed not to speak unless spoken to, to ensure breakfast was ready by six every morning, and to fold laundry specifically to minimize creases. I almost yawned at how boring it all sounded. And yet, I hadn't been here long, and I was already feeling frustrated. Especially since my first lesson was about obedience, my hopes weren't high. Give me biology, physics, or English any day. I'd love to be a doctor, teacher, or professor at a prestigious law school. But no, because of my genetics, this was the best I could expect.

It was sad to say that my dads would be proud that I was finally accepting my birthright. I scoffed to myself. They would be proud after what they did to my mother. But she'd grown to love them, they were kind to her, and loved her. But forcing an Omega to bond to a pack should never happen. I glanced around, feeling nervous about the idea of being connected to any of these jerks. If I hadn't found a pack by graduation, one would be forced on me.

I chewed on my lower lip, staring at a pack of four Alphas that were leering at me and shuddered. The thought of them made me sick, and when all of their scents mingled together, it smelt like a cat had vomited. At least, that's how it smelt to me. But, I'm sure some pretty little princess of an Omega that loved cat vomit was around here somewhere. I almost gagged as I edged between them. They clearly weren't moving out of the way!

My grandparents were to blame. The sadistic assholes. I wouldn't be surprised if they'd donated a huge amount of money to keep a place like this open for the greater good, as they would call it. Because I am oh so rare and have a duty to birth the next generation.

If I hadn't figured out that the man we treated at the clinic with the Doc was the one who tipped off the Taskforce about my location, I would have suspected my grandparents. My brothers were fond of them, and one of them, likely Kurt, might have mentioned my involvement at the clinic.

"Hey, you!" Janine said, standing up and clicking her fingers in front of my face. "Are you in there?"

I laughed and looked around. "Yeah, just noticing how much of a dive this shit hole is."

She winced. "Don't let the guards hear you swear again. You might not get away with it twice!"

I shrugged my shoulders. "Why? What are they gonna do? Throw me in the hole or spank me with a ruler?"

Her eyes widened. "No, but the Birthing Grounds are an

actual threat Amy, always remember that."

I nodded, then pursed my lips. "How do you know? Have you ever met anyone that's ever come back from there, or is it a myth?"

She sat down and patted the bench beside her. "Fair point, no. I've not met anyone that's made it back. But doesn't that make it even more alarming?"

I took a deep breath. "I guess so."

A girl that looked a year or two younger than me danced her way between packs, laughing as they spoke to her, and smirking at their remarks. Bright-eyed, with blond, bouncy hair, she made her way over to the table and Janine groaned.

"Hey, you two."

"Hi Nora," Janine said grimly.

I smiled at her. Her pale face was flushed with pink blusher and rosy red lipstick.

"Are you going to introduce me, Janine?"

Janine grimaced. "Sure. This is Amy Anderson. But I'm sure you already knew that."

The new girl grinned and nodded. She looked down in front of me at the blank space on the table. "Aren't you hungry?" she said.

I shrugged. I hadn't thought about it, to be honest. But just then, my stomach growled to betray me. She laughed.

"Janine, haven't you shown her where to get food from?"

"We haven't had a chance yet," she said, narrowing her eyes at her.

"That's fine. Allow me!" Nora grabbed me under the arm and yanked me up. She was surprisingly strong for a tiny Omega. She looked at me, studying my face. I frowned. "Come on, Cherry Red. Let's get you something to eat."

Huh! My brow furrowed. Cherry Red. What the hell? Who's Cherry Red?

I looked back at Janine as Nora dragged me along to find Janine smirking.

Nora finally loosened her grip, and I followed as we mingled our way through crowds of students. Some Beta, some Omega, some sniffing Alphas. I swear they all looked like they had a cold when they came near me. I seemed to trigger that response. Laughing under my breath, I knew full well the suppressants wouldn't allow them to scent me yet. I was sick of them scrutinizing me, though. I shuddered, shaking my head to myself. Like I'd ever be in their bed.

I didn't look like the average Omega thanks to the suppressants. I was taller and flatter chested too, and didn't quite fit the whole rosy Omega picture, either, but that was my personality. You can thank my four Alpha brothers for that.

I was a hardass, and I knew it. My brothers had taught me how to take care of myself, and I knew they'd kick anyone's ass that tried to hurt me. But I wanted to do that myself. Growing up, I'd always dreamed of being like them, like an Alpha. Had always hoped I would be until my designation came in. I was devastated, utterly destroyed. My dads, well, they were over the moon. They said I was following in Mom's footsteps. My mom cried for days. Like I said, she was happy, but she wouldn't have wished what happened to her on anyone. Although I know she wouldn't change it now, not for anything.

So, my brothers vowed to protect me, to look after me. And I'd made it clear to them, there was no fucking way I would be an Omega. They would laugh at this now, that's if they weren't trying to get me out of this hellhole. I hazard a guess why they hadn't already broken me out, and that was my dad's influence... or my sodding grandparents. They're the only ones who could stop and rein them in. They only ever listen to them. I can envision the conversation, or the shouting match, "She needs to master her way, and learn who she is. She can't pretend all her life." Yeah, I can see that happening. Heck, I expected that's already happened. I'd be surprised if Kurt wasn't waiting behind the gates right now, sniper rifle at the ready, to shoot any Alpha who looked at me the wrong way.

We stopped as we reached what I could only describe as a long rectangular buffet of fresh foods in silver pots with metal ladles, so you could help yourself. They didn't even have staff that served us here. Shit, this was worse than a prison, at least at prison, there were people to serve you.

"Right, pick up a plate, grab what you want, and then meet me back at the table. I'm going to perch my lovely bottom right there. All right, Cherry Red?" I growled at her and she giggled and headed back.

Frigging Cherry Red, I was gonna have to have words about that. She clearly lacks any clue about me if that's her new nickname for me. I'm the opposite of a nice and sweet Cherry Red!

I huffed, looking down at the selection of slop in front of me. The first bowl held a brown meat resembling mince; hopefully, it was. It looked pureed, and too much like diarrhea for my liking. Beside it lay tempting baked potatoes. So, I took one of those. Sachets of butter. Yep, check. Took one of those. Salad. It looked old and smelled funny... so I left that.

Pasta. Now pasta was usually my favorite dish, and this had some kind of tomato-based sauce with it, which was a good sign as you couldn't go too wrong with that. But there are some kinds of disturbing mushy green vegetables in it taunting me. I looked at the rest of the rubbish on offer, then grimaced. The pasta looked like my best bet.

I took a ladle full and placed it onto my plate, so it wouldn't touch the baked potato, just in case it was vile. I hated my food touching on the best of days, especially when I didn't know what it was.

Looking around, I decided I needed to make a wall between them, but there weren't any carrot sticks. Otherwise, I would have. My food choices were selective, especially when someone else prepared them. Next, I grabbed a carton of juice, an apple, and some utensils, and put everything on a tray.

The Omega behind me was staring at me, with her Afro hair wild and rampant. I smiled back.

"The pasta is alright, you know." She smiled. I smiled back.

"And they're zucchinis," she said, "just in case you were wondering." I sighed in relief.

"Thank you. I was wondering. They looked a little mushed."

"Yeah, it's not like how I would make it, either. But God help them. I don't know what staff they employ in this place. The food could do with a few Omegas making it. Don't you think?" I smirked and nodded. "I'm Ava. You're the new girl, aren't you?"

"Yeah, what gave it away? The zucchinis?"

She laughed. "No. I'd say, your table speech earlier. You've got some guts, girl!"

I smirked. "Thanks... I think."

She smiled, then placed her hand on my arm and said, "Don't worry, it takes some time to get used to this place. It can be hard at first, but you'll get there."

I nodded.

"Look," she glanced left and right, checking where the guards were. "There's a group of us that hang out. If you ever feel you want company, you're always welcome to join us."

"Thank you," I smiled. "I appreciate that."

"Anyway," she said, "I've got to get going. My pack is waiting for me."

I looked at her, brows furrowed. "You've found your pack?"

"Yeah, I met my scent matched pack here. I'm as surprised as you are!"

"So what happens now?" I asked, considering the entire purpose of this place was for Omegas to join packs and become respectful members of society.

"We're waiting to see if I can get an early release into their custody." I rolled my eyes. "Yeah, I know... It's stupid, isn't it?" I nodded. "It's the fact that the law says the pack will own me which grates on me the most. But I know my boys don't see it that way."

I smiled. "You wouldn't have scent matched if they weren't right for you," I said, trying to soothe her.

"True. So you, Amy Anderson, need to find a pack so you can get the heck out of here!"

I laughed. "I'm planning on bulldozing my way out, if I'm honest." She laughed.

"Ava! You coming, babe?" A gorgeous hunk of a man shouted.

She grinned. "I've been summoned," she joked. "See you later, Amy Anderson!" and with that, she waved and disappeared into the crowd.

I picked up my tray and started walking back to the table. Nora waved at me, and Janine rolled her eyes at her. I smirked, shimmying my way through packs in the cafeteria.

Returning, I resented the constant sniffing. It made me feel like I had a problem. But I knew it would stop when my suppressants wore off and they could scent that I wasn't their scent match. At least, I hoped it would.

Chapter 6

If I didn’t know better, I might have mistaken this place for a legitimate academy, albeit a shabby one, judging by the state of the cafeteria. But when you looked past the surface and into the hidden corners, you uncovered the reality of it all. Insincere smiles, the guards patrolling with batons ready to strike anyone who misbehaved, and Alphas lounging in groups, claiming tables and snarling at anyone who approaches. Next: Wannabes, nerds, dropouts—all with dismal expressions and attitudes. This table threatened revolt. These Omegas refused to conform. They glared at the staff and acted more like animals than the prim and proper Omegas they were meant to be. I watched as they flipped off a delicate young thing as she came too close to their table. They didn't care about others' opinions and didn't hide behind fake smiles, giggles, or hair flips. These Omegas were exactly what they appeared. They were genuine girls I hoped to befriend one day—if they didn't get thrown into the Birthing Grounds soon. Who knows, maybe I'll see them there. I shrugged and carried on walking.

I bit my lip, chewing it, as I shimmied between two Alphas who were barking orders at each other. Two rival packs, angry that the other had wandered into their territory. I almost laughed, watching as their Betas just stood there, shrugging. They were supposed to be the peacekeepers, but they couldn't be bothered anymore. I didn't blame them. Who wanted to deal with all this shit? I wondered why they were in here. It wasn't like Betas to be the rebels of society.

How did these Alpha packs end up here? Were they just packs that didn't have an Omega, and were hoping to be scent matched? Or were they the real, rough, vile, rancid members of society? Those that the academy hoped to restrain and reform?

I laughed to myself, causing an Alpha with carrot-orange hair to glare at me. "What?" I said, shaking my head and walking past. His eyes widened, and then he frowned. Clearly, he wasn't expecting an Omega to bite back at him. The Alpha next to him punched his shoulder and laughed. He growled at him, then looked at me with interest. I rolled my eyes.

As I reached the table, I placed my tray down next to an over-active Nora, who was patting the space next to her.

"Come on, sit here," she said. "I've saved you a space."

But before I did, I picked up the juice carton, squeezed it into the glass, and then walked over to the bin and threw it in. Then everything changed.

As I walked back, the room grew quieter. Whispers taunted the air. The midst of a darkened energy raveled itself around me, coiling and writhing against my soul, pulling me further into it. I stood frozen, unsure of what was happening. The scents. There were too many of them. All mixed, embroiled in candy floss and rainbows. Normally, I'd vomit at the thought of that, but right now, it was the best thing that could ever happen to me. It was the easiest way to describe exactly how it felt: candy floss and rainbows. Happiness, elated, pure and divine.

The surrounding air I breathed had turned into a mixture of perfection. The scent of the sea captured me. As though I was standing on a sandy beach watching the waves crash against the shoreline, driftwood aching to be sat on, to be caressed and touched, seemed to wrap itself around me. Chaotic sea water invited me in, pulling me closer. I wanted to reach out and touch it, but it wasn't there. I looked at Nora, whose face had paled. Her eyes widened. Janine too. Her mouth was agape. What was happening? Silence fell. Why was everybody staring at me? I was the new girl, but I was the new girl five minutes ago, and nobody stared at me that much anymore, not like this anyway. I gulped, still lost in the sweet shadows of succulence, groaning as the temptation of sugary delight teased me. Champagne and darkness, delicate bubbles, slithering their way throughout my body. I breathed deeply and whined, absorbed in its delight.

Then, a rough voice rumbled from where everyone was staring... behind me. "Are you going to move, Omega?" To say I jumped was an understatement. To say I gulped was another. I almost choked on my saliva when he tapped me on the shoulder. I wasn't expecting anyone to be behind me. But then did I really believe everybody had actually stopped to stare at me? No, of course not. They were staring at whoever was behind me.

Did I dare turn around? I bit down hard on my lower lip, the sharp allure of fear snaking up my spine, wrapping itself around my body, constricting me in its icy grip. Yet something so soothing caressed me alongside the darkness, encased within the fear, was something so safe that made me feel at home.

Two hands gripped my shoulders and spun me around. “Omega, move.” The raspy voice sounded as I came face to face with the chiseled, toned expression of a dominant, dreamy, but furious Alpha.

He was not an Alpha I'd ever seen before, or pictured, or ever even wanted. But since I'd laid my eyes on him, there was nothing more in my life that I wanted at this moment than to take his face in my hands and kiss his lips, hot and heavy.

His eyes narrowed into an almost psychotic glare. He tightened his grip on my shoulders. “You,” he said. His voice was deeper. “Who are you?”

“I?” I stammered, “I… I'm I?”

“Yes, you're?” he said, the corner of his lip rising.

What the hell was going on with me? Why couldn't I speak? Why did his presence affect me so much? It wasn't as though I was standing in the shadow of a God. He was a mere Alpha and nothing more.

“My name, it’s just Amy,” I said, finally finding the words.

“Well, just Amy.” He gripped my shoulders harder, forcing me backwards until I slammed against the wall of the cafeteria.

"Hey!" I yelled, My head hit the side. "What was that for?"

"You're in our way," he said.

I pushed him back, and his eyes widened. A slight smirk smothered his face as a collective gasp sounded across our audience.

"Haven't you ever heard of saying excuse me?"

"Excuse me," he said, smirking.

I narrowed my eyes. "Yeah, try that first next time!"

His hands still gripped my shoulders. "Why are you so tall for an Omega?" he asked.

"She's got to be on suppressants," another Alpha said, walking up to him, and placing his hand on his shoulder, "Come on, I'm hungry." The sweet smell of champagne wafted over me and I moaned. He looked at me and smirked, his sandy blond hair catching the light like sunlit wheat. "Something you want, Omega?"

The Alpha, with the psychotic glare, softened and loosened his grip on my shoulders, staring at me. I remained quiet, staring at the new Alpha as he edged his way closer.

"Who is this, Omega?" he asked his pack brother.

"This Cole is Amy. Amy Anderson, the new girl," the psychotic Alpha said. I narrowed my eyes. So, he knew who I was. I had never given him my surname.

My lips creased slightly into a smile edging across my face.

"What's so funny, Omega?" Cole said, moving closer to me, and gripping my arm. Now I had both of them touching me, their hands kissing my skin like the sun on a warm summer's afternoon. A delicate tingle slithered through my body, urging me closer and pushing me further into them. What was it about these Alphas? Who were they? Why did they feel like mine? Was it possible? I thought, an inkling of desire corrupting me. Could they be? I wondered. Breathing in their scent and letting it meld with mine. "Is this how it feels?" I uttered under my breath.

"What did you say, Omega?" Cole said, standing so close now, his chest pushed against my arm. His breath was a whisper in my ear, his fingertips curling within my hair as he breathed in my scent. "There's something about you, isn't there?"

The guy with the psychotic eyes that held me by the shoulders nodded.

"You two." Another Alpha said, walking over. "Have you finished playing with your food?" He smirked, then looked at me and froze, eyes widening, scenting the air and walking closer like a predator to its prey: me. I felt trapped amongst them, but not trapped in a scared-of-my-life way. Trapped in a keep-me-forever way. They were mine. I knew they were. Was it possible? It had to be, but they wouldn't be able to tell. The suppressants prevented it. A loud cough came up behind the psychotic Alpha as a guard walked up, hands on his hips, batten at the ready.

"What's going on here?" he asked.

The Alphas said nothing.

"Are they bothering you, Missy?"

I looked at him wide-eyed, still a deer in the headlights.

"She struggles to speak," the raspy voice of the psychotic one said, "but I can speak for her." He smiled, "And I'll tell you we're not hurting her in any shape or form, and she most definitely wants to be here with us."

The guard looked at me. I must have looked like a girl high on drugs while standing in the middle of a road with a seven-ton lorry hurtling her way. "I'm not sure that she does, boy," the guard said. The guard was an overzealous Beta, which was strange because, out on the streets, a Beta would never dare interrogate an Alpha. But here in the academy, the guards seemed to have all the power.

"She's fine, mate," the new Alpha said, with his blond hair curling around his ears. He gave a beaming smile and slung his hand around the guard's shoulders. The guard growled at him. "Oh, no need to be like that. You know who we are, don't you?" The guard growled again and nodded. "Then you'll want to scoot off before we contact the headmistress and have you fired."

The guard looked at me again and shook his head. Then walked off. These alphas had the control here. I'd got it all wrong. Who were they? "Who are you?" I stammered.

"They call us the Penthouse Alphas," the new guy said, bouncing over with a grin so wide it reminded me of a Cheshire Cat.

"Penthouse?" I asked.

"Yeah." He furrowed his brow.

"Why Penthouse?"

"That doesn't matter. What matters is who you are, and why can't I scent you," the new Alpha said, as he came over and started sniffing the surrounding air.

"Exactly!" the psychotic one said, growling under his breath. "It's strange. It's like, well, I don't know."

I rolled my eyes, then smirked.

The psychotic Alpha looked at me and glared. I gulped.

Regardless of who these guys were, or whether they were mine, I was tired of being put on display in this cafeteria with everyone staring. I glanced beyond the Alphas and finally noticed the hush and the occasional whisper aimed in my direction. Students sat with their mouths agape, eyes wide. What were they afraid of? Was it the Penthouse Alphas? I frowned. Well; it wasn't me!

Tired of being studied, I finally said, "Well, how about you get off me so I can go eat my food?" Then ducked under the psychotic one's arms, since he'd loosened his grip for long enough to allow me to do so. He growled as his touch left me. Cole folded his arms and narrowed his eyes.

"We will find out more about you, sweet girl," Cole said as he grabbed an apple off of another Omega's tray and walked out of the cafeteria. The psychotic one followed, with the bouncy guy jumping along afterwards.

I exhaled, realizing I'd held my breath for what felt like forever.

The whispers started in earnest throughout the cafeteria, people pointed, and packs of Alphas walked over, ready to try to scent me and find out what all the fuss was about. Screw that. I walked over to Nora and Janine, grabbed my bag and a few things off my tray, and left the cafeteria, heading up the corridor. There was no way I wanted to stay for the rest of this shit show.

I needed somewhere quiet, somewhere to think and work out what had just happened. "Hey, wait!" Nora said, with a groaning Janine catching up behind her. "Don't think you're leaving us behind."

I turned back to find both of them running after me.

"Here," Janine said, "I know a quiet place we can go."

I feigned a smile, unsure whether to scream, run away, punch something or swear. My anger boiled. It felt like whoever they were; they'd had full control over my every emotion as my body betrayed me, yearning for them, needing them. I shook my head as we turned the corner, listening to Nora bound on about how high and mighty the Penthouse Alphas were. It almost made me sick that I wanted them. I'd never desired anything more. Heck, I was Amy Anderson, the only daughter of the Anderson Alphas, and I never gave up control. Hell. Kurt would be furious knowing what had just happened; and that I didn't even try to stand my ground. What was this academy doing to me? And where the fuck was my brother? Why hadn't he stormed the place already?

Maybe he had. Maybe, all my brothers had, but they'd been sent on their merry way, manipulated by my fucked-up family, twisted into thinking they were doing what was right for me. My grandparents would have made certain of that! I looked down at the stone floor as we walked along the corridor. Does that mean I'm alone here? No one was coming to save me? I took a long, deep breath and balled my fists. Well, screw them. Screw all of them. I wasn't a damsel in distress. I'd save myself and every bloody Stepford Omega in this messed up place. I pursed my lips, thinking. I just needed a plan first!

Janine directed us along the corridor past pictures of dismal leaders and beaming Omegas with soulless eyes, showing what we could have, what we could be. I wanted to rip every snot-nosed face down from that wall and claw those fake smiles and stupid clothes off of every Stepford body. Then I'd drive my knife into every one of those Alphas for making those Omegas less of a person. I was more than that. I couldn't just be a bundle of emotion and desire, waiting for my men to come home. That wasn't me. That would be the death of me.

Who the hell were they to tell me how to live my life? I didn't want to make beds or wear stupid dresses and sing with the birds every morning. Have you heard my singing voice? I sounded like a strangled cat. No Alpha would want that in their life. Jeez!

Heck, I was the person who helped Omegas out on the streets. I was the one who helped keep them hidden and helped teach them to fight and hold their own.

My friends back home would wonder where I was, but they'd know. They would soon learn of my capture, and they would pray for me in their own twisted way. But I taught them well. They'd go underground. We had safe houses all over the city. Places no Alpha had ever touched, not even my brothers, who I trusted with my life. If only I hadn't been so stupid to think I could help others in the clinic. It was obvious now I thought about it; the clinic was one of the last ones that gave out suppressants. It was the perfect target. I wouldn't be surprised if they'd injured that Alpha and sent him in on purpose.

I was so sick of being 'rare.' Maybe we didn't want to birth their babies and be responsible for the next generation. Maybe all we wanted to do was live our own damn lives!

"It's just down here," Janine said, as we walked down past the classrooms and through the gymnasium to a little room at the back.

"Where are we?" I asked. Having not yet seen inside.

"You'll see," Janine said.

Nora grinned. "This place is where the cleaners hang out," she said.

Janine nodded. "Most of them are Omegas. They have to work to bring in extra money for their packs." She looked around to check there was no one watching. "They help hide us when we want space."

I nodded.

"You just can't ever let the guards see you come down here. We're not supposed to be back in this area. You'd be electrocuted for it."

I gulped and nodded as I walked in, closing the door to the hideaway behind me. I sure as hell didn't want that again.

Chapter 7

My first lesson of the afternoon was the Obedience Workshop. I stood in the middle of a sea of Omegas decked out in identical pleated skirts and tailored blazers, each of us an unwilling player in the Academy's twisted pageant. Our taskmaster for the day, Miss Elliot, paced the polished floorboards like a hawk circling its prey, her every movement precise and calculated.

"Backs straight, chins up, eyes down," she commanded, her voice slicing through the murmurs of unease. The irony wasn't lost on me; we were being taught to stand tall, just to learn how to bow lower.

Around me, Omegas dipped into submissive postures that would've made contortionists sweat. I caught my reflection in the room's ornate mirror, a façade of compliance painted across my features. Inside my head, though, it was a different story.

Oh, sure, let's pretzel ourselves into human doormats. Because nothing screams 'dignity' quite like groveling at the feet of some imaginary Alpha, I mused, my inner monologue dripping with sarcasm.

As if on cue, Miss Elliot showed the 'proper' way to bow, a deep, soul-crushing angle that suggested we were little more than slaves in a colonial court. "Your submission is your strength," she intoned, as if reciting from the Omega Taskforce's handbook of ironies.

"Right, because nothing says 'strength' like eating carpet," I muttered under my breath, mirroring her moves with mechanical precision. My muscles coiled with resistance, each bend an insult to the hours I'd spent learning to fight, a slap to the face of my very nature.

Miss Elliot straightened, her hazel gaze cutting across the room, searching for any sign of disobedience.

"Again," she demanded, and we complied. But with each motion, a silent vow etched itself deeper into my core: they could force my body to bend, but my spirit would remain unbroken.

"Pair up, Omegas! Time to practise your reverent whisper," Miss Elliot's voice sliced through the room like a whip, and I found myself partnered with a trembling girl who looked as if she might faint at the prospect of more drills.

"Watch me, and follow my lead," I murmured to her, adopting the most obsequiously demure posture I could muster without bursting into laughter. "Because nothing screams *competent adult*, like needing someone else to decide how you should stand."

She glanced at me, a flicker of amusement in her eyes, then quickly suppressed it. "Do you think they'll ever have us walk on all fours?" the girl whispered back, her voice barely audible.

"Only on Tuesdays," I deadpanned, straightening just in time to avoid Miss Elliot's roving gaze.

The drudgery of etiquette drills was mind-numbing, but soon we were released from the pathetic dance and herded toward the kitchens for a 'culinary arts' lesson. The sterile scent of disinfectant mingled with the rich aroma of spices as I stood before a stove, armed with a recipe that promised to 'seduce any Alpha's senses.'

"Remember, ladies, a way to an Alpha's heart is through his stomach," our instructor cooed, as if revealing the secret to eternal youth.

"Good thing I'm aiming for lower," I muttered, eyeing the pans with disdain. I reached for the heat dial, deliberately giving it a vicious twist. The flame roared to life, far too strong for the delicate sauce I was supposed to be simmering.

"Isn't that too high?" my partner asked, her voice tinged with worry.

"Probably," I agreed, dumping ingredients into the pan with reckless abandon. "But I've always preferred my meals with a side of arson."

Within minutes, the contents of the pan took on the color of tar, the smell of charred hopes filling the air. Smoke billowed, curling upwards in a desperate escape that I envied. A symphony of crackles and pops sang a tune of beautiful destruction.

"Oops," I said, not bothering to feign regret as I watched the dish morph into a culinary disaster. The smoke billowed thicker, filling the kitchen, and setting off alarms.

Miss Elliot stormed over. "My bad!" I said, shrugging.

“Miss Anderson!” she screeched over the noise of the extractor fans kicking in. “What on earth do you think you’re doing?”

“Following the recipe,” I replied, though the only thing I'd been following was my rising urge to rebel against every absurd rule this place tried to force down our throats.

The air in the kitchen had shifted, heavy with the scent of my rebellion. I could feel every pair of eyes on me, but none bore into me as sharply as Miss Elliot's. Her gaze cut through the smoke, zeroing in on the blackened mess that used to be food.

“Miss Anderson,” she began, her voice icy calm– a surefire sign of the storm to come. “Explain yourself.”

I straightened my spine, refusing to wilt under her scrutiny. “It seems I've underestimated the cooking time,” I said, my tone casual, as if we were discussing the weather and not the culinary catastrophe before us.

Her eyes narrowed further. “You lack the finesse required for such tasks,” Miss Elliot declared. She reached towards her wrist and pressed a button on her watch. As she did, a severe electrical shock screeched through every cell in my body, dropping me to the floor. Pain splintered through me, radiating from my neck where the collar clung like a serpent. It was as if lightning had struck, turning my bones to glass and my muscles to stone, all while I lay twitching, enveloped in a haze of charred dreams.

Don't give them the satisfaction, I coached myself internally, biting down on my tongue to keep from crying out. My body spasmed, an involuntary betrayal, but I kept my voice locked away. They would not hear my pain.

"Is there something you wish to say, Miss Anderson?" Miss Elliot asked, letting go of her watch.

"Nothing at all, Miss Elliot," I managed, forcing a smile that was more like a baring of teeth. "Just savoring the unique scents of my dish."

The dark humor was a thin veil, but it was mine to cling to. A shred of self in a place that sought to strip it away. The collar had done its job; the message was simple. But so was my resolve. They could try to break me, burn me, shock me into submission. But like the smoldering ruins of my culinary defiance, some things refused to be extinguished.

As Miss Elliot turned away, I could have sworn I caught a smirk cast over her lips. Did she enjoy the torture, or was it something else? Something more?

Chapter 8

"Fresh air time, ladies," announced Miss Elliot, clapping her hands to gain everyone's attention.

I pulled myself up off the floor, dusted myself off and checked I hadn't vomited or wet myself. I was lucky, this time. Leaving the classroom, I gave Miss Elliot a defiant glare, then continued being herded out to the courtyard, like sheep to pasture.

"Come on, chop chop!" she yelled, following us. "Omegas need their vitamin D!"

I growled under my breath. She'd pissed me off. I'd shove my vitamin D right up her ass if she came near me again.

Outside, it was cold, and there wasn't a sunbeam in sight. Vitamin D my arse.

The high stone walls loomed above, cold and unfeeling, their surfaces marred by the scars of time.

Long shadows stretched across the cobblestones as if the architecture sought to ensnare us in darkness. The gothic spires of the academy pierced the sky, oppressive and unwavering, their silhouettes overseeing our every move.

"Looks cozy, doesn't it?" I said under my breath to the Omega I'd been paired with, my gaze tracing the jagged outline of our prison. "Like a picture from a twisted fairy tale."

She smiled, looked around, and nodded. This girl was too scared to say boo to a goose. How would she endure a few more years in this dreadful place?

As I stood there amidst the other Omegas, breathing in the crisp outside air tainted with the stench of control, I felt something shift inside me.

The moment they stepped into the courtyard, it was as if the shadows themselves parted to herald their arrival. It wasn't just their uniforms that set them apart—the stark contrast of crisp pants and structured blazers against the dreariness of Stonehurst. It was the air around them. It crackled with an energy so palpable that even the ironclad discipline of the academy seemed to bend in its wake.

Nora had told me very little about who they were. She knew their names, and that they were from one of the more influential families in this shitty society, but besides that, they kept to themselves. What was it about these Alphas that had me all hot and flustered?

The psychotic Alpha, Draven Blackwood, led the trio, moving with a predatory grace that made my heart drum a frantic beat against my ribs. His jet-black hair framed his face like a raven's wings and flickered with hints of blue rebellion. And those piercing brown eyes held a depth that both enticed and unnerved. The scent he carried was a storm on the horizon, dark and electric, promising chaos that could tear down walls—or hearts—with ruthless efficiency.

Cole Hawthorne trailed a step behind, his presence a quieter threat that was no less compelling. Deep brown hair caught the waning sunlight, highlighting an almost purple tone to it. But it was the carnivorous desire in his brown eyes that beckoned me closer, that sent an involuntary shiver down my spine. Yet his champagne and darkness were the twisted bubbles I'd craved so desperately.

Finally, the shorter of the three, the wild Jake Sullivan, with his chestnut brown waves and eyes that danced with mischief. Where Draven commanded the shadows and Cole walked with them, Jake seemed ready to ignite them with a mere flicker of his grin. The laughter in his scent was a bright spark in the dim courtyard, as the scent of roses surrounded him wherever he walked. It reminded me of my mother's favorite flower, the white rose, a symbol of divinity that my Alpha fathers would give to her every week without fail.

"Great," I muttered, "the holy trinity of Alphas graces us with their divine presence." My sarcasm was a flimsy shield against the primal part of me that stirred an instinctive urge to bare my neck in submission.

But hell would freeze over before I'd bow down to anyone.

"Down, girl," I chided myself silently. They may be walking pheromone bombs, but I wasn't some starry-eyed Omega who swooned at a strong jawline.

A muscle twitched in my leg, betraying me. Watching them, drawn by their intoxicating scents, was like being caught between two opposing worlds. On one hand, I was expected to be the perfect Omega, adhering to their every expectation. On the other, a rebellious fire within me wanted to defy every rule this place represented.

A smirk played on my lips. It would be poetic to lead a rebellion right under their perfectly sculpted noses.

As they moved past, a gust of wind carried their mingling aromas towards me, a sensory assault that had my body tensing and my mind racing. I wrapped my arms around myself.

The crunch of gravel under their boots halted as Draven, Cole, and Jake stood a mere breath away from me.

"Is the Omega curriculum so fascinating that you find yourself lost in thought?" Draven's voice rolled over me, deep and unsettlingly warm.

"Actually, I was contemplating the irony of such perfect flowers," I retorted, meeting his gaze with an insolent tilt of my chin. "Being so dark and deadly in nature."

Jake snorted, a grin flickering across his face as he checked out the belladonna before us.

Their collective scents, the salt of the sea cradling the driftwood of the shore, the pull of the darkness that too much champagne offered a naïve Omega, and the sweet scent of roses as they promised a romance for years to come, threatened to undo the knots of resistance I'd tied around myself.

"Careful. Knowledge like that could be dangerous," Jake quipped, his tone light and playful.

"Only if one cannot appreciate it," I shot back.

Draven's eyes narrowed, a smirk tugging at the corner of his mouth. "Keep that fire burning, Amy. It might just keep you warm on the cold nights here."

Their laughter was a low rumble, a resonant sound that vibrated through the air already thick with tension. As they turned away, the crackle of their departure echoed in the enclosed space, leaving me with the ghost of their amusement.

I watched their retreating backs, muscles coiled tight, ready to spring into action or curl into defense. Confusion swirled my thoughts, each colliding with the next. How could these Alphas, with their calm confidence and unspoken power, see anything in me but another Omega to mold? Why did they seek me out again? Do they feel the pull that I feel? They can't scent me yet. My suppressants should still work... shouldn't they?

I was full of questions, but no answers. Each interaction with them was another puzzle piece, a fragment of a larger scheme I had yet to decipher. The idea of entanglement with any Alpha was enough to set my teeth on edge. But curiosity gnawed at me, as well as the urges I had to mount them every time I saw them.

After my afternoon classes had finished, I headed back to my apartment and kicked off my shoes. The oppressive grip of the academy clung to me, a second skin I itched to shed. So I did. Taking off my uniform piece by piece and throwing it across the room felt liberating. I didn't care that it would crease or not be 'perfect' enough for tomorrow's shit storm of a day. All I cared about was falling back on my bed in my sweats and screaming at the top of my lungs, because well why the fuck not.

Today had been shit. Eye-opening and shit.

I'd been pushed around, strangled, herded, told I was nothing more than a slave, electrocuted twice, and somehow, I'd still found what I think might be my scent matched pack. Well, screw them. Screw them all.

I wasn't some pretty primped-up princess, ready to get down on my hands and knees and present for anyone, let alone three Alphas I'd just met. Hell no. Who even knew where they'd been! Hasn't anyone heard of STDs nowadays? I just had to keep my pussy quiet down there, because if she yearned for the good stuff, I would be screwed, literally.

Chapter 9

The next morning, as the sun rose and bleached its way through the veneer blind, I sat up, stretching. Today would be my first full day in this crap hole of an academy. This was my life now. Locked up with a permanent shock collar strapped around my neck, and a school full of obnoxious ass hats to deal with. I wouldn't mind if they weren't so hot. But the Penthouse Alphas were goddamn breathtaking! It was a shame they didn't have the personality to go with the looks.

I grabbed breakfast on the go from the coffee shop and snuck it into my first class, which I was late for. Nora smiled and Janine smirked when I arrived. I shrugged. The teacher, however, was less than impressed and expected one hundred lines from me. I felt like Bart Simpson, writing I should not be late and disturb the class.

After an exhilarating class on female biology, the timetable said I had Communication 101. I yawned. Communication was not my strong point.

Nora waved goodbye and headed off toward the library. "Where's she off to?" I asked Janine.

"She gets out of all the Communication classes and helps in the library instead."

"Err, like how?"

"I have no idea. It's not like her communication skills couldn't do with a little finer tuning."

I laughed.

"Right, I'm in this direction," Janine said.

"What! You're going too?"

She laughed. "Yeah, and you'll be fine. I'm in Communication 102."

I smirked. "Seriously?"

"I kid you not. I actually graduated from your shitty class."

"Oh, the fun I have to look forward to!"

She smirked and waved bye as she left.

I stopped at the wooden door with the patterned glass window, then pushed it open to enter.

The heavy door of Communication 101 creaked open, announcing my entrance like some sort of twisted fanfare I neither wanted nor welcomed. With my heart thumping a rebellious beat, I stepped into the room.

"Amy Anderson, I presume?" I feigned a smile and nodded. "Here is your morning vitamin. Take it now, please."

"My morning what?"

"Vitamin Amy. You have one every morning."

"What? In class?" She nodded. I looked at the purple pill in my hand. "What's in it?" She shrugged. "Great," I growled.

"Now please, we do not have all day."

Placing the tablet in my mouth, I swallowed.

"Open wide."

"Are you being serious?" She nodded, so I did as I was told, sticking my tongue up so she could see I had swallowed the damn tablet.

"Okay, now take a seat."

I walked past two sniggering girls in the front row, and further down the far right to an empty seat.

"You can't sit there," a girl with long brown hair snapped. As she spun around to face me, I gritted my teeth. Damn, this was like being thrown back into the merciless world of school, where every glance and word felt like a battle for survival!

"Why?" I asked, huffing.

"The Stone pack sits there. That's their omegas seat."

"So where can I sit then?" I asked Miss know it all.

She pointed further to the right, three rows back. "There. That's where the unmatched sit."

I nodded, feigning thanks, as to be honest I couldn't care less where I sat. I just wanted to avoid a turf war in this shithole.

"Miss Anderson, have you found a seat yet?" The teacher asked in an irritated tone.

I quickly shuffled forward and sat in a seat in 'no-man's-land.'

"Yes, thanks."

Just as she said that the Stone pack walked in and took their seats, followed by the dickhead Alpha from yesterday's library encounter. Go figure, the son of the asshole that runs the Omega Taskforce, was a dick. He smirked when he saw me and zoned in. The rest of his pack fanned out behind him—a procession of tailored blazers and smug arrogance.

The scrape of a chair next to mine cut through the tense air like a knife. I knew immediately who it was.

"Nice of you to save me a seat," he sneered, close enough for me to feel the heat of his breath against my skin. I focused on Miss Harlow's doodles on the chalkboard, willing my heart rate to steady.

"I think you're confused about your seat," I said. "Surely you belong over there?" I motioned to the opposite side of the room.

The corner of his lips twitched upward. "I made an exception today. For you."

"Oh, I'm honored," I deadpanned.

I growled under my breath, taking out my notepad and pencil, knuckles whitening against the graphite, as I forced my gaze to remain fixed on the blank page before me.

He sat staring at me, licking his lips and scenting the air. For fuck's sake. I gripped my pencil tighter, listening to the teacher drone on about introductions. The Alpha edged his seat closer.

"Miss Anderson," the teacher said, and I just about jumped out of my skin. Too busy side-eying the dickhead Alpha to pay attention to class. "Will you introduce yourself to the class, please?"

I growled. This made matters worse as it only seemed to turn the Alpha on as he growled under his breath too. "Right, well..."

"No, Miss Anderson, when we introduce ourselves, we stand upright and smile. Please do so."

She was kidding, right? I gripped my pencil tighter and pushed myself up from my desk. The Alpha watched. His hand sneaked closer to my thigh as I stood upright. "Hi," I said. "I'm Amy Anderson, and I'm also a prisoner here." I immediately sat down as a few Omegas sniggered.

The teacher slapped her hand on her desk. "Amy Anderson, that is not how you introduce yourself, is it?"

I rolled my eyes.

"Beatrice, could you please show Amy how to make a formal introduction?" Beatrice, the brown-haired girl from earlier, stood up.

"Hello class, my name is Beatrice Dansmore," she said in a well-rehearsed exquisite voice. Like a toffee-nosed rich person would use. "I am delighted to be here with you all." She curtseyed and then sat down.

I think I vomited in my mouth a little.

"I can break in that pretty mouth of yours," the Alpha next to me said as the teacher continued her lesson. He leered closer.

"Eurgh gross! Back off, will you!"

"No one talks to me that way, princess," he said, leaning over and moving my hair out of the way so he could sniff me. His greasy nose and hot breath poisoned my skin. I shuddered, backing away into my chair.

"You've got a lot to learn. But with a firm hand." His thick, brutish hand gripped my thigh, squeezing it. I froze for a second. "I will teach you to obey me." His hand trailed up my leg, closer and closer, up and up, trying to cop a feel right in the middle of class.

I took a deep breath. No one touched me unless I said they could! "That's fucking enough!" I growled under my breath, at the same moment as I raised my sharpened pencil, moved and slammed it into his hand.

The howl that came from his mouth was followed by the largest grin of pure satisfaction on my face. Heads turned; hearts raced. He recoiled back in his chair, gripping his hand, knocking over books and scattering papers to escape the wooden stake I'd planted firmly in his hand.

"You fucking bitch!" he yelled, the pencil still sticking out of his hand.

I pushed him away.

The teacher looked up. "What on earth is going on?" she said in her exquisite voice, then, "OH, MY," she cried as she saw the blood.

There was no time for her to react as the dickhead Alpha Andrew ripped the pencil out of his hand and lunged at me, eyes ablaze with the kind of blind rage reserved for wounded predators. Clawing at the air, he aimed for my throat. I braced myself, leaning back enough to feel the rush of air as his fingers grasped nothing but space. Students scattered, their movements a chaotic dance of self-preservation as desks toppled and chairs skidded across the floor.

My chair toppled backwards, me still within it. Within moments, Andrew had leapt on top of me, his bloodied hands grabbing me by the neck, squeezing all the life out of me.

"You fucking bitch!" he yelled again. The rest of the class was yelling, and all I could see were stars as my world hazed into a shadowy darkness. "I'll teach you your place!" he screeched.

At that moment, the classroom door burst open with such force, it could've been a gunshot. Every pair of eyes darted toward the sound, and there he was—Draven Blackwood, an unyielding force filled with rage. Even through my barely conscious haze, I still recognized him, as his scent wrapped around me, the vast chaos of the ocean, stormy seas soothed by the calming nature of the driftwood beach. The psychotic Penthouse Alpha. He was here... and right now he was pulling the dickhead off of me and beating seven bells of shit out of him.

Draven tossed Andrew aside like a rag doll into the nearest row of desks. "Touch her again, and you'll regret it," he growled, looming over him. Their gazes locked, two Alphas with every line of their bodies drawn tight, a coiled spring of animosity between them.

"Blackwood." Andrew spat the name as if it were poison, scrambling to regain his footing and what was left of his dignity. "This is none of your business."

"Make it my business again, and you won't be walking out of here," Draven threatened, his voice low and dangerous.

Andrew rose, straightening his blazer with his bloodied hands. Hands that trembled just enough to betray his fury. But behind the rage, I saw it—the flicker of fear in those icy blue eyes. Draven had him spooked. And hell, I couldn't help the smirk that crept onto my face.

I leaned up on my elbows, still coughing from being choked. My heart was pounding like a train veering off the tracks. But as I watched Draven hold his ground, a twinge of admiration flickered within me. He had appeared from nowhere. Protected me. Not that I needed it. I clearly had it handled. I smirked, then coughed again, touching my sore neck. Shit. That was going to leave a mark.

Andrew retreated, growling and kicking a chair as he left the classroom. Draven turned to me. Our eyes met, and for a fleeting moment, I saw the man behind the Alpha—a hint of concern, maybe respect. Then, like a curtain falling, the mask of the indomitable Alpha slid back into place.

"Thanks," I murmured, almost begrudgingly. Draven moved toward me, picked me up into his arms and placed me on a chair.

"You should watch who you befriend around here," he said, still touching my shoulder, as he raised my chin to look at my neck.

I nodded once, lip wobbling, tears in my eyes. The entire scene had been a little too much, even for me to handle.

"Stay away from Calloway in the future. Do you hear me?"

"I plan to." He rubbed his thumb under my eye, catching a single tear before it dropped, then smiled and left the room. I wiped my eyes and bit my lip, forcing the tears back down.

Miss Harlow, who had been no more use than an ornament throughout my attempted murder, finally found her voice. She cleared her throat awkwardly. "If we could all take our seats."

Chapter 10

The rest of Communication 101 was a suffocating intoxication of whispers. Students stared at me, sniggered and some even stopped by my desk to check how I was. Those, at least, well, they were the nice ones. The Alphas were all in cahoots with the dickhead Alpha, Andrew Calloway, and the Omega Taskforce. However, the Omegas, well, they still hated him.

The classroom door banged open with such force that the leering portraits on the walls rattled in their frames. The air, previously thick with the scent of aggression and blood, now carried a new fragrance—one of impending doom as the tall, imposing figure of Warden Xavier Gray filled the doorway. His shadow loomed over us like an eclipse, darkening the room and quelling the storm of tension with a cold, hard silence.

"Quiet!" His voice was a whip-crack, instantly slicing through the noise. The room fell silent. Even Miss Harlow paled at the sight of him.

Warden Gray's eyes were as sharp as shards of ice, flickering from one student to the next until they met mine. "YOU!" he bellowed. "STAND IMMEDIATELY!"

I groaned, still weak from earlier. Using the desk, I rose, albeit a little wobbly. "What's wrong with you, girl? Stand still!"

"I am trying to!" I stated, already pissed off at how this day was turning out.

He stormed over. His heavy footsteps pounded the floor. "YOU DARE ANSWER ME BACK?"

I nodded. Obviously, I did. I just had. I rolled my eyes at him while wobbling some more.

"TO MY OFFICE! NOW!"

"Where is that?" I asked.

He growled, grabbing my arm and forcefully gripping it, dragging me out of the classroom. I normally would have kicked and screamed and beat seven bells of shit out of him.

But right now, I was happy at the free ride to his office, as I doubted my legs would carry me there alone.

Draven walked out of another classroom, being ordered out by another faculty member. He growled when he saw me, stormed over, and picked me up in his arms.

Warden Gray was about to say something, but even as tall and butch as he was, he was no match for the likes of Draven, and he knew it. He backed down and let Draven carry me.

I fell into Draven's chest, soothed by the warmth of his skin through his shirt, and the scent of the beach as I closed my eyes, imagining the waves crashing against the shoreline. The sandy beach was always my favorite place. My safe place. My mother used to take me there for day trips as a little girl. We'd sit for hours building sandcastles, or dipping our toes in the ocean water as it lapped around us, caressing us, protecting us. That time was ours. It was perfect. Draven reminded me of those happy memories. He reminded me of my safe place.

"Amy?" a soothing voice said, as a hand brushed the hair from my eyes. "You need to wake up now."

Then growling. More growling.

"If you touch her, you will have me to deal with."

A male voice began shouting, and the door slammed.

"Amy?"

I groaned, rubbing my eyes and smacking my lips as I yawned.

Light streamed back into view.

"You nodded off," the chest that reverberated against me said. I sat up on his knee and looked up into the eyes of Alpha Draven.

"Oh, shit! I'm sorry!" I said, almost jumping off of his lap. Thankfully, we were sitting down. He laughed.

"It's fine. You took quite the hit today."

"Yes," another more annoyed voice said. I turned to see the Headmistress. "Take a seat, Amy," came the steely command from behind her desk, as large and as cold as the woman who sat behind it. I sat in an empty seat beside Draven. "And on this occasion, I shall forgive that swear word." I nodded. She sat forward, her fingers steepled like the arches of a cathedral. I shifted in my seat, the fabric of my uniform skirt covered in droplets of Andrew's blood. "Draven has explained what happened." My brow furrowed, and I looked at him.

Draven smirked. "Yes Amy, I told the Headmistress how Andrew was trying to force himself on you against your will, and you took the actions to defend yourself." I nodded. That was correct, after all.

"Then you saved me," I said, wide-eyed and still sleepy.

Draven grinned. "Yes, well, I'm sure you could have handled it yourself. But I didn't want to see that pretty neck of yours get throttled anymore."

I smirked.

The Headmistress narrowed her eyes. "I don't know how I am going to tell Mr Calloway about this."

"Who?" I asked.

"Andrew's Dad, the reason you're in this place," Draven explained.

"Oh..." I pursed my lips and huffed.

"Well, tell him if he touches me again, I will press charges," I said, sitting upright.

The Headmistress sat up straight. "But you're an Omega without a pack, you do not have any rights."

"I can damned well try, can't I."

She narrowed her eyes. "Fine. I will tell young Mr Calloway to stay away from you."

I nodded and stood up. Draven stood up too, steadying me. But before I could leave, the Headmistress called out, "But Ms Anderson, make sure you lock your doors at night."

I stared at her for a moment, my mouth agape. Draven took my hand and pulled me out of the office. "He wouldn't dare touch you. Not when he knows you're under the protection of the Penthouse Alphas."

I narrowed my gaze. "But, well, don't get me wrong, I'm thankful for it. But, why am I?"

He stopped in the corridor, pulled me into his arms and scented me. His lips were so close I could feel every breath as he spoke. "You're mine, Amy Anderson," he said. "I know it." The heat from his body up close unraveled me. My legs weakened, my heart pounded, and a needy whine escaped my lips. He chuckled.

"Is it playtime?" Cole asked as the scent of champagne and darkness tickled my taste buds. Within seconds, his body was against me, holding me in his arms. "I heard what happened with you today, sweet girl. Would you like me to finish him for you?"

I groaned. Draven held me up, placing soft kisses along my sore neckline.

"Should I take that as a yes?"

Jake laughed as he walked over. "I think you're teasing her too much, boys," he said, grinning. Draven and Cole pulled back, smirking. My eyelids fluttered, and I regained some level of dignity again as I found myself once again able to stand on my own two feet.

"What did you do to me?" I asked Draven.

"Oh, I can do a lot more than that if you'd let me."

I narrowed my eyes, pursed my lips and backed away. What was it with these three? Every time I saw them; I lost my damn mind!

"Until next time, sweet girl," Cole shouted as he grabbed Draven and Jake around the shoulders and the three of them walked off, leaving me behind to watch my future walk away.

Chapter 11

The door to the hideaway creaked, and I stepped into its colorful embrace. Lamps without shades illuminated the corners, giving birth to dancing shadows as I shut the door behind me.

My heart thudded like a drumbeat in my chest. The day had been a relentless storm, and each beat echoed its fury. In the room's dim light, Nora and Janine were already hunkering down on the tattered old sofa.

"God, you look like hell," Janine commented without lifting her gaze, a deck of worn cards forgotten in her hand.

"Thanks, I aim to impress," I shot back, my voice still jittery with leftover adrenaline.

I sucked in a breath, letting the memory flood back. Draven's looming figure, the way he'd swooped in. It was straight out of some twisted fairytale. Only there were no heroes in Stonehurst Academy, just varying shades of tyrants.

"Okay, spill it Cherry Red," Nora urged, her voice feather-soft but insistent.

I rolled my eyes at the nickname.

"Draven happened," I said, and even as the words left my mouth, they tasted like someone else's story. "He just... appeared." My mind spun, reeling from the insanity of his intervention—the way he commandeered the chaos with that predatory grace Alphas were cursed with.

A shiver crawled up my spine, but whether it was fear or something far more dangerous, I couldn't tell.

I launched into the tale, my voice a low hiss as I skirted around the edges of the forbidden. Nora's presence calmed me as she leaned forward, the blue of her gaze bright and earnest in the lamp's soft light, absorbing my every word.

"Andrew had me cornered," I confessed, the words scraping against my throat like gravel. "Thought he was the big man, ready to put another Omega in her place." A bitter laugh eluded me, dark with the memory. "But, well, after I stabbed him, Draven just materialized. Like some demon of vengeance."

Nora flinched, her gentle soul recoiling at the violence implied, yet she remained steadfast, her curiosity a beacon that beckoned me to continue.

"Woah, hold up. You stabbed Andrew?" Janine said.

I nodded, smirking in delight at my victory.

"Damn girl, I like you even more now!"

"What happened after?" Nora asked. "After Draven appeared?"

"Everything went still for a second, you know? As if the world held its breath." The image of Draven stepping through the chaos flickered through my mind. "It was surreal. He grabbed Andrew and pulled his bloodied hands off of my neck."

Janine launched forward and checked my neck over. "Shit girl, that looks sore!" I nodded. Nora winced.

"Draven threw Andrew aside like a rag doll, then beat seven bells of shit out of him!"

The relief of that moment slithered through me again, unexpected and disorienting.

Nora's hand found mine, a sliver of comfort in a world that sought to chain us. Her touch was feather-light, but it anchored me back to the here and now, away from the maelstrom of what-ifs that threatened to engulf me.

"Draven was a force of nature, all snarling power, contained in human skin." My words tumbled out as I tried to paint the picture for them. "He loomed over us—over Andrew—like some avenging angel. It's like, he wore that Alpha aura like a damn crown."

"Did it come with a sword and shining armor too?" Janine quipped; her smirk almost audible in the dimness of our shared space.

"More like psychotic fury," I shot back, a wry smile pulling at my lips despite the gravity of the memory. "No one dared move. It was like he had this gravitational pull, you know? Everything and everyone just orbited around him."

"Sounds less like gravity and more like everyone needed a change of pants," Janine said, her grin wicked as lamplight glinted off her teeth.

"Quite possibly," I conceded, a chuckle escaping me despite the tight knot of emotions in my chest. "But when he spoke, he didn't ask, he commanded. Andrew backed off as if struck, and I felt this strange mix of relief."

"Classic damsel in distress," Janine teased, her eyes dancing with mirth. "But with more stabbing and less swooning. Our Amy doesn't swoon."

"Damn right, I don't," I affirmed, the laughter bubbling up, feeling strangely cathartic. "But there's something about Draven. It's unsettling, how safe I felt in that moment—and how much I hated that safety."

The silence felt heavy after my last words, like a curtain of darkness descending on us. Nora squeezed my arm. "You're sure you're okay, Amy?" Nora asked. "Andrew has hurt so many of us; I can't bear the thought of—"

"Hey," I cut in, my tone gentle despite the adrenaline still coursing through me. "I'm here, aren't I? And yes, Draven swooped in like some kind of avenging angel. But I had it handled." I smiled, trying to reassure her. She nodded.

"Avenging angel? More like a brooding dark knight, if you ask me," Janine interjected, her voice rich with that brazen humor that made light of our grim reality.

"Brooding is right," I agreed, but then my voice faltered, memories of the confrontation flooding back with palpable intensity. "He was there, all righteous fury, and everyone else just vanished into the background."

"Sounds like someone's got a bit of a hero complex going on," Janine said, her words slicing through the room's tension. She fixed me with a knowing look, as though she could see the conflict warring within me. "You're acting like you don't know what I'm talking about, but we both know you weren't just relieved by his sudden appearance."

"Janine—" I started, my protest weak even to my ears.

"Come on, Amy," she pressed, her tone earnest beneath the sharpness of her words. "It's written all over your face. You're drawn to him, whether or not you want to be. And it's not just because he saved your ass from Andrew's clutches."

I opened my mouth to deny it once more, but no sound came out. It was true, wasn't it? Draven's sudden intervention had left a mark on me, one that I couldn't easily scrub away. The very notion stirred a rebellion within me, but Janine's unwavering gaze demanded the truth—even if only acknowledged silently between us.

A tremor ran through my hands as I clutched them together, fighting the riotous swarm of butterflies in my stomach. Draven Blackwood—my supposed savior, my potential undoing. The memory of his scent, a mix of driftwood and the ocean, lingered in my senses, stirring something primal deep within. A dangerous allure that resonated with the very Omega nature I'd spent years trying to suppress.

"Are you okay?" Nora asked, her concerned gaze probing.

I forced a half-smile, a brittle facade. "Just thinking." My words trailed off as I grappled with a truth too raw to voice aloud. Draven had swooped in like some brooding force of nature, and part of me—God help me—wanted to lean into that storm, to let it consume me. But no, I was Amy Anderson, not some damsel waiting to be claimed. I was steel wrapped in flesh, not easily bent or broken.

"About Draven?" Janine's eyebrow quirked, a smirk playing on her lips.

"Give it a rest," I muttered, though her teasing tone somehow made the heaviness in my chest lighter.

"Here, this will help." Nora produced a half-eaten bar of chocolate from the folds of her skirt, her blue eyes twinkling with mischief. It was contraband here, where our bodies were policed as strictly as our behaviors—no sugary foods allowed for Omegas-in-training.

"Where did you—" I began, but she cut me off with a conspiratorial grin.

"Let's just say the Omega cleaners are good at finding unexpected treasures." She broke off a piece, offering it to me. I took it, letting the rich, forbidden flavor melt on my tongue.

The laughter bubbled up among us then, low and secretive, a shared delight in this small act of rebellion. We passed the chocolate between us, each bite a silent oath of solidarity. Here in this shadowed room, huddled close, we found solace in one another. No matter how suffocating Stonehurst Academy became, they couldn't crush the spirit we shared—the unspoken pact of defiance we nurtured like a flame in the dark.

"Guess we're all partners in crime now," Janine whispered, a playful lightness to her words that belied the steely determination in her eyes.

We were three Omegas against a world that sought to shape us into perfect, pliant dolls. But as long as we had each other, as long as we could cling to these stolen moments of joy and unity, they hadn't won.

Not yet, at least.

Chapter 12

My shitty alarm clock droned on like a pillar drill in my head as the worst headache in the world destroyed every brain cell I had left. Which, considering what they were teaching me in this place, wasn't many.

I groaned as I rolled out of bed, kicked the alarm clock across the room to shut it up and headed for a nice warm shower. It helped. It always did. That, and a large glass of water and I would feel better soon. At least I hoped I would. It didn't help that since I'd been here, my temperature kept rising in the night, and I woke up covered in sweat.

After washing and dressing, I stripped the sheets and changed them again. This was now a daily occurrence. Plumping the cushions, I created a nice little nest in the center, a place of pure comfort. When I realized what I was doing, I stopped, took a step back and mentally smacked myself. I was seriously acting weird lately!

I picked up my bag and headed downstairs to meet Janine and Nora for breakfast. I was determined not to be late for a change and sit down and eat with them.

Leaving the Omega complex was easy today. There were no conversations about how late I was with the guards. Instead, I strolled right past them and even waved when they glared at me. They loved me really. I thought, rolling my eyes.

This morning, crowds of Omegas were all heading in the same direction. I was on time for once! But, as I entered the woods, I had this strange feeling I was being watched. It wasn't a dark romance stalker vibe or a man with a mask that you wanted to take home to meet your mama. No. This was a creepy serial killer vibe, and someone with revenge on his mind. I turned around and found the brutish Alpha Andrew leering at me. He was leaning against a tree, waiting for someone. I narrowed my gaze. Wait. Was he waiting for me?

I hurried along the path after a group of Omegas. The darkness of the woods seemed to coil over my body, taking it hostage as I entered deeper into the shadows of the trees. My breathing faltered, and with each step, my chest tightened.

I quickened my pace, trying to keep up, but they were moving too fast. Soon enough, I was alone in the darkness of the woods.

I stopped to catch my breath. The silence was deafening, broken only by the rustling of leaves and branches in the wind. The trees towered above me, their thick trunks casting eerie shadows on the forest floor.

Laughter sounded behind me, and I almost crapped myself at how close he was.

"I'm coming for you, Amy..."

My mouth had all but dried up as I struggled to swallow. My heart thundered in my chest, my throat constricting like a noose tightening. Eyes wide with terror, hands slick with sweat, I realized with bone-chilling clarity that if I didn't escape this instant, I would fall victim to his sinister game.

"Leave me alone," I croaked.

Laughter cackled all around me.

He wasn't alone.

He'd brought his entire pack to come and play, too.

My breath came in ragged gasps, my legs begging for respite as I stumbled through the underbrush. The morning light fought to breach the thick canopy above, casting blinding streaks across my path. Fear clawed up my spine as shadows danced around me—each rustle of leaves and snap of a twig sounding out my impending doom.

I dared a swift glance over my shoulder; their silhouettes ghosted between the trees.

"Run all you want, Amy! You can't escape us!" Andrew's voice was tainted with anger.

Panic continued to surge within me; raw instinct screamed to keep running, but it wasn't enough. They were faster—the gap between us closing too quickly despite how much energy I spent in blind terror-induced flight. Then, out of nowhere, an arm whipped out from behind a tree trunk, catching hold of mine and violently spinning me to an uneven stop that nearly knocked the air straight from my lungs.

They dragged me back towards a clearing where dim light filtered down through tangled branches overhead. Kicking wildly didn't help; they were too strong, even with my Beta strength, which was waning without the suppressants. Their grips were ironclad, as multiple sets of hands grasped at me greedily from every angle imaginable amidst thunderous laughter echoing throughout the cursed woods.

Absolute terror broke free when coarse hands clutched at my shirt, tearing it to shreds, and exposing the skin beneath, as shivers ran down my body.

Andrew towered over me, licking his lips, as his pack mates held onto either arm tightly enough that their sharp nails bit painfully against my skin underneath torn sleeves of what remained of my Omega uniform blazer and shirt.

"You're not so tough without your Alpha guardian," he sneered, kneeling between my legs and pulling down his pants.

My eyes widened in horror. "Get the fuck away from me!" I screamed, arching back into the ground as much as I could. But despite my protests, I couldn't move. His three pack mates had me pinned to the muddy ground.

He laughed, and pulled at my skirt, ripping my tights to give him easy access to my underwear.

"Get off me!" I yelled, tears brimming my eyes. "If you touch me, I'll kill you. I swear I will kill you!"

He leaned forward and grabbed my chin. "Such foul words for such a pretty mouth. Maybe we should cut out your tongue first," he said. "Knife!" he demanded, holding out his right hand. The stocky guy to his right produced a flick knife. Andrew flicked the blade open and waved it around, allowing it to shimmer under the speckles of daylight that fought their way through the treeline.

He laid on top of me, with his pants still down. His cock was already hard and twitching against me as he shoved his vile fingers into my mouth, trying to grip my tongue.

I bit down hard. Blood spurted out, and he screeched, dropping the knife and grabbing his hand. One finger was hanging on for dear life.

"You fucking bitch!" He yelled.

I spat his blood at him and grinned.

"Touch me again and it won't be your finger next time!"

He growled at me again, then raised his fist and punched me in the face. Specks of sparkling silver filled my vision, dancing before my eyes like the stars twinkling in the night sky.

I could hear him talking to me, saying something, then laughing. But I couldn't understand what. My grip on reality was waning as my mind threatened to delve into a deep sleep and leave this nightmare as concussion took over.

"She's losing consciousness!" One of the pack mates said.

Andrew laughed and fiddled around with his pants and then my underwear.

"Hold her down. I want to savor this!"

Just when my tears threatened to break free, a crescendo of storming footsteps crashed at a breakneck pace into the clearing.

"AMY!"

Draven burst into the clearing, plowing straight into Andrew, knocking him right off of me. I groaned, feeling the freeing nature of all the hands releasing my body at once.

Cole and Jake rushed forward, tackling the three pack mates between them. Punches were thrown, blood sprayed and in a fit of rage, Draven forcibly broke Andrew's arm, releasing an audible bone-crushing snap.

I couldn't stop shaking as reality sank in. My head pounded; my body ached. Even my pride had taken a hit this time. Still lying on the floor, I curled up into a ball and let the tears fall. I was half-naked, freezing cold, and had almost been raped by the vile Alpha Andrew Calloway. Every part of me felt disgusting right now. Every inch he'd touched needed bleaching. I would never get his scent, his stain off of me.

The tears continued to fall, soon turning into heart-wrenching sobs. I was so caught up in my vile existence that I hadn't noticed the surrounding violence had stopped.

"Amy," Jake said, his soothing scent of roses washing over me. "I'm going to cover you over with my coat."

I nodded, sniffling, trying to look through the tears at their concerned faces. They were discussing something through whispers. Then the next thing I knew, I was wrapped half-naked in Draven's arms and being carried away from the bloody scene of my trauma.

Draven's arms were a fortress, his grip unexpectedly gentle for someone with his fierce demeanor. I curled against him, the fabric of the coat brushing softly against my battered skin. My mind was foggy, with a blend of fear and exhaustion that clouded my thoughts.

The world blurred past me as Draven carried me away, his stride unyielding. The cold air of Stonehurst Academy's gothic corridors whipped around us, but the warmth radiating from Draven's body offered a stark contrast to the chill gnawing at my skin. I tried focusing on anything other than what had happened. On his scent as it soothed me, or on his chest as the beat of his heart lulled me to relax.

Cole glanced back, his eyes scanning for any signs of further danger while Jake murmured soothing words into my ear now and then, trying to distract me by talking about mundane things like campus gossip.

Finally reaching their penthouse, nestled in an exclusive section reserved for high-ranking students, I was placed onto a plush couch in their expansive living area. My mind reeled, still partly trapped between that horrific moment and this sanctuary they'd brought me into. I couldn't talk, couldn't form a word to explain the horror of what I felt. For if I did, if I heard it aloud, it made it real. It made everything real.

Without missing a beat, Jake disappeared momentarily, only to return, announcing that he'd run a bath filled with lavender bubbles aimed at soothing nerves. "Gonna wash all those bad vibes away," he said softly before guiding me towards an exquisite marble bathroom glowing under warm light.

Meanwhile, Cole vanished through another door, quickly returning with a soft dressing gown which felt like pure cashmere against my raw skin.

I locked the door, took off my tattered clothes, and slipped into the frothy lavender embrace. Each bubble seemed to absorb a fragment of my unease. The sensory overload was hypnotizing, the warmth enveloping me like a gentle cocoon. It was then that I looked down at the scratch marks on my arms, the bruising that was already appearing on my pelvis where he'd held me down, and I cried.

I cried more than I would normally have allowed myself to, but nothing mattered. My body had been violated. I had been violated. I'd been trained to protect myself. But when it came down to it, my training meant nothing. I was still just a victim, a deer in their headlights. If it hadn't been for the Alphas, I wouldn't have survived their attack... not mentally, anyway.

Is it possible to be broken? Separate from your own body? That's how I felt. The frame I saw under the water had been abused. It wasn't mine any longer. It was theirs. Tears streamed down my face as I looked around to find something, anything, to scrub my skin. I spotted a loofah, took it and covered it in body wash, standing up, trembling, I washed every inch of myself over and over again until I was red raw. Then I rested, tears slowing to a stop, eyes stinging, face swollen, lip split from when he'd punched me. I sank under the water and let the warmth soothe the pain away.

Half an hour later, I emerged from the bathroom. Wrapped in the soft layers provided by Cole. Draven was waiting for me. He reached out. His touch was both a balm and an ache as he wiped away the lone tear with his thumb, his gestures tender but loaded with unspoken promises of vengeance. "You're safe here, Amy," he murmured against my cheek, each word imprinted like a vow. His lips briefly pressed where the tear had trailed, folding comfort into my skin alongside that peculiar heat only he could ignite.

He led me to the lounge area we had originally entered through. It was a sanctuary pieced together by muted colors and soft textures designed to shield us from Stonehurst's sharper edges. The couch swallowed me whole in its cushions as I sank into it; opposite me sat breakfast savories arrayed on aged wood. The simple aroma of buttery pastries battled relentlessly against lingering shadows clawing at the edge of my senses.

Cole stood near one of the tall windows which overlooked the sprawling academy grounds. He had said little since what happened in the clearing. He just kept looking over at me with sadness in his eyes. But that sadness was bound by something else, a blood lust, a pure defined anger for Andrew's head on a spike.

"Come sit down, Cole," Jake said. "You're scaring her."

I looked at Jake and smiled weakly.

"I..." I tried to speak, but my mouth was so dry and full of unspoken screams I dared not open it for fear I'd never stop screaming.

"It's okay," Jake said, sitting on the other side of me. He placed my hand in his. "We are here for you."

I frowned. But why? I wanted to scream. Why?

Draven smiled. "You know why," he said, anticipating my question. "We know you're ours."

I swallowed what felt like sandpaper and winced. Cole walked over, kneeled in front of me, and passed me a drink of water. "Here, drink this sweet girl."

I nodded. "You can talk to us. There is nothing you cannot say to us, Amy."

I nodded again, taking a large drink of water and finishing the whole glass. Cole laughed. "You were thirsty."

"Blood," I said, regaining my voice. "All I could taste was his blood."

Draven smirked. "Now, did you stab him again?"

I pursed my lips. "I, I bit his finger off."

"That's my girl," he said, laughing. "See boys, I told you she's a fighter."

"Good! We didn't want to end up with one of those prim and proper snobbish Omegas."

I laughed. It felt good to laugh.

Chapter 13

The following day, I awoke bright and early in my room, having finally drifted off at about three in the morning. I turned over to find Nora and Janine hogging the bed. Draven had demanded they look after me because of yesterday's unfortunate turn of events.

When I told them what happened, Nora cried. That's when I found out the vile scum Andrew Calloway had attacked and raped her during her first week here at Stonehurst Academy. Apparently, after he got his fill, he'd leave you alone. I felt sick to the stomach. No one was there to protect my friend, and I almost wished I'd been caught sooner so I could have murdered Andrew in his sleep.

Janine found out that the dickhead Alpha was residing in a private hospital, and under the protection of his father; who would soon visit the academy to look at its security measures.

Apparently, Andrew's attack was unprovoked, and they were determined to find the culprits who'd done it. It sounded like Daddy Dearest hadn't been told the truth about what his son had been up to. I just hoped it would stay that way. The last thing I wanted was the Penthouse Alphas getting into trouble for saving me... again.

After my shower, I wiped the steamed-up mirror and saw that I was sporting a black eye. "Wowsers!" Nora said. I jumped as she appeared from nowhere. "You're gonna get pulled in to see the Headmistress with that!"

"With what?" Janine shouted from the bedroom.

"My eye," I said, walking in while pulling my top over my head.

"Bugger me, that's a corker!" She laughed. I pursed my lips and smacked her on the shoulder.

"Not helping!"

She laughed some more.

"Here," she said, pulling me to the sparse vanity unit. "Sit your ass down. We've got work to do!"

Over half an hour later, and layers upon layers of foundation and concealer, you could hardly notice the bruise. It looked like eyeshadow. Although, it was hard to match the color of the other eyelid. Still sore too, especially after the constant sponges worked their magic.

The girls showed me another path to the Academy. One that walked around the outside of the wood. Granted, it took fifteen minutes longer, but I didn't fancy being in the dark anytime soon. It didn't matter though, because as soon as we made it around the wood, the Penthouse Alphas were there waiting for me.

"Going somewhere?" Draven asked, while leaning against the stone wall, arms crossed.

I smiled.

"Looks like that black eye is covered up nicely," Jake said, throwing his arm around my shoulder, smothering me in the scent of roses. I groaned, and he chuckled. The girls laughed, following behind. "Let's get you some breakfast," he said, pushing me towards the cafeteria.

Cole and Draven followed, continuously checking the area and surveying the hall for any issues.

Draven even walked with me to get breakfast... albeit silently. But he never took his eyes off of me. As we approached the end of the cereal, he poured me a coffee and our fingers touched. Sparks ignited between us and I almost dropped the coffee. He smirked, steadying it. "Feeling a little clumsy?"

I shot him a narrowed glare, my nostrils flaring in frustration. "Will you be shadowing my every step now?" I demanded, leaning forward to snatch an apple from the bowl at the end of the row. He stood behind me, leaned over my body and in one swift motion, he grabbed me around the waist and pulled me flush against his chest, inhaling my scent with a possessive hunger. "We will follow you wherever you go, Amy Anderson," he growled, his voice sending shivers down my spine. I arched back into him, tilting my head to give him access to my neck, and he took full advantage, trailing fervent kisses along my neckline and down my collarbone. His teeth grazed along where my mark would one day be. "You're mine," he asserted. "Always and forever."

I wanted to ask why, but was interrupted by an angry giant.

"Come on!" A giant Alpha with a grumpy attitude said. "You're holding up the line!"

Draven whirled around, still holding me, and growled at him. I shook my head, pulled out of Draven's arms, grabbed my tray, and walked over to the table. I was sad to admit that I already missed his touch, his warmth, his scent. The way he'd held me just now possessed me. I wanted more of it. I scoffed at the thought of it. I, Amy Anderson, the girl who never aspired to be an Omega, the girl who took suppressants to be an average Beta. Was I giving in to my Omega instincts? I wasn't... was I?

Sitting down in silence, I noticed that the Penthouse Alphas were all staring at me, making sure I ate something. I pursed my lips. Why were they insistent on following me around? Granted, I was happy about it. Who wouldn't be? They were drop-dead gorgeous! But why were they interested in me? I wasn't the cream of the crop around here.

They can't scent me yet. Can they? Had the Doc given me the full dose at the clinic? I chewed on my lower lip. Even if she had, it would buy me a few weeks.. But then again, with how my body had been reacting, I doubted I'd last a week without another dose. Was it possible I was starting to scent?

I curled up next to Janine. She nudged me back. "Boundaries love. I'm trying to eat this delicious piece of, well, whatever it is." I chuckled at her words.

"Janine, can you scent me yet?"

"That's a rather personal question," she said, laughing.

"And no, but I'm not an Alpha. Those assholes have noses trained for smelling out Omegas a mile off. Why?"

"I'm wondering why the Penthouse Alphas are watching my every move."

Nora bounded over and sat opposite me. She looked over at the Alphas, smirked, and then said, "Isn't it obvious, Cherry Red? They're your scent matches."

"Well, obviously!" Janine rolled her eyes, then swatted Nora on the arm. "But I was waiting for our little miss here to come to that conclusion herself."

Nora huffed at her.

My mouth remained open. I'd considered it. I knew that deep down. But to hear someone else say it out loud made it even more real. I looked over at Draven, Cole, and Jake. They were my scent matches, and that meant, goodbye Beta existence, hello Omega servitude. I bit my lip again. Was I ready for that? Ready for being a possession? A nobody? Surely, they wouldn't see me like that though? Aren't Omegas supposed to be scent matched with an Alpha pack that would be perfect for them? I tapped my fingers on the table, all while Janine and Nora looked at each other and shrugged. But what if the goddess thinks I need reigning in? I looked over at the Alphas, my Alphas, and sighed. No matter how attracted I was to them. I couldn't risk them controlling me. I had to get out of this place and save other Omegas, just like I had before. No Omega was property; mistreatment, confinement, and enslavement were unacceptable terms to live by.

"Are you okay?" Nora asked.

"Yeah, just thinking."

She smiled. "Having a scent match is a good thing,."

I took a deep breath. "I know, but ultimately, I need to escape this place and continue my work on the outside. There are too many Omegas that need my help."

Nora leaned forward and placed her hand on my arm.

Within a split second, Draven was behind me, his hand on my shoulder. "Is everything okay, Amy?" he asked, glaring at Nora. Nora sat back and paled.

I rolled my eyes. "Yes, I'm fine. You don't need to babysit me."

Cole and Jake walked over, hovering over me. Janine edged to the side.

Three glorious scents intermingled, making me gasp, and biting my lip, I edged ever closer to them. Draven growled when I licked my lips. Their combined scent threatened to send me over the edge.

Janine's eyes widened as she watched me. She nodded at Nora, and they both got up, making a lame excuse to leave, giving us space. I huffed, annoyed at my friends bailing on me.

Jake sat beside me and slung his arm around me. "What's wrong, baby?" he asked.

Baby? I wasn't sure about being seen as an infant who couldn't do anything for herself. But I'm sure he meant it in his own affectionate way.

I sat up straight, trying my damned hardest to ignore their panty-wetting scents that curled up my nostrils and caressed my body, promising climatic screams of pure bliss.

Draven scented the air, and the corner of his lips raised when he looked at me.

"Are you scenting me?" I asked. It seemed best just to get it straight out in the open.

Jake smirked and Cole kneeled in front of me, placing his hands on my thighs, trailing his fingers up and down the inside of my thighs. "Did you think your half-hearted attempt at a suppressant could stop us sweet girl?"

I growled under my breath. "So does this mean..."

"Yes," he said, his eyes dark and hooded. "We're your scent match."

Chapter 14

I wasn't proud of my next move. I bolted up from the cafeteria table, my chair clattering to the ground with a betrayal as loud as the chaos in my head. The revelation slapped me across the face like an unwelcome gust of winter wind: I was a scent match for the Alphas. The very fabric of my being recoiled at the thought. For a long time, suppressants had protected me from a world determined to confine me. And now? Now, that armor was dissolving, leaving me exposed and raw.

"Damn it," I muttered under my breath, my feet already carrying me away from the sea of blue and white uniforms, away from the suffocating reality they all accepted without question. My past life—a meticulously crafted lie of being a Beta—crumpled like a discarded piece of paper within my clenched fist. What did this mean for me, Amy Anderson, the girl who could outmaneuver any Alpha with a sharp tongue and sharper wits?

The corridors stretched endlessly as I sprinted, each echo of my footsteps a drumbeat to my rising panic. 'Just breathe,' I told myself. But oxygen seemed scarce when every breath was laced with fear. Fear of becoming just another Omega possession, locked away in a golden cage.

“Where are you going?” someone called after me, but I didn't turn back. Couldn't. The walls of Stonehurst Academy closed in, gothic and suffocating, as if the gargoyles perched on high had come to life, their stone eyes tracking my desperate flight.

Students blurred past, constant chatter, doors banging. It was almost like a regular old school, except it wasn’t.

As I weaved through the maze of Stonehurst Academy's oppressive stone halls, each whispering portrait of long-dead Omegas seemed to mock me with their painted-on serenity. 'You're next,' their eyes seemed to say.

“Over my dead body,” I shot back, my voice barely above a breath. The last thing I needed was some nosy student reporting my mutterings to the Warden.

I slipped past a group of Alphas, their postures radiating arrogance and entitlement. They didn't even notice me, too caught up in their self-importance. Good. Let them ignore the Omega who'd bring their world crashing down around them.

"Out of the way," I growled when a younger student stepped into my path, her eyes wide with surprise. She scurried aside.

Bursting through the heavy doors, I stumbled into the Academy's pristine gardens. The place was a cruel joke. A splash of color in a world that preferred its shades of control and conformity. Rose bushes clung to carefully sculpted trellises, their thorns as sharp as the reality slicing through my chest. Leaves rustled in whispers of pretend freedom, while the neatly trimmed grass seemed to laugh at the very idea.

"Great," I muttered, the words catching on a ragged breath. "Even the damn flowers are in on it."

I stalked past a fountain, its water dancing in the sunlight. How many Omegas had sat here before me, contemplating a life bound in invisible chains? My shoes crunched over the gravel path, each step an echo of my frantic heartbeat.

The further I went, the more the garden walls seemed to close in. I knew I should be grateful for the solace, yet all I felt was trapped, ensnared in a reality I'd never asked for.

That's when I saw it again. A flower so dangerous it should never be allowed to grow in areas such as these. With its deep purple bell-shaped flowers and dark green leaves, it stood testament to the fact that perhaps there was a little luck on my side after all. Belladonna, or deadly nightshade, as some might know it. It was the perfect poison for the pack that had caused me so many problems. I would sleep better at night knowing they no longer walked these corridors. I just needed to take some without touching the stuff. Easier said than done.

I ended up using a page I ripped from one of my class books to cover my hand and pick the herb, placing it inside the book for safekeeping.

A secluded bench beckoned me like a siren's call, tucked away beneath a weeping willow whose branches swept the ground with a sorrow that matched my own. I dropped onto it, the weight of this new Omega identity crashing down on me like a ton of bricks.

My hands shook, lips trembled. I needed to think, not full-on sob my heart out, which was exactly how I felt right now. My chest squeezed beyond belief. Even the open air became claustrophobic.

The poison would wait. I had bigger problems. I'd found my scent matched pack, and they knew it.

The bench was cold against my back, the wrought iron as unforgiving as the society I was up against. I took a few deep breaths, unclasping my hands and concentrating on calming my racing heart down. From Beta to Omega—just like that. All because of a scent match. A damn scent that had lain dormant, hidden beneath layers of suppressants and false bravado.

My mind raced back to simpler times, to laughter in the training ring with Kurt, to that spark of pride in my brother's eyes when I landed a solid punch. They'd taught me to fight, but how do you throw a punch at your own biology?

How was I supposed to live a life of servitude? Being controlled not just by an electric collar, but by three entitled men who would use and abuse me? The salty taste of tears caressed my lips. I sniffled, wiping them away, trying to stop them from flooding out, but it was too late. Too much had happened, too much was going to happen. How was I meant to help the Omegas I was taking care of? What about the Safehouse? The birthing grounds? It was all real. I needed to warn them!

I was cracking, splintering under the pressure of a truth I could no longer hide. The expectations, the rules, the destiny I was supposed to fulfill as an Omega. It was all bearing down on me, threatening to crush the spirit I had fought so hard to protect.

"Mom," I whispered, her memory a balm and a curse. She'd been caught in this same snare, and I'd be damned if I let history repeat itself. Her strength was mine; her fire burned in my veins.

I hiccupped back a sob. "Guess it's time to burn it all down," I decided, a wry smile pulling at my lips despite the tremor of fear. "After all, what's a revolution without a little flame?"

The crunch of gravel underfoot snapped me back to the present, a jolt tearing through the fog of my thoughts. I jerked upright, my heart slamming against my ribcage. Three figures emerged from the shadowed archway, their Alpha uniforms crisp against the twilight.

"Easy, Amy," Draven said, his voice a deep timbre that seemed to resonate with the garden's silent hum. His hands were raised in a calming gesture. Beside him, Cole mirrored the action, an ocean of concern washing over his features. Jake trailed behind, eyeing me cautiously.

"We didn't mean to scare you," Draven added, his tone gentle as if he were coaxing a wild animal not to bolt.

I eyed them warily. My body tensed for flight. "What do you want?" The words came out sharper than I'd intended, but vulnerability had no place here, even less so now.

"Only to talk," Draven assured, taking another careful step forward. His gaze held mine, steady and sincere. "We didn't mean to scare you." I nodded, sniffling, regretting crying in front of them. Draven sat beside me and wiped my tears with his thumb. He placed his arm around me and pulled me into his chest. "We're here for you, Amy," he soothed. "Always and forever."

Cole sat on the other side of the bench and placed his hand on my thigh, stroking me gently. Jake joined from behind, but instead of carefully wrapping his arms around me, he grabbed the three of us in his arms and yelled, "GROUP HUG!" I burst out laughing.

Draven swatted him, and he went flying backwards. "What? It made her laugh, didn't it?" I smirked again, turned around on the bench, and offered my hand out to help him up. "Why thank you, baby!" I rolled my eyes.

"I'm not sure about the whole 'Baby' nickname."

"But..."

"But I guess I'll get used to it."

He grabbed me from behind and squeezed me way too hard. I coughed. "That's my girl!"

I pursed my lips together for a moment. Cole was watching me. He smiled softly. "We're not here to claim or control you, Amy," he said. "We just want to talk."

"Talk?" I asked, brow furrowed. "What do you want from me? I'll have you know I'm a terrible cook."

Draven laughed. "We don't want you to cook for us."

"Or do any of the other shit they teach you in this awful place!" Cole said.

My eyes widened, and I turned to look up at him. "You disagree with the way Omegas are taught to provide for Alphas?"

"Heck, yes!" Jake said. Cole nodded in agreement.

"Of course we do, Amy! Look, there's a lot you don't know about us."

"I'm beginning to see that."

Cole squeezed my hand. "We see you as our equal, sweet girl."

My jaw dropped. I don't think I'd ever heard an Alpha, including my brothers, call an Omega an equal.

"We do," Draven said.

"But, why?"

Draven sighed. His brown eyes seemed to see right through me when he spoke. "There's something we need to tell you," he began, his voice steady but laced with an undercurrent of pain. "About my sister, Scarlett."

"Our sister," Cole corrected. "Just because she's not my blood, your family is my family Draven!" Draven nodded in thanks.

"Scarlett?" I repeated. Her name seemed so familiar.

"Yes, she's an Omega too," Cole said. "The Taskforce took her." He squeezed my hand a little tighter. "She was too fierce for this world. Too much fire and spirit. They said she was a threat to the *natural order*."

"Because she fought back," Jake continued, the muscle in his jaw ticking. "Like you, Amy. She wouldn't be broken. And now, we're trying to find her, rescue her from wherever they've stashed her away."

Then I remembered. Scarlett. There was a girl called Scarlett who had been staying in my room and was taken to the Birthing Grounds.

My brow furrowed as I recited what Janine had told me when I'd first arrived. Draven hugged me, pulling me in tight to his chest. His oceanic scent washed over me, cleansing me with memories of pure happiness.

"Is that why you're here?" I asked them.

They all nodded. "Because everyone says you don't need to be here."

"No, we rebelled against taking an Omega, so our parents sent us here to 'improve' before forcing one on us."

I shook my head. "Why weren't your parents trying to help Scarlett?"

Jake sighed and placed his hand on Draven's shoulder as Draven looked down to the ground. "Draven has never had a great relationship with his parents," he said.

Draven looked up, his brow furrowed, anger framing his features. "Not when they believe in chastising females and using them as nothing more than breeding machines."

I chewed on my lower lip. "So, let me get this straight," I said, looking at Draven. "Your parents are working with the Taskforce."

Cole shook his head. "No sweet girl, they are the Taskforce."

My eyes widened. "But Andrew? His dad runs it… doesn't he?"

Draven nodded. "He does. He's a founder, as are our parents."

"Well fuck me!"

Jake smirked. "If you're asking nicely, then bend over, love."

I rolled my eyes and swatted him on the arm.

"So, how are you going to find your sister?"

"We're not. At least not while we're stuck in this place. We need to get out."

"Now you're talking my language," I said, smirking.

"There she is," Jake quipped, monkey scrubbing my head.

"Hey!" He grabbed me and started tickling me under the armpits. I couldn't stop laughing, which of course set Cole and Draven off too.

By the time we'd settled down, I was lying on Draven, my legs up on Cole, with Jake sitting on the floor against us. It felt like heaven. Perhaps the goddess had got it right after all.

"How did you get caught?" Cole asked me.

I sighed, the weight of years bearing down on me. I told them about the clinic and the suppressant run. Jake nodded. "You see, my mom wasn't given the choice to fight or flee." My voice wavered, spilling secrets I'd hoarded like stolen treasure. "The Taskforce paired her with my Alpha fathers when she was eighteen. Luckily, they treated her well. But she still was never given the choice."

"Your fight—it's personal," Jake said, looking back at me. I nodded.

"Personal doesn't even scratch the surface. It's ingrained, etched into every cell," I admitted. "I refuse to wear her chains."

"Nor should you," Draven murmured, his hand finding mine, a simple touch that spoke volumes. "We will always protect you, Amy. And we will never force you to do anything. We will wait for you to say you're ready." I smiled at that.

"So, you'll protect me against the world?" I half-joked, though the prospect seemed less daunting with these three at my side.

"Especially against the world," Cole affirmed, his grip firm on my other hand. "Together, we'll rewrite the rules."

"We hear you, Amy," Draven said, his voice as steady as bedrock. "Your fight is our fight."

"Equality isn't just a dream," Cole added, the intensity in his gaze igniting the air between us. "It's a birthright, one we'll claim for every Omega. No matter the cost."

I nodded, my heart hammering a frenzied beat against my ribs. "Good," I breathed out, a smirk tugging at the corner of my lips despite the gravity of our pact. "Because I plan on being a damn nightmare for anyone who thinks they can put chains on us again."

Jake chuckled, the sound a low rumble that vibrated through my bones. "Well, nightmares are our speciality."

Draven's hand brushed a strand of hair from my face, a touch so tender it threatened to unravel me. "Let them try to tame you. They won't know what hit them."

At that moment, the garden's lush prison melted away. The towering walls of ivy and the wrought-iron gates seemed less like barriers and more like challenges waiting to be conquered. As the Alphas stood with me, I realized I wasn't just an Omega or a rebel. I was an inferno waiting to set their world ablaze.

"Okay then," I said, letting out a long breath I didn't realize I'd been holding. "No more running. From now on, we'll take the fight to them."

"Exactly," Jake said. His voice melded into a harmonious promise of defiance.

Draven's arms encircled me, an embrace that was anything but confining. It was strength, warmth, and an unspoken understanding that here, in this secluded pocket of rebellion, we were equals.

As I leaned into his hold, my body relaxed, each muscle unwinding from its coiled readiness. In the quiet comfort of their presence, I allowed myself to be vulnerable, to be comforted without losing the essence of who I was—an Omega, yes, but also a force to be reckoned with.

"Thank you," I whispered, my voice barely audible over the rustling leaves. "For seeing me. For standing with me."

"Always and forever," Draven responded, his words a gentle wind chasing away the last of my hesitation.

Chapter 15

The next morning, I traipsed down the corridor after my first class of the day. Homework. I was given homework! I couldn't help but scoff at the absurdity of what it was. Smirking, I continued walking towards the library. My homework was to learn how to make a bed. I coughed out a laugh. I mean, that's something kids learn at home. But no, not any kind of bed, but a bed with hospital-style corners, folded at a forty-five-degree angle, and tucked under the mattress. This was to ensure the sheet would never move beneath the person sleeping in the cozy nest of a bed.

I turned the corner, passed the canteen, and dodged an Alpha pack that leered for a little too long.

So, I was tasked with changing my sheets. I shook my head. I'd been doing that daily because of bloody night sweats! This place was a joke!

The second lesson had proved to be just as challenging.

The sharp scents of herbs and spices filled the air, making my nose twitch in response. But amidst the chaos and confusion, I found solace in cooking. As I mixed ingredients, memories of my mom came flooding back. Her graceful movements around the kitchen, and her polka-dot dress as it swayed to an invisible beat when she baked bread or my dad's favorite cakes. They all had a notorious sweet tooth. I often perched on a stool, observing her techniques or playfully sifting through flour, most of which covered me instead of the cake tin. Despite the mess, those were some of my fondest memories.

"What's so funny?" Cole asked as he started walking beside me after class. I jumped when he appeared, sneaking along like a shadow in the darkness, unseen and unheard.

The air twisted and writhed, a suffocating weight pressing down on my senses. Each breath required immense effort, like inhaling through a straw while being crushed by a boulder.

I swallowed; my mouth was drier than the Sahara Desert.

What the hell?

He brushed his fingers through his deep brown hair, twinges of purple catching under the light. His brown eyes bore holes into my soul as his tanned skin and muscular body made me all sorts of giggly inside.

Damn it, Anderson! Get a grip! He may be my scent match, but I was still in control of my body, not these damn Omega hormones!

I sighed. Damn, he was hot.

He watched me as we continued to walk in silence. I still hadn't answered his question. But by the frown on his face, he was studying me, probing, searching, working something out. I wasn't sure if it was something good, or something I should run from.

Reaching the library, he grabbed my arm and swung me into his chest. I gasped. His scent was everywhere, dancing all around me, washing over my entire body. The sweet floral scent of champagne, a favorite of mine. One my family would have on summer afternoon picnics when all of us would come together, laugh, joke and have fun. Wonderful memories were made with champagne. It felt like home.

He grinned at me, yet his eyes spelt mischief as he looked down from his six-foot-four appearance.

"Why are you following me again?" I asked when my constricted throat finally relaxed.

"Why wouldn't we be? You're our Omega."

I rolled my eyes.

"Plus, I want to know what you found so funny?"

I stopped outside of the door to the library, my eyes widening. "You were watching me?"

"Was that a question?"

I narrowed my eyes. "The homework."

It was his turn to frown now.

"You asked what I found so funny. It was the homework."

"And why does your homework amuse you?"

I sighed, staring at him. His scrumptious scent wrapped me in its sweetness, promising me bubbly highs. "Because they want me to change my sheets."

He smirked. "Really? That's the type of homework you Omegas get?"

"Exactly. It's stupid!"

He laughed. "You're not much of an Omega, are you?"

"Rude. But no, I never wanted to be one. I'd much rather take your role. Tell you what, let's swap!"

He laughed again, placing his hand on my arm. "Sweet girl, you wouldn't last five minutes with a pack of Alphas like ours."

"I fear you underestimate me, Alpha."

"I fear you overestimate your skills, Omega." He stood watching me for a moment. "I say we put those skills to the test."

"Hey no thanks, I'm not into any of your weird shit."

"I'm sure Omegas aren't supposed to say shit."

"I'm sure the Omegas you've been hanging around with have been boring then." Grinning, he nodded.

"So, how about that test, sweet girl?"

I bit my lower lip, which made him growl, and as he did, shivers ran through my body, pulling me closer to him. I shook it off. "An arm wrestle now, in the library," he demanded.

Laughing, I nodded in agreement. With my Beta training, I had to have half a chance... didn't I?

The library was a grand chamber, lined from floor to ceiling with books that seemed to breathe the dust of centuries. Ancient wooden ladders leaned precariously against dark oak shelves, reaching up to the domed ceiling that arched overhead, painted in a glorious symphony of colors that swirled together to create an enchanted sunset sky.

Sunlight filtered through the long ornate windows, finished with iron hinges, just like the doors.

"Heads or tails?" he asked as we whisked past a row of tables towards a cleared space where two leather armchairs sat opposite each other invitingly.

Positioning ourselves before one another, his eyes twinkled mischievously under the chandeliers and he rolled up his sleeve, revealing a monotone tattoo that snaked up and around him.

His firm hands clamped around mine, sending currents racing up my spine; our gazes momentarily locked, hinting at far deeper contests stirring within. An intense connection sparked between us as electricity sparked upon our touch. He pulled back and looked at me, then smiled and nodded. "Ready, Sweet girl?"

I grinned. "Are you ready, Alpha?"

I managed initial dominance, courtesy of my Beta training kicking in. I'd trained most days with my brothers, even though they were dead against me leaving my true nature behind. But they knew they'd never stop me.

I gritted my teeth as he applied more pressure and smiled some more, watching me. He wasn't even breaking a sweat! And here I was, huffing and puffing like I was trying to pull a brick wall down with my pinkie finger!

A playful smirk teased the edges of his features and he pulled down harder, seeming to enjoy making me sweat for him. I caught his scent as it bellowed out of him, engulfing me once again, teasing, tantalizing, until all I wanted to do was snuggle in his arms and let his hands roam over every part of me.

He chuckled, breaking his concentration, losing crucial seconds. So, I took advantage and mustered all my strength into pulling him down. I made him budge ever so slightly, but not before his other hand slid under the table and on top of my knee, eliciting an unintended jump from me and a sharp slam down for him. He smirked in triumph.

Instant heat flared through my face, matched by pouting as I accused him, "You cheated!" His laughter echoed throughout the eaves of the library.

His delicious smile remained, "Oh no sweet girl, I didn't cheat. I just redirected your focus!"

He extended his hand, helping me to stand, and what did I do, but stumble over the table leg and fall flat into his arms.

He laughed, holding me upright. "Perhaps you need to sit down for a while longer?"

I shook my head. "No, I'm fine, thank you. I wouldn't want to be seen with a cheater, after all." He laughed again, then looked at me.

"So, why did you want to come to the library?"

"Err... for a book."

"Well, that's obvious. But which one? Surely it's not how to make a bed, is it?"

"Ha, ha!" I stuck my tongue out at him. "No, I'm looking for something to read at night."

"Oh, I see. Well, I'm all out of ideas for that. But I know Jake likes to read fantasy romance."

I laughed. "An Alpha that likes romance! Whatever next!"

"No. 'Fantasy' romance."

"Ohhh, well okay then," I smirked.

"Come on. Last time he was here, he went down this aisle." He took my hand and pulled me after him. Sparks tingled beneath our fingertips again, igniting the bond we both felt between us.

Entering the aisle, two other female Omegas were there. But when they saw him, they soon fled.

I rolled my eyes. Why did everyone run from him? I pursed my lips as he scanned the books. I mean, I guess all of my Alphas gave off that asshole attitude. And they were all strong, stronger than any Alpha I'd met before. I wouldn't be surprised if they'd give my well-trained brothers a run for their money.

"Here," he said, handing me three books. One had a half-naked man and woman on the front cover. The other two had symbolic covers, but all three sounded action-packed, with a romantic plot line and the promise of a happily ever after... at least I hoped they had.

"Have you read these?" I asked.

He grinned. "No, I don't read books. It's movies for me, sweet girl. But you're welcome to stop by anytime and join me."

I smiled. "I'll think about that. After all, you did cheat."

He laughed.

"So, are these books Jake has read?"

"Yeah, he wouldn't shut up about them."

I smirked. I could imagine that would annoy him. "Well, tell him thanks. I'll give them a go." He beamed.

"I will do. Now scoot, sweet girl. The bell will ring soon, and you don't want to be late for class, do you? You need to learn how to be the perfect Omega."

I frowned, turned away, and flipped him off. He laughed as I left him behind.

Chapter 16

The door to the classroom creaked open, and I stepped through like a ghost haunting its own funeral. Stonehurst Academy was good at making you feel six feet under before your time. The air hung thick with tension, the kind that stuck to your skin and didn't let go. I scanned the room, found Nora's mop of curly blond hair, and made a beeline for her.

"Hey," I murmured, sliding into the seat beside her.

"Morning," she whispered back, her blue eyes searching mine for any sign of trouble brewing.

I couldn't help but smirk. Trouble had been my shadow since the day I'd popped out of the womb with more attitude than society cared to handle. The Penthouse Alphas were nearby. I could sense their presence. They were like static on a TV screen, impossible to ignore.

As if summoned by my thoughts, the door banged against the wall, announcing them. Silence clawed its way through the students, the kind of quiet that comes before a storm. Heads turned as they entered, all posturing and power. Draven led them. He locked eyes with me, and I felt a jolt down my spine. Not fear. Anticipation, maybe? I'd never been one to shy away from a challenge, and Draven Blackwood was challenging.

"Amy," he said, his voice deep and certain. It rolled over the room, commanding attention. "You're sitting with us now."

My heart kicked against my ribs. This wasn't just about seating arrangements; it was a claim, clear as day. Sitting with the Alphas meant protection, but it also meant being marked as theirs. Independence had always been my battle cry, but these days it seemed to echo back at me, distorted and strange.

"Is that an invitation or an order?" I shot back, tilting my head. My voice dripped with sarcasm, a weapon I wielded better than any blade.

"Consider it both," Draven replied, the corner of his mouth lifting slightly. He extended a hand, an offer, a command, all wrapped up in one gesture.

With a sigh that was part annoyance, part resignation, I stood up. Nora gave me a small nod—her way of saying, 'Go on, I've got your back.' And damn, I believed her.

"Fine," I conceded, matching Draven's smirk with one of my own.

As I squared my shoulders, ready to cross the room, the room became an arena of eerie silence. All eyes were on me, wide with a mix of shock and morbid curiosity. This wasn't just a walk across the classroom; it was a ceremonial march into a new reality where every step declared my allegiance.

"Go on, Amy," Nora whispered, her fingers brushing against mine in a fleeting moment of solidarity.

I took a breath, letting it out slowly, measuring my next move not in distance, but in the weight of consequence. The air bristled with unspoken warnings and whispers of a destiny rerouted. Every instinct screamed for me to dig in my heels, to resist the tide pulling me from the shore of who I was into their turbulent sea.

As I approached Draven, Cole, and Jake, they all sat smirking. I narrowed my eyes, considering throat-punching every one of them for making me walk the room like that. Assholes.

"Ah, there we go," Jake chuckled, a spark of mischief dancing in his eyes. "The Omega with enough backbone to make us all look soft."

"Watch it, Jake," I shot back. Jake's laughter, a rumble of genuine amusement, cut through the tension, a lifeline tossed into a stormy sea.

Sitting down amidst the Alphas, I allowed myself one last glance at Nora. Her smile was small but fierce, a beacon of encouragement. In that split second, her blue eyes seemed to say, 'You've got this.'

And maybe I did.

The drone of Mr Harkness's voice faded into the background as I settled into my new, unwanted throne among the Penthouse Alphas. My fingers tapped an anxious rhythm on the desk, betraying the calm I fought to maintain. The room had fallen into a routine hum. Textbooks scraped against the wood, pens scratched onto paper. It was bloody boring.

Then an Omega I didn't recognize stumbled in. A girl with tear-streaked cheeks and a blouse that hung off one shoulder, torn and telling a silent story of strife. Her breaths came out in ragged gasps, eyes darting around the classroom like a cornered animal seeking an escape that didn't exist.

"Miss Carver," Mr Harkness's voice cut through the air, laced with disdain. "Your disregard for punctuality is as glaring as your attire." The collective intake of breath from the class was almost imperceptible, but I felt it, electric and charged with fear.

"Please, sir, I—"

"Silence," he snapped. His thumb hovered over the button on his watch with a casual cruelty that made my skin crawl. Before anyone could react, he pressed it.

Her body convulsed, her cry a jagged edge that tore at the silence. The sound burrowed deep, igniting a fury within me. Fury at the academy, at the Omega Taskforce, at every oppressive shackle they clamped onto us. She crumpled to the floor, blouse agape, revealing a canvas of reddening flesh beneath.

"Let that be a lesson," Harkness declared, voice as cold as the stone walls encasing us. His gaze swept over the class, a warning to any who might have harbored thoughts of dissent.

The girl's body stilled, her whimpers tapering off into a silence that was worse than the screams. Before I knew it, my chair was scraping back against the floor, the noise jarring in the aftermath of her torment. I strode towards her, every muscle in my body coiled tight with anger and purpose.

"Miss Anderson, where do you think you're going?" Harkness's voice was like the crack of a whip, but I didn't flinch. The threat hung in the air between us, his finger itching to teach me a lesson too. But his eyes flicked past me, to where the Penthouse Alphas sat, and his confidence wavered.

"Helping someone in need. Isn't that what we're taught?" My words were laced with venom, daring him to contradict me.

"Sit down," he spat, but there was uncertainty behind the command, his hand lowering ever so slightly from the control panel.

Ignoring him, I knelt beside the girl, whose breaths came in shallow gasps. "Hey," I murmured, my voice a stark contrast to the harshness that had filled the room seconds ago. "You're safe now."

I glanced up as Jake sauntered over. His green eyes were dark with concern, despite the smirk dancing on his lips. "I can't leave you alone for a moment, can I?" He slipped off his sweater and draped it over the girl's shoulders, hiding the signs of the academy's cruelty.

"Consider it a loan," he quipped, trying to coax a smile out of her. It was a minor act, but it spoke volumes of the protective nature that lay beneath his playful exterior.

"Thanks, Jake," I said softly.

"Let's get you seated, okay?" I helped the girl to her feet, feeling the weight of her reliance on me. She nodded, her tear-streaked face contorting in a grimace as she moved. I shot Harkness a defiant look as we passed him, the unspoken challenge clear: try it, I dare you.

He didn't.

She settled into the seat beside mine. Jake moved to sit on the other side of me. The girl's breath hitched as she leaned closer, her voice a secret meant only for me. "It was Andrew Calloway," she whispered, a tremor lacing her words.

The name struck me like an ice bath, sending a jolt through my veins. That bastard—his very existence was a poison in our already toxic world. My hands clenched into fists beneath the desk, nails digging crescents into my palms. Anger flared hot and fast within me, a wildfire threatening to consume everything in its path.

"Hey, it's okay." My voice was steel wrapped in velvet as I turned to her, trying to infuse my words with enough conviction to chase away her fear. "He won't touch you again. Not while I'm here."

Before she could reply, a shadow fell over us, and the temperature in the room plummeted. Draven stood there, his presence commanding silence without a word being spoken. His brown eyes found mine, and in them, I saw the storm brewing.

"Repeat what you just said," he demanded, voice dangerously low, every syllable a thunderclap waiting to break.

"Andrew Calloway did this to her," I echoed, the name tasting like venom on my tongue.

A roar erupted from him, so primal and ferocious it vibrated the windows. Chairs screeched against the floor as students recoiled, their faces masks of shock and awe. Draven's fury was a living thing, a beast unchained, echoing off the stone walls of Stonehurst.

"Draven, hey!" I shot up, concern etched across my features. I placed my hands on his chest, moving into his embrace.

His chest heaved, eyes locked onto mine, the air sizzling around us. I knew then I'd reached him; my words were the tether holding him back from the edge. Slowly, the tension ebbed from his frame, though the promise of vengeance never left his gaze.

"He needs to know not to touch any Omega again!" he growled, the words laced with a protective menace that was oddly reassuring.

"Damn straight," I muttered under my breath, casting a sideways glance at the girl who now clutched Jake's jumper like a lifeline.

Without another word, Draven kissed my forehead and turned on his heel, a silent signal to Cole, who was already at his side. The door slammed shut behind them, leaving a void that sucked the air out of the room. Jake settled back into his seat, an unspoken guardian as he shot me a glance that said, 'I'm here.'

Mr Harkness, a Beta with more ambition than sense, tried to wrestle back control, his voice brittle with the effort to seem unfazed. "Let's continue," he spat, though his eyes kept darting to the door, betraying his unease.

As the lesson droned on, I could hardly focus on the words spilling from his mouth. They fell like dead leaves, brown and crumbled, discarded by the wind. My thoughts churned, caught in a whirlpool of worry for Draven and Cole. Where had they gone? What demon had Calloway's name conjured this time?

"Are they going to be ok?" I whispered to Jake.

He smiled and placed his arm around my shoulders. "Of course they will be. It's Andrew who should be scared, not you."

I smiled and nodded.

Absently, my fingers sought the penknife in my blazer pocket, its metal cool and familiar. Twisting it between my fingers, I felt the etched patterns, the vestiges of my father's touch. It was a talisman, grounding me to a time when things were simpler, when being an Omega wasn't akin to wearing a target on your back.

"Miss Anderson, are you even listening?" Mr Harkness's voice cut through the fog of my musings, sharp and jarring.

"Every riveting word," I muttered, the edge of sarcasm not quite concealed. My grip tightened on the penknife.

Mr Harkness's shadow loomed over me, his hand outstretched and demanding. "Give it here, Miss Anderson," he ordered, words clipped with cold authority.

"Give what?" I shot back, my voice laced with feigned innocence, though the metallic taste of adrenaline was already flooding my mouth.

"The knife, Amy. Now." His eyes were cold, a reflection of the institution's suffocating grip. I hesitated, the penknife in my hand feeling like the last shred of my autonomy.

"Or what? You'll zap me into submission?" My retort was a half-choked laugh, but the defiance in my gaze didn't waver.

"Your choice," he replied curtly before snatching the penknife and tossing it aside. A swift press of his remote, and pain exploded through my body, an electric fire that seared every nerve ending. I heard the collective gasp ripple through the classroom, yet all I could see was white-hot light.

"AMY!" Jake's voice was a distant roar as I convulsed, my muscles betraying me. Then, his hands were on me, steadying me even as they balled into fists, ready to strike.

"Touch her again, and I swear—" Jake's threat was cut off by the sound of the door slamming open.

Draven and Cole stormed in, their presence sending shockwaves through the charged air. Blood stained their knuckles, dripping onto the polished floor like rubies in a monochrome world.

"WHAT THE HELL DID YOU DO?" Draven's voice was thunderous, a primal growl that vibrated through my bones.

The teacher retreated a step, his earlier bravado dissolving under Draven's incensed glare. "She was... disruptive," he stammered, eyes flickering to the discarded pen knife.

"Disruptive?" Draven repeated, stepping closer, the threat in his posture unmistakable. "You hurt my Omega!" he growled.

Cole picked up the penknife, turning it over in his hands, his expression unreadable. The tension coiled tight; a spring ready to snap.

"Where we come from," Draven continued, his tone deceptively calm, "we protect our own. And you just attacked part of my pack."

I struggled to my feet, leaning heavily on Jake. Bile rushed up my throat and I gagged. Jake gripped me. "Draven, she needs to rest."

My legs wobbled and Cole came over and picked me up, allowing me to snuggle into his chest.

Draven roared, punched Mr Harkness, knocking him out cold, and said, "Class dismissed."

Chapter 17

The days rolled into weeks. Weeks of shitty lessons, sub-standard food and tearful Omegas. The only positive thing about Stonehurst Academy was having met my scent matched pack and two best friends that I owed my sanity to.

It had been another dull day, one where I had seen little of my Alphas. Sadly, we'd had no lessons together, and since the dreaded asshole, Andrew Calloway had been put back in his place. Which was, back in the hospital. I had little else to concern myself about. As long as I followed the rules. I smirked.

The last bell of the day faded as Janine materialized at my side, her ginger hair a flame in the sterile light of the classroom. "You serious about getting out?" she whispered, her voice slicing through the hum of departing students like a blade.

"Dead serious," I replied, my heart skipping a beat, adrenaline already coursing through my veins.

"Meet me after dinner in the hideaway. I have a plan!" she grinned. My eyes lit up. "But hey, watch you're not followed!"

"Yeah, yeah, I know the drill. Keep to the shadows and all that shit."

She rolled her eyes and smirked, then melded into the crowd.

Dinner was a bland affair. Even my Alphas weren't there. Where were they?

I pushed the soggy vegetables around on my plate, my mind elsewhere, waiting for the clock to signal the end of the day.

As the hall emptied, I pushed my dinner aside and smiled. It was time.

Slipping away from the remnants of chitchat and clinking cutlery, I headed down the uninviting corridors of the Academy that stretched before me like the belly of some ancient beast. My pulse hammered in my ears, and I kept my head down, making no eye contact as I drew closer to the hideaway, and the secret meeting that held the key to my shackles.

The door loomed before me, and with a last glance, I pushed it open and stepped inside.

The flicker of light greeted me first, casting long shadows that danced across the walls in a silent waltz with the darkness. Hushed whispers filled the space. My eyes adjusted, and I took in the sight before me. A collective of determined Omegas who carried the scent of defiance like a badge of honor. Who were all these girls? I recognized a few from classes, but not all of them. Which made me nervous.

And there she was, Janine Johnson, standing at the heart of it all.

"Hey, Amy," her voice sliced through the murmurs, commanding immediate attention. "So, everyone! Shut up!" Janine began, silencing the room. I smirked at her boisterous tone.

"Why are we here, Janine?" one girl said.

"Yeah," another girl asked. "It's dangerous to all meet together!"

Janine rolled her eyes. "Obviously! Which is why we have Ava's pack and Amy's standing guard."

"Wait, what?" I asked. How come I hadn't been clued in on this?

"Listen," Nora said. "We have a way out!" whispers traveled throughout the room.

"We tried your 'way out' last time and we nearly got caught, Nora!" groaned a red-headed Omega. I recognized her from the rebel's table at lunchtime.

Nora smiled. "Well, this time we have a map."

"We don't need a map, honey; we know the grounds."

"But you don't know the patrol routes and shift changes, do you?"

The rebel quietened; her lips pursed.

Janine smiled. "So, last month's attempt was a reminder," she said, her gaze sweeping over us. "They're watching closer than ever. But it's also proof that their grip isn't as tight as they want us to believe."

I edged closer, drawn in by the gravity of her words. "We've learned from those who dared before us. Their sacrifice won't be in vain."

My eyes narrowed. Sacrifice? Had there been more Omegas sent to the Birthing Grounds?

"Like Nora said, we've mapped everything out, memorized it." She tapped the side of her head as she said the word. "But it won't be easy."

"It never is," the rebel said, sighing.

I rolled my eyes. Janine continued. "Timing is everything. We must move under the cloak of night."

"Isn't that too risky?" someone whispered from the back.

"It's riskier to stay and hope for a mercy that will never come," Janine shot back, sharp and sure.

Then Ava Montgomery stepped forward. "Shock collars," she began, her voice low but clear. "They think it's what keeps us tamed. But they have flaws—weaknesses my pack and I have discovered."

Heads turned; attention rapt. Even in the dim room, I could see the spark in her eyes, the kind that ignited revolutions. "A quick burst of electromagnetic interference, timed correctly, can fry their circuits."

"Electromagnetic... you mean like a pulse?" I asked, my mind racing with the implications.

"Exactly," she affirmed, a smile touching the corner of her lips. "And I've been working on something. A gadget not much bigger than your palm."

"Does it work?" Another Omega asked. It was the girl I recognized as having sat with me during my culinary disaster. The question came from a trembling lip, a hope as fragile as glass.

Ava nodded. "It does. And I'll teach you all how to make one."

The room crackled with a new energy, electrified by the promise of Ava's words. It wasn't just a plan; it was a lifeline, a crack in the walls of our prison. I felt it then, the birth of something fierce and uncontainable within me, a determination that clawed at the confines of my chest, desperate for release.

"Then we prepare," Janine declared. "And when the time comes, we strike."

The echo of Ava's conviction still reverberated in the room as my pulse thrummed with a cocktail of adrenaline and dread. Possibilities tangled like live wires in my mind, sparking with each rapid heartbeat. My chest tightened with the gravity of what we were about to undertake. Was this hope or just another brand of fear? I wasn't sure anymore. But damn it, I was ready to find out.

"Listen up," Janine's voice cut through the excitement of escape. "There's talk. Rumors of a place beyond the reach of the Taskforce. A sanctuary for Omegas like us."

A collective inhale swept the room as if the very air we breathed had turned electric with promise.

"Somewhere out there," she continued, the lights casting shadows that danced across her determined face, "is a refuge where we're not pawns or prizes. Where we're people. Free to live without collars, without fear. It's uncharted and off the grid."

My imagination reeled, painting vivid strokes of a world unfettered by the iron grip of the Taskforce. A haven draped in the lush embrace of the wilderness, where laughter was unpoliced, and dreams uninhibited. Could such a place exist? Or was it an illusion, a mirage for the desperate?

"Does this place have a name?" someone asked, their voice barely above a whisper, as though too loud a word might shatter the possibility.

"Eden," Janine said, and the name fell upon us like a sacred decree.

"Janine," I spoke up, my voice steady despite the storm brewing within. "I want in. Whatever it takes."

"Good," she replied, a smirk tugging at the corner of her mouth. "Because it's going to take everything we've got."

After the meeting, I snuck out of the hideaway. My footsteps were silent against the cold stone floor.

"Running off to your little fantasy land?" Draven's voice startled me, a low rumble of amusement that echoed in the hollow space of the gymnasium.

He emerged from the darkness, his presence commanding the shadows to dance at his feet as he moved closer to me. The sight of him—tall, dark, and infuriatingly perceptive—sent a shiver up my spine that wasn't born of fear.

"Thought I might stretch my legs," I retorted, sarcasm wrapping around my words. "You know, before the curfew strangles all the fun out of the night."

"Curfew is for your safety, Amy," Draven said, smirking. Stepping closer, his brown eyes fixed on me with an intensity that felt like a weight I was too stubborn to carry.

"Right. Safety," I scoffed, crossing my arms. "Because nothing screams 'safe' like being caged."

"Listen, Amy," Draven began. There was an uncharacteristic hesitance in his tone that pricked at my curiosity. "This Eden, it's a gamble. It could be everything we've hoped for, or it could be a trap. But I swear if anything happened to you—"

"Then I'll have to be smart enough not to get caught," I interrupted, because I couldn't afford the luxury of his worry, not when it threatened to unravel me. "And strong enough to handle it if I do."

"Strength isn't always enough," he murmured, stepping closer.

"Good thing I've got you three then, isn't it?" I said, injecting bravado into my voice. The proximity was intoxicating, his scent a heady drug that dulled my senses.

Draven's lips twitched, a semblance of a smile that didn't quite reach his eyes. "Just don't forget you're mine, Amy."

"Never," I promised, though I wasn't sure whether it was to him or myself. I sidestepped him. His gaze followed me, heavy and heated, a brand upon my skin.

I slipped past Draven, and my steps carried me toward Cole, who was leaning against the cold stone wall by the entrance to the Academy. In the dim light, his eyes found mine—warm, brown, steady.

"Hey," he said softly, pushing off from the wall to meet me halfway. "You holding up okay?"

"Define 'okay,'" I replied, feeling the coil of anxiety in my gut loosen ever so slightly at his calm presence.

Cole's lips quirked in understanding. "Well, you haven't stabbed anyone else yet, so I'd say you're doing better than expected."

A chuckle eluded me before I could clamp down on it. "Give it time. The night is still young."

"Save some of that fire for when we really need it." He reached out and took my hand. "I'll walk you back to the Omega complex. Make sure you're safe."

"Thanks, Cole," I said, though the words felt inadequate for the gratitude swelling within me.

Before the moment stretched too long into seriousness, Jake bounded over with that irrepressible energy of his. "Are we plotting revolution or exchanging secret love letters?" he teased, green eyes alight with mischief.

"Both," I shot back, the edge of my nerves smoothed by his levity. "The love letters are written in code. Didn't you get yours?"

"Damn, must've been intercepted by the Alpha Post," Jake jested, winking. "I'll have to lodge a complaint with the mailroom."

"Good luck with that," I said with a snort. "You know how they love to meddle with our correspondence."

"True," Jake agreed, his smile softening into something genuine and warm. "But hey, if they're reading our mail, at least we're giving them something interesting to look at, right?"

"Always keep them guessing," I affirmed.

"Exactly!" Jake exclaimed, throwing his arm around my shoulders. "Now let's go show them what Omegas are really made of."

As we walked, Cole on one side and Jake on the other, I couldn't help but feel a surge of defiant hope. With Draven's strength as my foundation, Cole's empathy and Jake's playful spirit lifting the darkness, maybe—just maybe—we can turn this rebellion into something real. Maybe we'd escape this shithole of a place!

Draven joined us as we walked through the grounds, towards the creepy woods. "You're not seriously considering going through with this, are you?" His voice was a low rumble of concern.

"Considering? Heck, I'm all in!" I quipped, feeling the familiar itch of defiance under my skin. "Besides, I thought you'd appreciate a girl who can think on her feet."

His frown deepened. The protective furrow in his brow, as endearing, as it was infuriating. "Amy, this isn't a game. If they catch you—"

"Then I'll tell them the dark side seduced me. You know, led astray by a band of charming Alphas." My lips twisted into a smirk, even as my heart hammered against my ribs like a frantic bird seeking escape.

Draven growled.

Cole's hand brushed mine—a silent offer of solidarity that sent an unexpected shiver down my spine. "We will have your back, no matter what you choose to do," he said, his serene gaze holding mine.

"Thanks," I nodded, entering the woods, a shiver running down my spine.

Draven picked me up and pulled me into his chest. "You're cold," he said. I sighed, snuggling into his muscular body. I would not correct him and tell him the shiver was my fear clawing at my backbone. A fear of entering the woods for the first time since my attack. Janine, Nora and I had taken the longer route around the side ever since. I hadn't been ready to face it.

I bit my lower lip, looking around at the dark, looming trees, and the promise of violence, blood, and pain. Gripping my nails into my palms, I took a deep breath.

"You're safe now," Draven whispered to me, kissing me on the head as he continued walking.

"Thank you," I said. He had realized. I almost swooned at how he'd given me a way out of my anxiety without me even realizing it.

Taking a deep breath, I settled into him, listening to the sound of his heartbeat, as he carried me back to safety, to my apartment, to my home.

Chapter 18

Huddled in the shadowy corner of Stonehurst Academy's common room, we were a cluster of whispers and wide eyes. Ava was trembling, her usual unshakeable composure fractured by an all-too-familiar warmth that left no room for doubt. "Someone tampered with the vitamins," she hissed.

The air hung heavy with a sense of impending doom, thickened by the Gothic chill seeping through the stone walls. I could feel my panic rising like bile, realizing this wasn't an accident but a strategic move by the academy, a sinister plot to see us bound and claimed. It set my heart hammering against the tailored blazer of my Omega uniform—a symbol of subjugation that suddenly felt like a second skin, too tight around me.

"Stay calm," I urged, my voice low and fierce. Kurt's training whispered in the back of my mind, reminding me that panicking was what they wanted—an Omega in distress was easy to manipulate. But I wasn't just any Omega; I was Amy Anderson, and I'd be damned if I played into their hands.

As the others murmured about stolen futures and broken dreams, I swallowed the knot of fear in my throat, my determination hardening like steel. We had to fight to outsmart them at their own twisted game. But even as my brain whirred with strategies, my body began its own rebellion.

I felt it first as a mere spike of heat, a ghost of a touch that brushed against my senses, igniting something primal within. The sensation crawled beneath my skin, a slow burn that promised to erupt into an inferno. *Damn it, not now.* My breath hitched, and I pressed a hand against the cool wall, willing the creeping warmth to recede.

But it spread, relentless and consuming, like wildfire racing across a parched field. My skin flushed, betraying the battle raging beneath the surface. Pheromones, invisible yet potent, wove their treacherous scent into the air, marking me, claiming me as what I feared most, a beacon for Alphas.

Each breath felt laced with kindling, stoking the fire that threatened to engulf my senses. I leaned heavier against the wall, seeking solace in its unyielding coldness. I recognized the irony, seeking comfort from the very stones that formed my gilded cage.

My fingers curled into fists, nails digging into my palms in a futile attempt to anchor myself to reality.

The air shifted, signaling the arrival of my Alphas. Their gazes locked onto me like predatory animals zeroing in on a rabbit too dumb to realize it was meant for dinner.

"Damn it," I hissed under my breath as their combined scent hit me, the unmistakable musk of my Alpha's coiled around my body. Their arrival was like a punch to my gut, rattling the iron bars of my resolve.

Draven took the lead, his nostrils flaring as he inhaled the charged atmosphere. His eyes, dark and probing, never left mine.

Cole was more reserved, his gaze sweeping over me with a discernment that suggested he saw through the sarcasm-lined armor I wore better than anyone else.

And then there was Jake. "Looks like someone turned up the heat," he quipped, chuckling at his joke as if we were all in on some grand cosmic prank.

"Only you would find this entertaining," I shot back. My mouth felt dryer than the Sahara, the heat spike clawing its way through my veins.

"Can't resist a hot situation," Jake replied, winking.

"Shut it, Jake," Draven growled, his protective stance tightening around me.

"Relax. I'm just keeping the spirits up," Jake said, raising his hands in mock surrender.

"Enough," Cole interjected. His eyes met mine, steady and reassuring, somehow grounding me amidst the maelstrom of instinct and rebellion churning inside.

Draven pulled me close, and the intensity of the heat spike dimmed just a little.

Cole's hand brushed against mine. He watched me, reading the tumultuous waves that threatened to drag me under. There was no need for words; his presence alone spoke volumes, a muted strength that anchored me to the here and now.

Draven and Cole flanked me, their stances a silent vow against any Alpha who dared approach. It was a protective formation that both irked me and provided a measure of relief. I hated that I needed it, yet part of me clung to the safety it promised.

"Stick close," Draven instructed, his gaze scanning the room like a hawk. "We'll get you out of this."

"Out of the frying pan and into the fire?" I quipped, trying to keep the edge of panic from creeping into my tone.

"Something like that," he responded, the ghost of a smile fleeting across his face as his eyes met mine. In that moment, the world narrowed down to the charged space between us, a dance of wills and desires poised on the knife-edge of control.

The tension in the room coiled around us like a living thing, an electric current charged with primal instinct and unspoken threats. Draven's resolve was a tangible force, and Cole's silent support a steady pulse against the chaos that threatened to erupt.

But even as I acknowledged his steadfastness, a fresh wave of heat surged through me, a cruel reminder of the predicament we were in. My body began its treacherous rebellion, warmth spreading under my skin, igniting nerves and waking desires I'd fought so hard to suppress.

"Damn tablets," I muttered, clenching my fists at my sides. I knew those purple pills were all kinds of wrong. Why were we having heat spikes? We'd all taken one that morning.

Were they meant to bring on everyone's heat early? Or had someone tampered with them?

Draven's gaze sharpened, catching the subtle shift in my stance, the restless energy that vibrated just beneath the surface. "Amy?"

"I'm fine," I lied through gritted teeth, the word tasting like ash on my tongue. My mind raced, desperate for control, for a way to quell the rising tide that threatened to sweep me away.

"Sure you are," Jake chimed in, though his voice lacked its usual buoyancy. "And I'm the next Alpha Prime."

"Shut up, Jake," I snapped, the edge of desperation creeping into my voice. My independence was a fortress I'd painstakingly built, brick by stubborn brick, but now the walls shook with the force of my instincts. Every fiber of my being screamed to yield, to seek solace in the strength of the Alphas before me, but I couldn't—I wouldn't. But I knew I had no choice. Soon I would be out of control, and the pain would be unbearable unless they helped me. I growled under my breath, pissed at having my freewill taken from me. Again.

"Easy, Amy," Cole murmured, a note of caution threading through his words. "We're here for you. You're not alone."

But alone was exactly what I wanted to be, free from the smothering concern, the intense scrutiny, the undeniable pull of their presence. I needed space to breathe, to think, to fight the primal urges clawing their way to the surface.

Bursting through the double doors, I gulped in the frosty night air as if it were pure freedom. My boots thudded against the frost-kissed grass, each step propelling me deeper into the academy's manicured prison they called a garden.

"Your heart's racing," Draven observed, his predatory grace making my skin prickle with awareness.

"Maybe it's the thrill of impending doom," I snapped, desperately clinging to sarcasm like a shield.

"Or maybe..." Draven's voice trailed off as he closed the distance between us, "...it's because your body knows what you need even when your mind fights it." The charged air zapped with electricity as he inhaled deeply, a low growl vibrating in his chest. "You're having a heat spike, Amy."

"Observant much?'" My humor was a flimsy attempt to deflect from the truth, clawing its way out of me.

"Stop," I wanted to yell as his hand reached out, but my body swayed toward the warmth of his touch, yearning for the promise of safety and pleasure that came with his knot.

Internally, I was screaming—a desperate plea for him to stake his claim, even as my mind revolted against the very idea.

"Still so defiant," he murmured, thumb brushing against my jawline, sending sparks of unwanted desire down my spine.

"Always," I choked out, my words a mixture of pride and panic.

We were two magnets being pulled together by an unseen force, the invisible strings of biology and pheromones tugging at us with relentless determination. Every cell in my body was rebelling, eager to submit, to be claimed, while my spirit, fierce and unyielding, fought tooth and nail against the surrender.

"Draven," I whispered, the name a barrier against the wave of heat crashing over me. But it wasn't enough to drown out the primal part of me that craved his dominance, that wanted nothing more than to let go and let his scent envelop me, marking me as his.

"Why are you fighting it?" Draven's voice was gentle now, a stark contrast to the intensity burning in his gaze. "For them? For you? Or is it against something inside you can't control?"

"Maybe it's a bit of everything," I admitted, breathless with the effort to stay standing, to remain myself. And for a moment, the garden blurred, the world reduced to the space between us, electric and alive with our struggle.

I exhaled deeply, falling into his arms. "Control is overrated anyway," I added with a forced laugh, my last line of defense before the fortress of my will shattered completely.

Chapter 19

Heat. It slammed into me like a freight train, its fiery tendrils clawing at my insides, pulling at the threads of my composure until they frayed and snapped. Sweat beaded on my forehead, a treacherous giveaway of the battle raging within.

"Damn it," I muttered, willing my legs to stay rooted even as my body screamed for something else entirely.

Cole's gaze locked onto mine, his brown eyes steady pools of understanding in a sea of chaos. He knows, goddamn him. Without a word, he grasped my hand.

Cole guided me down, and the cool blades of grass kissed my skin through the fabric of my academy-issued skirt. I collapsed onto the grass, breathing ragged and heavy, the heat turning my bones to molten lead.

"Easy, Amy," Cole whispered, his voice low, grounding as he sat beside me.

I wanted to lash out, crack a joke, and do anything but admit how much I needed him right then. Needed all of them. Fear began to gnaw at the corners of my mind while longing built a nest in my chest. "I hate this," I confessed between labored breaths. "I hate how it makes me feel... vulnerable."

Cole's hand found my arm, a touch so gentle it set off crackles of energy across my skin.

Draven knelt beside me, his eyes held mine, his breathing heavy. Was he holding back too? But that thought was soon ripped away as a sudden, sharp pain speared my abdomen.

"Shit," I hissed, doubling over as my surroundings spun dangerously. The only thing grounding me was my nest of grass and leaves that I gathered to calm my tremulous thoughts.

"Breathe through it," Jake said, mimicking breathing in and out. I wanted to slap him. He stopped when he saw me glare.

If this is the sensation of a heat spike, then entering heat would be like a raging inferno consuming me. My hands flew to my midsection, trying to quell the fire that threatened to consume me from the inside out.

"Easy, Amy." Cole's voice was a distant echo, concern layered beneath the calm. Jake's hands were on my shoulders, a grounding presence amidst the chaos unfurling within me.

"Back off," I managed between gritted teeth, even as my body betrayed me with another wave of searing agony. It was a primal scream locked behind the walls of my chest, begging for release. But I clamped down hard on it, refusing to give in. Not here. Not in front of them.

"Let us help," Draven said, moving closer, his hand hovering just inches from my arm, poised to provide support or restraint—I couldn't tell which.

"Touch me, and I swear..." the threat died on my lips as another jolt of pain surged, stealing my breath and my bravado in one fell swoop. Tears fled down my face, and my hands fisted the grass, body slick with sweat. Pride be damned when your body declared mutiny.

The world tilted, a disorienting spin that had my senses reeling, each breath was an effort as Draven moved closer. His shadow looming over me. He pulled me into his chest and wrapped his arms around me with a force that was both ironclad and tender. It was like being caught in the eye of a storm, his embrace a barrier against the chaos that raged inside me.

"Got you," Draven murmured, his voice a deep comfort that vibrated through my bones. It reassured me, I knew that, but it also sent a thrill of something more primal skittering up my spine. My body responded before my mind could catch up, leaning into the solid wall of his chest as if it belonged there.

Stupid, stupid hormones. I mentally kicked myself, even as I burrowed closer, seeking the comfort his strength offered. The heat clawed at my insides, demanding attention, recognition, submission. But I wasn't some damsel in distress, ready to swoon into the nearest set of Alpha arms. Except, apparently, I was exactly that—at least physically.

As heat churned within me, relentless and demanding, I realized that maybe, just maybe, there was strength in this surrender. But I would never say it out loud.

Another spasm cut my thought short, a white-hot lash searing through my core. I doubled over, gasping, my nails digging even deeper crescents into my palms. Sweat beaded on my forehead, and I could feel the insidious pull of my Omega nature, begging for more of my Alphas' touch.

"Keep your damn hands off me," I gritted out, the words a garbled mess of pride and agony. But it was like arguing with the tide, the pull too strong, my resistance crumbling like sandcastles against the waves.

"Stubborn woman," Draven murmured, a ghost of a smile flickering across his lips. Even so, he held me close, knowing it would ease the pain, if only a little.

"Look at me, baby," Jake's voice broke through the fog of my pain, the usual jest gone from his tone. He was on his knees before me, his green eyes earnest and filled with something that looked a lot like fear. "You're not alone in this. Let us help."

"I can handle this," I rasped out, hating the way my voice cracked.

"Of course you can," Draven said, and I could hear the smile in his voice, the unspoken challenge.

I wanted to laugh, to make some cutting remark, but the next wave of heat stole the breath from my lungs. I clutched at my stomach, nails biting into the fabric of my shirt.

But hell, perhaps there was some merit in not facing everything by myself. Maybe there was a sliver of power in allowing myself this moment of vulnerability. Maybe, I thought, as Draven's arms tightened fractionally, the real strength lay in choosing which battles to fight and which to let someone else shoulder alongside you.

"Fine," I gasped out, hating the desperation in my voice. "But listen closely, you three. No bites. You hear me? We're not there yet!"

Their nods were almost imperceptible, a synchronized movement. Draven's gaze held mine for a moment longer, as if searching for any sign of retreat. But I was done running.

"Agreed," he said, his voice a low rumble that seemed to vibrate through the charged air. Cole's hand was steady on my shoulder, grounding me even as my body threatened to tear itself apart from the inside. His presence was like a shadow, cool and enveloping, as he leaned against me. He brushed against the fabric of my uniform in a touch so light it barely registered as contact.

My breath hitched, and for a second, I allowed myself to lean on him, to feel the solid reality of another person who didn't want to cage me. It was terrifying and soothing all at once, a flicker of hope dancing in the back of my mind, daring me to grasp it.

The heat surged through me like a tidal wave crashing against the cliffs of my willpower. I felt every blade of grass beneath me. Each one became a lifeline to cling to as my body convulsed with an instinctual need for relief. Draven, Cole, and Jake circled me, their movements attuned to the distress signals of an Omega in turmoil.

"Easy, Amy," Draven murmured. I laid back against his chest as his fingers trailed along my arm, igniting pathways of fire that both scorched and soothed.

Cole sat to my left, an immovable presence, his eyes locking onto mine with a clarity that seemed to pierce through the chaos. His quiet strength was the eye of the storm, a place where the wind held its breath and the world paused.

Jake's levity lingered in the air like a promise that not everything had to be a battle—a strange comfort amid the minefield of emotions inside me. He knelt and brushed his fingertips across my cheek, drawing a shuddering breath from my lips. The playful glint had vanished from his eyes, replaced by an intensity that pierced through the haze of my pain.

I fought to keep my mind above the waves of heat that sought to drag me under. But the primal urges within me were relentless, clawing at the edges of my self-control. My skin was ablaze. Sweat beaded on my brow.

I pulled my top over my head, struggling as another pain ripped through me. Draven ripped my top in two, pulled his top off and lay beside me, our skin touching, sparks igniting between us.

I groaned as I felt his hot breath on my neck, his fingers tracing invisible lines down my spine.

Cole growled, and I shivered in anticipation as he made his way between my thighs, pulling my skirt off and revealing my academy-issued lace underwear. One of the few luxuries we had.

His hand found its way to my thigh, tracing lines to my panties, teasing my clit through the fabric. I groaned, and Draven tilted my chin, our lips crashing together in a fierce kiss that left me breathless and wanting more.

"Mmm, you're soaking for us!" Cole said, as he gripped my underwear and ripped it in two. "Such a good girl!"

I moaned, squirming beneath him.

"You don't have to be scared, baby," Jake said, joining us. His hands roamed my body with expertise as he growled with desire, his lips sucking my nipple, before playfully biting and dragging his teeth over it.

Cole pinned my thighs down and lowered his head, running his tongue up and down my slit. I cried out, throwing my head back and grasping onto his hair. Cole groaned.

"Mmm! You like that, don't you, sweet girl," Cole said, then continued to suckle on my clit.

My hips involuntarily moved upwards, grinding against him in a frenzy. The sound of him drinking from me only added to the intense, erotic experience.

His tongue was skilled in the art of pleasure, never too hard or soft, always keeping me on the brink of climax. Every purr that escaped his lips sent ripples of sensation through my entire body.

"My turn," Draven said, stripping off and revealing his hot, throbbing cock. Cole pulled back, moving up my body, keeping his body next to mine. "Are you ready for me beautiful?"

"Mmm," I groaned. I could feel his growing erection pressing against me as he ground his hips into mine with intentional slowness that drove me wild with desire.

"More," I said, and Draven chuckled seductively.

Chapter 20

I wrapped my legs around his waist as he lifted me effortlessly and impaled me on his throbbing cock with one swift thrust that made me cry out in pleasure.

His thrusts were hard and unforgiving, each one hitting my G-spot with a surgical precision that had me seeing stars. I clawed at his back as I came hard, my juices flowing down my legs as he continued to pound into me.

Their hands were everywhere, pushing me to an edge I hadn't known existed. My breath hitched as waves of pleasure crashed over me, a crescendo of release that shattered the chaos into starbursts of clarity.

His release came soon after, filling me up with his hot, sticky cum that dripped down my thighs as his knot held me in place. Draven kissed me softly until his knot softened. We lay there, panting and sated, our bodies glistening with sweat as we basked in the afterglow of our raw and uninhibited encounter.

Draven eased out of me, and Jake moved in, when another flush of heat triggered throughout my body. "More," I moaned. He spun me over and pulled my ass in the air, slapping it.

"Such a tasty ass you have," Jake said, pretending to bite it. He pushed his fingers into my hole. I groaned. In and out, his fingers tempted and teased. Then the next thing I knew, he removed them and slid the tips of them into my bottom. I gasped and groaned. My head was low to the ground, presenting for him.

"Mmm," he said, pushing them in further, stretching me. My fingers tore at the grass beneath me.

"More!" I demanded, pushing back into him. I heard him laugh.

"Quite the impatient Omega we have here!"

Draven and Cole laughed.

"Come here," Draven demanded. I bit my lip and followed his gaze. Cole was sitting on his heels, his thick cock hard and ready for me. "Face Cole and mount him," Draven directed. I took pleasure in his dominance, giving in to the lack of control.

As I sat on Cole's cock, I kissed him hard and fast, our tongues grazing one another, searching deep inside. Sliding on, I cried out, biting my lower lip. The thrill was immense.

But Cole didn't move. He lent back a little. I gripped on to him, my legs wrapped around his waist, my core throbbing from his touch.

The next thing I knew, Jake pressed up against my back, the blunt head of his cock pressing against my anus.

"You're ours, Amy, completely," Jake breathed into my ear, his voice a velvet threat that made my skin tingle with anticipation and need.

I couldn't respond. The overwhelming sensations and the dire need to please them consumed me. My world narrowed to right now. To the taste, touch, and scent of these men who'd claimed me as theirs in every sense.

Then I felt it. Jake's cock pressing, seeking entrance beside Cole's. "Fuck, Amy," he groaned as he pushed the tip inside, his voice tight with restraint. "You're so fucking tight." A challenging stretch, a delicious burn as he pushed inside, made me feel even more owned, even more full.

I didn't care. I needed them. Needed all of them now! Pushing back against Jake, I urged him on. "I need you to fuck me, Jake. I need to feel your cock deep inside me too."

He pushed forward, and it burned, but the pain quickly gave way to pleasure as he filled me up, his thick cock stretching me wide open. A shiver of desire ripped through me and I moaned from the friction as Jake began to move.

He thrust his hips, slapping against my ass as he fucked me with long, deep strokes. I moaned with every thrust, my body quivering with intensity as he claimed me.

At the same time, Cole kept pace, thrusting harder and harder into me as I drove my hips into his lap.

"Mmm, look at all that slick!" Draven said, his hand around his cock, getting himself off.

Their movements became a synchronized chaos—pushing and pulling in a rhythm designed to break down any remaining barriers between us. Pain mixed indistinguishably with pleasure; it overwhelmed my senses until tears pricked at the corners of my eyes. Not from sorrow but from an overwhelming burst of every emotion possible spun together by their relentless loving.

"I need more!" I screamed, watching Draven and licking my lips.

Draven laughed, moving closer. "I need to taste you," I cried while screaming out in ecstasy at being fucked so hard.

Draven's eyes widened, and he licked his lips, moving closer so his cock was at the level of my mouth.

I eagerly snatched it up and licked the end. He moaned in response as I took his enormous shaft into my mouth and flicked my tongue around the head. It filled my mouth, almost making me gag with its size.

"You're doing great, Amy," he whispered as his hands entwined in my hair. "Just relax your jaw and take me all the way."

I wanted him. All of him. All of them. I needed them.

I parted my lips further, trying to take in more of him until he was thrusting against the back of my throat. Almost choking, I refused to pull away.

A primal growl escaped Draven's lips, "Fuck me, you look hot taking my cock like that!" His hand formed a fist around my hair. "Now be a good girl and suck my cock for me."

I growled, moving in and out, wanting more, sucking his length deeper, faster. Draven growled and responded by thrusting his hips back and forth, fucking my mouth.

I struggled to keep him in my mouth, coughing and choking as I tried to take him deeper. More saliva dripped from my lips.

"Fuck!" Draven yelled, gripping my head tighter.

Cole and Jake forced themselves into me faster and faster. Ruthlessly picking up pace, as Jake tweaked my nipples and Cole sucked at my neck. I moaned, more arousal pooling between my legs.

"You like that, don't you, sweet Girl?" Cole groaned. "You like when we're all fucking you together."

I moaned, taking Draven in more, gagging on his cock, my nails digging into Cole's back as I tried to force them all deeper into me.

The insatiable feeling of fullness spread throughout my body, each movement sending sparks of pleasure coursing through my veins.

The sensation of being utterly consumed by them blazed through me, a wildfire that left nothing untouched. Draven's grip on my hair tightened, the thrill of dominance clear in the way he commanded my actions. His sharp groans were like fuel, igniting an even deeper desire within me to please him. To please all of them.

Then, as if sensing my approaching edge, Jake leaned forward, his lips brushing against my ear. "Let go, Amy. We've got you," he whispered, his voice a soothing balm even as his movements remained relentless.

That was all it took. His words shattered the last of my resistance, and I spiraled into an explosive climax that tore through me like a storm. I screamed out in ecstasy, arching back into Jake as I quaked and convulsed around them.

Jake gave one last deep thrust before groaning loudly and spilling warmth inside me; his seed claiming me in a primitive act of possession. Cole wasn't far behind, each movement more determined until, with a low shout, he too surrendered, adding to the intoxicating sense of being owned.

Draven watched us with dark eyes, his breaths heavy as he pulled back from my mouth momentarily. Then, with a primal grunt, he pushed deep into my throat one last time before finding his own release, throbbing against my tongue.

I savored the plentiful amounts of hot cum spurting out of his cock as he exploded down my throat. He grabbed onto my hair tightly, intensifying the pleasure. The sheer volume of it made me gag, as it spilt down my breasts, and was lapped up by Cole, causing my body to tighten and release in waves of pleasure, again and again.

It was so hot to see him lick me clean. Draven pulled out, and I swallowed back, before he stooped to kiss me. Jake pulled me back to his chest, giving Cole's tongue access to the cum that had dribbled down and over my slit. I cried out at the sensation overwhelming me. He sucked hard, forcing my legs open, his fingers pushing inside, his mouth hungry for more.

"I can't," I cried.

Draven chuckled. "You can, one more time." he gripped my face, kissing me hard, absorbing my screams of ecstasy into him, tasting himself as my tongue found his.

Cole pulled away and fell beside me.

As my breathing steadied and the intense wave of fulfillment ebbed away, Draven leaned down and brushed a kiss on my sweaty forehead. "You are so incredibly strong and beautiful," he murmured with genuine awe, intertwined with lust in his deep voice.

Cole ran his fingers through my damp hair while Jake kissed along my shoulder blade.

I drew a ragged breath, feeling the weight of their gazes like a tangible caress. Draven's intense eyes seemed to pierce through my armor, seeing the turmoil within me. Cole's hand lingered on my arm, his touch grounding yet light enough to remind me he wasn't caging me in. And Jake, with a smile that held both mischief and understanding, sat back just enough to give me room.

"Looks like someone's coming back down to earth," Jake quipped. But his voice was softer, his words laced with an undercurrent of concern that didn't match the grin still playing on his lips.

"More like crashing back down," I muttered, pushing myself up to sit straighter, determined not to show weakness even as my strength waned.

I could feel the pull of their support. It was unnerving, this sense of connection, of belonging. The very thing I had fought against—this bond with Alphas—threatened to undo me in ways no suppressant ever could.

"Space. I need space," I said, more to myself than to them, but they heard the unspoken plea behind the words.

Draven nodded; his jaw set in a line of silent respect for my wishes. He took his shirt and placed it around my shoulders, helping me into it. "Here, your clothes are ruined. Take ours."

I nodded, thanking him and fastening the buttons.

Cole withdrew his hand, but his eyes stayed locked on mine, offering silent reassurance. Jake stretched his legs out before himself.

"Take all the time you need, Amy," Draven's voice rumbled, a deep sound that vibrated through the ground beneath us. "We're here when you're ready."

"Thanks, I guess," I grumbled, not quite ready to admit how much their understanding meant to me. A part of me wanted to rail against it, to fight the comfort they offered. But another part, a part I was only just beginning to acknowledge, craved the solace they provided.

As the last remnants of the heat spike dissipated, leaving behind a dull ache, I lay back on the grass, staring up at the sky where stars were peeking through the darkening veil. My mind raced with possibilities, choices stretching out before me like the endless night sky. Each path was fraught with its own dangers, its own promises.

The gentle whisper of leaves brushing against each other filled the night air, while the distant, mournful call of an owl echoed through the woods nearby. The Alphas, their eyes reflecting the moon's glow, settled into a respectful silence, giving me the space I needed, while remaining a steadfast presence.

As the cool breath of night drifted through the garden, it carried with it the scent of earth and the intoxicating promise of freedom. I closed my eyes, contemplating the path ahead, a path adorned with both thorns and blossoms alike.

As I drifted between wakefulness and sleep, I couldn't shake the feeling that whatever choice I made, it wouldn't be made in isolation. These Alphas, these infuriating guardians of mine, they had woven themselves into my story, and I into theirs.

"Tomorrow," I promised the darkness. "Tomorrow, I'll decide."

But as the moon rose high, casting silver beams across my face, I already knew that some decisions had already been made.

Chapter 21

I blinked awake, the last tendrils of sleep retreating like shadows at dawn. There was a thrumming under my skin, an electric buzz that felt like it could power the entire Omega Complex if I let it. Last night had been my first proper heat spike, and it was a bitch of one, but this aftermath was something else; it was like I'd swallowed the sun, and now its rays were leaking out of my pores.

My limbs stretched out on the bed, muscles tensing and flexing as if testing their newfound strength. The intense heat had scorched away more than just weakness; it had left behind a sense of clarity, a sharpened edge to my will.

Shuffling out of bed, I looked at the clock; it was lunchtime already, thankfully it was a Saturday, and I hadn't missed any classes! Still, I threw on my spare uniform, making a mental note to order another one after my boys had shredded my last one. I smirked, remembering all the juicy details.

When I was ready, I headed out of my apartment into the sunshine. Each step in the midday air was crisp but kind. As I reached the gates, I punched in the code, and the door to the outside world swung open with a reluctant creak, while I stood hesitating at what lay beyond.

Draven, Cole, and Jake were already waiting. Draven's piercing brown eyes met mine first, his gaze fierce enough to burn holes into the stone walls that caged us.

Cole's warm eyes held a softer flame, but the set of his jaw spoke volumes about his commitment. This was a man who rooted himself in the earth, steady and enduring. Yet the slight tension in his shoulders told me he was prepared for whatever hell we might have to walk through today.

And there was Jake, leaning casually against the gate. "Morning, baby," Jake called out, a smirk playing on his lips. "You look like you ate a guard for breakfast."

"I considered it," I shot back with a grin, stepping out into the crisp air. "But I figured I'd save my appetite for the big fish."

"Let's hope they're biting today," Cole said, his voice a low rumble that seemed to vibrate through the ground beneath us.

"Trust me," I replied, squaring my shoulders as we started walking through the woods and into the academy, "they won't know what hit 'em."

When we entered the academy, the rhythmic clack of our shoes on the polished floors set a cadence for the silent solidarity that bound us together. Draven's presence was a fortress beside me. His broad shoulders angled toward any potential threat. "Anything happens in there," he muttered, his voice low enough for just us to hear, "I'm right here."

"Wouldn't dream of it any other way," I said, the corner of my mouth twitching up.

Cole's hand brushed against mine, a fleeting but grounding touch. "Stay sharp," he advised, the undercurrent of concern barely hidden beneath his stoic exterior.

"Always am," I quipped, but the flutter in my chest acknowledged the weight of his words.

Jake's chuckle cut through the tension like a knife. "Just remember to duck if the food flies," he winked, and somehow, the idea of a full-blown food war didn't seem impossible.

"Only if you're cooking," I shot back, earning a snort of laughter from him.

We rounded the corner, and the cafeteria doors loomed ahead, a gaping maw ready to swallow us whole. With a collective inhale, we pushed through into the fray.

The clamor hit me first; Omegas darted between tables like spooked deer, their blue uniforms a blur of fear and confusion. Alphas squared off with the guards, the air thick with testosterone and aggression.

"Dammit," I muttered, taking in the chaos with a sweep of my gaze. "It looks like a battlefield." The perfect environment to sprinkle a pretty little topping on a certain pack's food, I thought. I dug my hand in my pocket for the bag of ground-up belladonna I'd prepared days ago. Those assholes weren't getting away with what they did to me. It wasn't just Andrew. It was his pack too.

"Stay close," Draven growled, moving instinctively to shield me as we navigated the bedlam.

With each step, the protective circle of my Alphas tightened around me, a living barrier against the turmoil. We moved as one, a unit carved from necessity and bound by an unspoken vow: to weather the storm together or not at all.

Amidst the uproar, my mind churned like a storm-swept sea. Omegas, usually so composed in their tailored uniforms, now thrashed against the current of control, their faces twisted with panic and desperation. Alphas, usually the picture of stoic authority, were now baring their teeth and bristling with dominance. And the guards, those pawns of the regime, stood rigid, batons at the ready. I spotted Andrew and his two pack members two tables down and made my way towards them. Draven stopped me when I reached the table. Andrew stood up. His pack members too.

"Something's not right," Draven murmured, his voice barely audible above the fracas.

"Understatement of the century," Jake shot back from somewhere to my left, but I hardly heard him.

My eyes narrowed on the telltale glint of purple—the pills. They were everywhere, crushed under boots, clutched in trembling hands. A pattern clicked into place, the source of the chaos as clear to me as if it had been scrawled across the walls. The heat spikes weren't random; they were orchestrated, the academy doling out doses of hell like candy.

"Those damn pills," I hissed, rage simmering hot beneath my skin.

Andrew stood in front of Draven, growling.

"Let's get out of here Amy," Cole urged, a hand on my arm, attempting to steer me away.

But no, retreat wasn't an option. Not today. I had a mission to complete.

"Watch this," I said, shaking off his grip. I stepped forward, vaulting onto Andrew's table and kicking aside someone's forgotten breakfast. As I did, I bent down, turning and sprinkling belladonna into their food.

"Hey!" I shouted, standing tall, my voice a blade slicing through the turmoil. Heads turned; eyes wide as they found the anomaly—an Omega standing tall amidst the bedlam.

"I hope all the Omegas are enjoying Stonehurst's special purple pills with a side of betrayal," I called out, my tone dripping with acid sarcasm.

A hush fell over the crowd; even the guards seemed taken aback by my audacity.

"Ever wonder why these flare-ups happen when they do?" I continued, sweeping my gaze across the sea of faces. "It's not just bad luck or poor timing. It's them!" I jabbed a finger toward the nearest guard, his face a mask of confusion and dawning fear.

"They think they can control us. But guess what? We're not puppets. We're not their playthings. And we are damned well stronger than their damn drugs!"

Murmurs rippled through the crowd, a tide of unrest turning to understanding. I could see it in their eyes—the flicker of defiance, the kindling of outrage.

"Time to wake up and smell the manipulation," I finished, my heart hammering against my ribs like a war drum.

For a moment, silence reigned, punctuated only by the distant echo of my last words. Then, like the first crack of thunder before a downpour, applause erupted, fierce and resonant.

"Damn straight," someone yelled from the back, and that was all it took. The cafeteria exploded into cheers and jeers, a chorus of resistance that would not be silenced. Not this time, never again.

The thunderous applause was still reverberating in my ears when I felt Draven's hand clamp down on my shoulder as he joined me on the table, his touch grounding me. I swiveled to meet his gaze, the fury burning in his brown eyes mirroring the fire in my own.

A guard walked towards me. Draven growled as Cole and Jake stood in front of me in a protective stance. The guard stopped and narrowed his eyes.

"Spot on, Amy," Draven growled, the sound rumbling from deep within his chest. "We can't let them keep playing God with us." His stature seemed to swell with each word, a towering bastion of defiance.

I could feel the heat of his anger like a physical force. Yet, beneath that wrath, there was an unyielding shield—his resolve to protect me.

"Thanks," I muttered, squeezing his hand briefly before turning back to the crowd, "but it looks like this is just the start."

"Get off my fucking table!" Andrew growled, pushing his food aside and walking off. I huffed, what a waste of poison! His pack members looked hungrily at their breakfasts, both grabbed a cob from their plates and ate them as they ran after Andrew. Well, that's two down at least!

Before another word could be exchanged, two figures broke through the throng of Omegas, their hurried steps drawing our attention. Janine's ginger locks were a wild cascade around her shoulders, her face flushed with urgency.

Beside her, Nora's blond curls bounced with each stride, her blue eyes wide with concern.

"Guys," Janine panted, barely catching her breath, "the Headmistress. She's called an emergency assembly in the Grand Hall. Now." I pursed my lips. The Grand Hall was an area rarely used. Unless there was some kind of emergency. Thankfully, there hadn't been one since I'd arrived.

"Seems she wants to address the 'unrest' personally," Nora added, her usually soft voice tinged with a sharpness born of necessity.

I cocked an eyebrow, the taste of rebellion still sweet on my tongue. "Well, isn't that timely?" My words came out laced with a dark chuckle. "Guess she's not too keen on Omegas thinking for themselves."

"Then let's not keep her waiting," I said, rolling my shoulders back in anticipation.

"Right behind you," Draven affirmed, his presence reassuring, as we navigated through the chaos towards the ominous doors of the Grand Hall.

The corridors seemed to pulse with tension, the very air thick with it, as if the academy itself were holding its breath. We marched onward, our expressions etched with determination, a shared understanding that this wasn't just another assembly. This was a declaration of intent, a prelude to the storm that would follow.

The Grand Hall loomed before us, its towering arches and ornate pillars casting long shadows across the polished marble floor. The cavernous space thrummed with the low hum of whispered conversations and the soft shuffling of feet against the ground. As I stepped over the threshold, the cold air brushed against my skin, heightening my senses. The atmosphere was charged with an electric tension that made the hairs on my arms stand on end. I quickly scanned the room, taking in the clusters of people gathered in tight circles, their faces a mix of apprehension and resolve.

The scent of anxiety hung thick in the air, mingling with the underlying resolve, a potent concoction that lingered on the tongues of my fellow Omegas. Their faces were an open book of emotions; eyes wide with anxiety, yet glinting with a rebellious fire that mirrored my own. Some clutched their messenger bags like lifelines, knuckles whitening against the worn leather, while others stood tall, shoulders squared as if ready to charge at the first sign of trouble.

Before I could dissect another wavering Omega's steely resolve, the room fell into an eerie silence. All eyes snapped to the entrance as the headmistress, Lucinda Stone, glided into the hall like death incarnate—if death wore tailored suits and looked over thin-rimmed glasses with soul-piercing ice-blue eyes.

Her voice, devoid of warmth, sliced through the heavy stillness, turning my spine to steel. The words were simple, but they carried the weight of a thousand chains—a challenge, a command, a cue for the curtains to rise on the scene she'd so meticulously set.

"Shall we begin?"

Chapter 22

Headmistress Lucinda Stone stepped up to the podium, her icy demeanor chilled enough to frost the ornate windows. I swear the temperature dropped a few degrees just from the glacial sweep of her gaze.

"Students," she began, her voice slicing through the murmur like a blade. "As you know, the Initiation ceremony is a cornerstone of our proud tradition here at Stonehurst Academy." Her words, cold and commanding, sent a ripple of dread that washed over the room like waves lapping at my sanity.

I could feel every pair of eyes around me, wide with the same fear, but I made sure mine were narrowed slits of defiance. They wouldn't see me break. Not now, not ever.

"The Initiation serves as the sacred binding between an Omega and her Alphas," Lucinda continued, detailing the barbaric ritual of mating before the whole academy. "It is a time-honored celebration of the natural order, ensuring the strength and purity of future generations."

My chest tightened, rebelling against the very idea. A 'celebration' she called it—as if being cornered and claimed because we'd been told to, was anything but a glorified caging. They might as well have paraded us in chains. We should be able to choose our packs, and bond on our own terms. Not with an audience.

"Let us remember it is both an honor and a duty for each Omega to birth the next generation," she said, her tone brooking no argument. "And the Initiation is to ensure all Omegas can present for their alphas."

As Lucinda laid out the timeline for the ceremony, ticking off each step like a judge enumerating charges, I could practically hear the shackles closing around me. The rest of the world faded into a distant hum, and all I could focus on was the thunderous pounding in my chest, reminding me that time was running out.

The Warden joined her on stage and called out the names of Omegas with their packs. Those without packs were given one. Finally, my name was called. My eyes widened. Why was my name called?

"Amy Anderson. You have found your scent matched pack and will perform the Initiation to birth the next generation immediately," the Warden said, sneering at me.

I looked at Draven. Immediately? What? Like now?

He growled.

"You and the Penthouse Alphas Draven Blackwood, Cole Hawthorne, and Jake Sullivan will ready yourselves for after dinner tomorrow," the Headmistress said.

The clang of dismissal couldn't have come soon enough, but as I shoved books into my bag, Andrew Calloway made his presence known, his two pack brothers following behind him. "Looking forward to the ceremony, Amy?" he drawled, voice dripping with condescension. Draven launched at him and he stepped back.

Cole pulled Draven back as the Warden watched. "Not here," Cole said.

I leveled an icy stare at Andrew, wishing I had another pencil to stab him with, in the eye this time. He turned and walked away, laughing to himself. Asshole.

As I left, each step echoed through the dimly lit corridors. The shadows curled into the corners of the corridors, dark tendrils that seemed to whisper insidious doubts into my ear. The Initiation loomed over me, a nightmare that haunted the edges of my consciousness, now stepping boldly into the light.

I stepped out into the cool air, the last vestiges of sunlight trying to escape the impending night. The sense of entrapment pressed closer, the weight of impending inevitability wrapping around my chest like a vice. But so long as there was breath in my lungs, the fight in my soul wouldn't be extinguished—not by the likes of Andrew Calloway, not by the Omega Taskforce, and certainly not by some archaic initiation ceremony.

I'd burn the whole damned order to the ground first.

Outside, Draven caught up with me. His gaze met mine, the silent exchange heavy with unspoken resolve. His protective instincts were palpable, a fierce energy that crackled in the space between us. But beneath that, I glimpsed something raw... fear? Frustration? Perhaps both, mingling in the depths of his unwavering stare.

"I won't let the whole academy, all of those Alphas see our Omega, my Amy, naked. It can't happen!" Draven growled, pummeling his fists. I took his hands and placed them on my chest.

Cole's words cut through the heavy silence that had settled over us, as sharp and clear as a blade. "We need a plan," he stated, his voice a low thrum of urgency that seemed to resonate with the very stones beneath our feet.

"We escape," I said, thinking back to what the resistance had spoken about.

"It's too dangerous," Draven said.

"No. What's more dangerous is staying here!" I almost yelled back in frustration. He held up his hands. I pursed my lips and took a deep breath. "Look, Ava can remove my collar, and Janine knows the guards' routes. We've got to try!"

Cole nodded, taking my hands and kissing the backs of them. "First, we disable the surveillance cams in the west wing—there's a blind spot," he said. "Then we exploit the shift change at midnight. That's our window."

I watched him, impressed despite the fear knotting my stomach. Cole always had a way of distilling chaos into action, turning our collective panic into something resembling hope.

"Brilliant," I managed, my voice dry but earnest.

"That won't mean jack if we can't get past the Omega Complex's outer fence," Jake chimed in, his attempt at levity falling flat in the thick atmosphere of dread. His usual spark was dimmed, the twinkle in his green eyes now just a flicker.

“Maybe we can charm the locks into submission?” he suggested, a brittle smile cracking his lips. His laughter followed a hollow echo that didn't reach his eyes.

“Charm?” Cole shot back; his gaze sharp on Jake. “If it were only that easy.”

“Hey, a dash of humor doesn't hurt,” Jake defended.

“Let's go over it again,” Cole ordered, his tone leaving no room for argument. “No detail is too small. Our lives depend on it.”

“Right, I’ll find Ava and get her help with the collar. While you check the guards’ schedules,” I said, looking at Cole. He nodded. “Jake, you need to find a way through the lock.” Jake sighed.

“The receptionist has a key. I was being serious about using charm to get through the lock.”

I smirked.

“But Amy, it's risky,” Draven interjected, his broad shoulders rigid with tension, as if he were trying to hold the weight of the world steady. His usually confident stance seemed to waver, betraying the worry etched across his brow. He was the rock, but even rocks could crumble under enough pressure.

"Everything worth doing is risky," I countered, feeling a surge of defiance ignite within me as if a fire had been lit in my chest. My hands clenched into fists at my sides, and my voice echoed with determination. "You think I don't know that? You think I haven't been engaged in this chess match since the day I swallowed my first suppressant and felt the world shift beneath my feet?"

"Chess match?" Jake raised an eyebrow, his tone laced with playful sarcasm. "We're talking about breaking out of Stonehurst, not sneaking an extra dessert past the dining hall guards," he quipped. But the laughter died on his lips as he caught my glare.

"Damn right we are," I affirmed, my eyes boring into his. "And we have one move left before checkmate."

"Fine. But say we make it past the walls. What then, Amy? We're fugitives. They'll hunt us down like—" Draven didn't finish, his jaw clenched tight enough to shatter teeth.

"Like animals?" I finished for him, my eyes blazing with a challenge. "Guess what, Draven? That's exactly what they think we are. But I'd rather be an animal on the run than a caged bird awaiting slaughter."

"Okay, okay," Cole interjected, his hands raised in a gesture meant to temper, not surrender. "Let's focus. We need to be smart—smarter than they expect us to be."

The surrounding air charged with electricity, every breath, every heartbeat syncing into a rhythm of rebellion. We were a pack, bound tighter than any chain or ceremony could forge. And together, we would tear down the walls that dared to confine us.

Draven's silhouette loomed like a storm cloud against the sky, his usually steady voice rising in a crescendo of frustration. "We can't just run headlong into the unknown," he growled, the primal pull of our bond sending tremors through his frame. He was the immovable force, the protector—the Alpha who never wavered, except for now, as his gaze flickered with an unfamiliar uncertainty.

"Draven," Cole said, turning to address the brooding mass beside him, "your need to protect is what makes you strong, but let it drive us forward, not hold us back."

"Fine," Draven conceded, dragging the word from the depths of his chest. His eyes locked with mine, a silent pledge that he would follow, even though every fiber of his being screamed to take control.

Cole nodded once, his warm brown eyes scanning our huddle of rebellion. "We use the academy's structure against them. They expect obedience and predictability. We give them chaos."

"Chaos," I murmured, tasting the word, letting it roll off my tongue like sweet blasphemy. "I like the sound of that."

"Then it's settled," Cole stated, his voice leaving no room for doubt. "Tonight, we turn their world upside down."

Chapter 23

I pulled open the small backpack and started shoving clothes in with a kind of desperation that had become second nature. My fingers fumbled over the fabric, every fold and crease an obstacle in the race against time. I could feel my hands trembling, a telltale sign of the adrenaline that was pumping through my veins like a siren's call to action.

"Are you... are you leaving? Tonight?" Nora's voice cut through the thick tension of my bedroom as she burst in, her eyes wide with a mix of fear and hope.

I didn't trust my voice, so I just nodded, feeling the weight of my fate settle on my shoulders. In an instant, she was at my side, her arms wrapping around me in a quick, fierce hug that felt like the warmth of the sun in this cold, unforgiving place.

"Okay, let's do this," she whispered, pulling away just enough to look me in the eye before diving into the task at hand. She grabbed a handful of shirts from the dresser, her movements echoing my own urgency as she stuffed them into the bag beside my haphazardly packed jeans and jumper, back from when I was abducted at the clinic.

The door creaked open, barely a sliver of movement, and for a fleeting moment, the oppressive silence was a welcome reprieve from the tumult of my escalating rebellion. Janine slid through the narrow opening like a wraith fleeing the glare of daylight, her ginger hair a subdued ember flickering in the dimness. The door snapped shut with a soft click that thundered through my mind like the relentless pounding of my heart as it threatened to give us away.

"I'm coming with you," she declared, her voice a low thrum of determination. "We all have to go. Tonight's the night they plan to..." she trailed off, her jaw setting hard enough to rival the stone walls of Stonehurst. "I won't be paraded in front of those Alphas. Not like some prize to be claimed."

"Escaping is dangerous," I warned. Nora's hands froze on a sweater, her knuckles whitening.

"Staying is death," Nora whispered, her voice cracking like thin ice underfoot. Tears brimmed in her eyes, spilling over as she turned toward me.

Without hesitation, I wrapped my arms around her, pulling her into an embrace that was part bear hug, part fortress. We were standing on the precipice of hell itself, and if we didn't leap now, its fiery maw would swallow us whole.

"Everything will be alright," Janine murmured, grabbing us both and crushing us into a hug. She was surprisingly strong for an Omega.

With our silent pact sealed in the strength of our embrace, we broke apart, resolve etched into every line of our bodies. My bag lay open, half-packed, on the bed. I looked at it and bit my lower lip. Tonight was going to be hard, hard on all of us. I just hoped we'd get through it in one piece.

The last few items—crumpled shirts, a spare pair of boots—found their way into the backpack with hushed thuds, as if even they knew the stakes.

"Okay," I said. "Let's talk exit strategies."

Nora nodded, and I explained what my Alphas were doing to secure our exit from this hellhole. My Alphas, I thought. I hadn't called them that before. But they were mine.

Always and forever, as Draven would say. I smiled, thinking back to his touch, his kiss, his...

Janine clicked her fingers in front of my face. "Amy, where did you wander off to?" she smirked.

I laughed. "Ah, nowhere." She rolled her eyes.

"Well, as I was saying. The North wall is our best bet." She leaned in close so her words would not reach beyond the confines of these walls. "There's a section where the guards change shifts. A ten-minute window."

"Ten minutes to reach freedom or be captured," I muttered, the irony not lost on me. Janine's lips twitched.

"Guess we better be punctual then," she quipped, her humor a flicker of light in the encroaching gloom.

"Timing is everything," I agreed, nodding once, sharply. "We must be in position to meet my Alphas as soon as the clock strikes midnight. No sooner, no later. We can't afford mistakes."

"Midnight," Nora repeated, her voice steadier now, the tears drying in the fire of our collective determination. "Let's take back our lives."

"Let's," I echoed, closing up the backpack with a finality that seemed to echo through the room.

This was it. Our moment of truth. And heck, we were ready to seize it.

I pressed my back against the cold wall, my breath fogging in the air of my cramped apartment. My fingers trembled, though I willed them to be steady; they had no right to betray us now.

“Clear.” Nora's whisper brushed through the room like a secret wind, her eyes scanning the world outside our barred window. She pushed the heavy drapes back into place, her hands careful not to make a sound. It was almost laughable how soft and gentle she could be in a world that begged for anything but.

“Good.” My voice clawed out from somewhere deep in my chest, more growl than word. “Fewer obstacles between us and the other side of hell.”

Janine caught my gaze then, a silent conversation passing between us—a language honed in the trenches of Stonehurst's cruelty. Her eyes, dark green and unyielding, held mine. I saw the reflection of our shared past; the nights spent plotting under the guise of innocence, the days we masked our fear with bravado.

“Ready?” I asked, my eyes never leaving hers.

“Born ready,” Janine shot back, a smirk dancing on her lips. A lie, maybe, but who cared? We were a heartbeat away from defying every chain they'd tried to lock around us.

“Let's burn their expectations to the ground,” I said, the words tasting of iron and resolve.

I caught the flicker of hesitation in Janine's movements as she paused, her hand hovering over a small, tattered photograph nestled in her blazer pocket. It was a candid snapshot, edges frayed from being handled too often, bearing the faces of people I knew she held onto like a lifeline.

“Keep this safe for me,” Janine said, the usual fire in her voice tempered by something raw, vulnerable. She slid the photo into my backpack, her fingers brushing against mine. “Just in case!”

I took her hand and placed the photograph back in it. “You keep it. You will see them again. One day, you will.”

She nodded, her lower lip quivering. She immediately straightened her back, coughed quietly, and placed the photograph in her pocket.

Nora drifted closer, her presence a soothing balm even as the storm brewed in her sky-blue eyes. She wrung her hands, the delicate knuckles white with the grip of inner turmoil. “We know this won't be easy,” she murmured, the tremor in her words betraying the steel in her spine. "There's a world of dangers out there—more than just the Task Force. But staying here..." Her gaze darted to the door, then back to us, a silent scream echoing in the depths of her stare. "This is no life at all."

"Damn right," I responded, clenching my fists until I felt my nails bite into my palms. "We've had enough of their torture, their rules."

We pressed into a tight circle, the heat of our bodies mingling with the electric charge of rebellion. I locked eyes with Janine and Nora, their faces etched with shadows and defiance.

"Remember this," I said, my voice low and steady, "we're leaving behind more than these stone walls and ironclad rules. We're shedding the life they forced upon us. The one where being an Omega means living on our knees." I paused, letting the weight of my words settle. "Out there is a chance for something real, something ours. A place where we're not pieces in their sick game."

Janine snorted, her ginger locks swaying as she shook her head. "Yeah, 'cause we all know how much fun it is to be paraded around like prized poodles, right?"

Nora let out a choked laugh, the sound brittle yet liberating. The absurd image clashed against the gloom, shattering it for a fleeting second.

"Spot on, Janine," I quipped, the corner of my mouth twitching upward. "I always fancied myself more of a rottweiler, anyway."

Our laughter was a flicker in the dark, a spark that ignited a shared courage. It warmed us, if only briefly, before the cold reality seeped back in.

"Let's do this," Nora breathed, her resolve hardening like steel.

"Let's," Janine echoed, her grin fierce as she tightened her grip on the backpack.

Together, we were more than the sum of our parts—more than what they wanted us to be. We were Omegas, yes, but on our feet, with our heads held high, ready to run towards the dawn of our own making.

Janine checked the clock. It was past eleven at night. "Ready?" Janine's voice was low, a conspiratorial whisper that held the weight of our collective fears.

"Let's not keep freedom waiting," I replied, mustering a smirk as I gave the room a cursory glance. The stark bed, the desk littered with books that preached subservience, the wardrobe that had housed my Omega uniform—my cage without bars. "Good riddance," I muttered, sticking my finger up at it. Janine smirked.

Nora's hand trembled as she reached down and pulled out her go bag she had stashed under my bed. "Hey," I said. "How long has that been there?"

She smiled weakly. "Ever since we knew you were in," she said. "We've been prepared."

Janine nodded, taking the bag off of Nora and slipping it over her shoulder.

"We're really doing it, aren't we?" I said, eyes widening as reality hit me like a ton of bricks.

"Damn straight." Janine grinned. "Just imagine being able to do what the fuck you want whenever you want to!"

"And," Nora said. "Getting these damn collars off!"

My eyes widened, and I nodded. Damn, that would feel good!

I looked at the clock; it was time. Taking a deep breath, I picked up the backpack and walked over to the door. "Are you both ready?" I asked. They smiled, ushering me forward.

"Remember," I whispered, "stay quiet!"

Together, bound by defiance and hope, we stepped forward, ready to claim the night as our own. My hand lingered on the cool metal doorknob, the chill seeping into my bones.

"Wait," Nora breathed, her voice barely more than a whisper, as if even the walls had ears.

We turned to each other, the gravity of the moment pulling us into a tight embrace. My arms wrapped around Janine and Nora; their bodies solid yet shaking against mine. The hug was a silent pact, each of us pouring our fears and hopes into the collective strength we shared.

"Alright, let's tear this place down," I murmured.

"Metaphorically, for now," Janine quipped back, her breath warm against my neck.

"Definitely metaphorically," Nora chimed in, a soft giggle escaping from her lips, betraying the steel beneath.

We broke apart, and with one last glance at my friends, I faced the door, my heart thudding against my ribcage. Slowly, cautiously, I cracked the door open—a sliver of darkness greeting me, the silent stairwell stretching out like a challenge.

"Coast is clear," I whispered. It was way past curfew, and even though the guard change would be at midnight, we still had to watch for patrols around the Omega Complex.

Nora nodded, biting her lip in a valiant effort to quell the fear dancing in her eyes. Janine squared her shoulders, her gaze fierce and unwavering, as if she could will the dangers away with sheer force.

With a deep breath, I stepped out, listening to the sound of silence. We tip-toed down the staircase, passing four more apartments until we came to the exit on the ground floor. We would soon be Omega fugitives in a world that hunted us, but tonight, we were the predators, stalking towards freedom on silent feet. Tonight, we would not be prey.

The open grounds stretched before us, a black wall of darkness hiding our fears, dreams, and nightmares. I gulped, took Nora's hand, and slipped into the depths of the unknown. Side-stepping beside the walls of the buildings, ready to duck down behind the bushes if a guard walked by.

Nora's breath was a whisper beside me, her steps so light they barely kissed the ground. Janine moved with lethal grace, eyes scanning the darkness, ready to face whatever might emerge from the gloom.

"Remember," I breathed, the words a prayer of sorts, "the moment we cut through the fence, we're officially AWOL Omegas."

"AWOL has a nice ring to it," Janine murmured, a smile in her voice despite the tension that held us captive.

“Better than 'property,'” Nora added, her tone defiant, as if daring the world to claim her again.

We crept along, our trio a single entity, bound by the impending thrill of freedom. The academy slept, giving way to the pattering pulse of our escape. Every movement, every distant footstep, felt magnified, yet we navigated the grounds of the Omega Complex with precision, thanks to Janine's memorized map.

“Almost there,” Janine whispered.

The last stretch loomed ahead, the threshold to our new beginning. My chest tightened, a cocktail of exhilaration and dread swirling within. We reached the barbed fence that marked the first stage in our plan to regain our freedom.

“Here goes nothing,” Janine said, reaching for the snips, a smaller version of side cutters that Janine had buried out here weeks ago. “You can do the honors,” she said, smiling, and passed them to me.

I nodded, took them in my hand and took pleasure in snipping away the first section of metal. Fifteen minutes later and I was still at it, my hand shaking as the thick wire seemed more and more difficult to cut every time I tried.

"Here, let me," Janine said, taking the snips and continuing. I stretched out my hand a few times and caught my breath. Bloody fence. Why did it have to be reinforced?

"There," she said, minutes later. "Come on!" She pushed her bag through and then crawled through to the other side, turning back and smiling. I mirrored her actions, then helped Nora up.

With a collective breath, we kept to the shadows, and ran into the woods. Our forms melded with the darkness, three Omegas no more, just a trio of rebels with hearts ablaze, sprinting towards hope. Leaving Stonehurst—and all its nightmares—in the dust behind us.

Chapter 24

The stone halls that confined us, now protected us like old friends as we crouched in the corner of Stonehurst Academy's dimly lit passageway, our breaths shallow whispers against the stone-cold air. I felt Janine's hand, firm on my arm, her green eyes ablaze with that spark I admired. Nora was there too, her features flickering with fear and determination. In this Gothic fortress designed to break us, we clung to each other, awaiting stage two of our escape to commence.

"Eden or bust," I muttered, looking around the corner, waiting. I pulled them both into a hug that spoke volumes of unspoken promises. "We're not just sneaking out for midnight snacks."

"Damn straight," Janine replied, her voice barely above a hiss. "If there's a place where Omegas can be more than just...

this," she gestured at her tailored blazer with a scoff, "then I'm all in."

Nora nodded, her curls bouncing. "I want to see it, Cherry Red. If it's real, I'm coming to find it with you." Her voice quivered like a leaf in the wind, but her resolve was ironclad. I smiled, tugging her to me for a hug.

"We will find it," I said. We had to. Because when we did, we'd bring back an army and shut down this academy forever. This was just the start. I had plans. Big plans and the damned Taskforce had seen nothing yet!

"Right. Are you ready?" I asked Nora, holding out the device Ava had given us. She winced.

"It's okay, do it on my collar first."

"But what if it alerts the guards?" Shit, I hadn't thought of that!

"Then we've got to be quick!" Nora nodded, took a deep breath, and then zapped my collar with the device. I convulsed, drool escaping my lips, but by the time it was finished, the clasp clicked open and it dropped to the floor.

I grabbed my neck. The skin, red and sore, blistered from it constantly rubbing. Tears pricked my eyes, threatening to spill. But I swallowed them back, grabbed the device and slammed it into Nora's collar with no forewarning. I knew she'd back down if I did. She shook, her eyes rolled back in her head, and her legs gave way. But just as they did, her collar unclicked and fell with her. Janine pulled her up and smiled.

"Now me," she said, bracing herself for the searing pain. I nodded, pushing the device onto her collar. The same happened again, but she didn't falter and caught her collar as it fell, tossing it in the bin beside her. "Fucking thing," she said, rubbing her neck.

"Let's go," I said, hiding the device behind the chalkboard in the classroom for Ava to find it.

The clock chimed midnight, and everyone was in the cafeteria. That meant it was time for the guards' shift change.

"Keep quiet," I breathed, casting a glance down the corridor, its oppressive silence hanging thick in the air. "Remember, stick to the plan."

We moved, our bodies synchronized in urgency, our backpacks thumped gently against our backs, the academy crest mocking us one last time before we attempted to strip away its hold on our lives.

"Remember, act natural if anyone spots us," I instructed, my voice low. "Just a few Omegas out for a late-night study session."

"Because cramming for subservience exams at midnight is absolutely riveting," Janine snorted.

I rolled my eyes. "And keep your hair over your necks." Nora gulped, but nodded.

As we made our way down the corridor, a shiver skated down my spine. Not from fear, but anticipation. The darkness was thick and suffocating, yet it grounded us and cloaked us in its murky embrace. I could barely see the faces of my friends, but their presence was a constant reminder of why I was doing this. Not just for me. For them.

Nearing the meeting point, the scent of the beach drifted over to me. I almost groaned at my need for him.

Draven emerged from the gloom ahead. He turned, his piercing brown eyes scanning ours, and raised a single hand, ensuring we remained silent.

"Showtime," Jake said, joining us and pulling me to his body for a kiss.

Draven licked his lips. Cole joined him. Their scents were enticing me, intriguing me, needing me. I whined. Jake pulled back and chuckled. "Come on baby, it's time we taught these assholes who they're messing with!"

I grinned and nodded.

Watching, my breath hitched, held captive as Draven approached the control panel nestled in the wall. His fingers were artists, defusing the alarm system with an ease that belied the complexity of the task.

With the distant hum of surveillance systems falling silent behind us, it was Cole's turn to shepherd us deeper into the academy's grounds. His eyes, those pools of warm brown that seemed to pierce through the darkness, were alert for any flicker of movement, any hint of danger that might lurk in the shadows.

"Left here," he murmured, his voice a low rumble that barely reached our ears.

We followed, our footsteps muted against the cold floors, threading through corridors that felt like the belly of some slumbering beast. I could see Cole's profile, the tension in his jaw that spoke volumes of his focus. He paused at every corner, every intersection, with the precision of a seasoned hunter.

"Watch out," he'd say moments before a faint shuffle would reach our ears, steering us away from a patrol's path before they even knew we existed.

A sudden stop had us freezing in place. Cole held up a hand, and we held our breaths. Seconds stretched like hours until he gave the signal to proceed. Our collective relief was palpable but short-lived as tension once again mounted with each step toward freedom.

That's when Jake decided the silence was too thick, too heavy to carry without cracking it open with his humor.

"Anyone else feel like we're in a posh version of hide-and-seek?" he quipped, his green eyes dancing in the low light.

Despite the gravity of our situation, chuckles rippled through our group, soft and stifled, but enough to remind us that fear hadn't claimed our spirits—not yet.

"Only if you're it," I shot back, earning a mock bow from Jake that somehow didn't trip him up.

He chuckled.

Our brief smiles were fleeting, lighting up our shadowed faces before fading into the grim reality of our escape.

We were so close to the outer perimeter that I could practically taste the tang of freedom on my tongue, a wild, metallic flavor. Then, without warning, a shadow materialized into form—a patrolling guard, his steps measured and lethal as the hands of a clock inching towards our doomsday.

"Down!" My whisper was a knife's edge, slicing through the tension as we collapsed against the cold stone wall. The world shrank to the space of shared breaths and racing hearts.

Janine's hand found mine, her grip tight enough to send a silent promise between us. We were more than our Omega uniforms; we were alive, bound by the desperation to evade the chains meant for us. Crouching there, we barely dared to breathe, while the guard's boots whispered across the floor like the grim reaper deciding where to cast his shadow next.

Time became viscous, every second stretching out like an accusation. I held my breath, counting the beats of my heart to calm my screaming mind, each thump a silent plea for mercy. The guard's presence was an oppressive force, the embodiment of every fear we sought to escape, yet he remained blissfully unaware of us, mere feet away from him.

And then, as if blessed by some divine power with a twisted sense of humor, he turned a corner, his silhouette dissolving into the darkness.

The air left my lungs in a rush, a gale-force relief that might as well have been a hurricane for all the noise it didn't make. We rose, stealing glances at one another. Draven kissed my forehead and held me to his chest. "Nothing will happen to you while I'm here," he whispered in my ear. I nodded and kissed him before Janine grabbed my hand and pulled me away.

"Come on, he'll be back!" she whispered. I nodded, trying not to laugh at Draven's grumpy pout I'd left him with.

"Close one," Nora murmured.

"Could've kissed him for being so blind," Jake said.

"Later, Casanova," Cole interjected, his tone low but urgent. "We're not out yet."

Right, not yet. But soon. I straightened my spine, my resolve hardening like the walls that tried to confine us.

We continued, the last barrier looming before us, as we ventured into the open air once again, making our way across the grounds towards the main gate. There were no guards in sight, which I thought was odd, but maybe it was all part of the shift change. I shrugged to myself and continued walking.

As we reached the gate, I remembered the last time I was there. Experiencing a fleeting moment of freedom, under the subterfuge of the collar, while I was shocked repeatedly until I threw up all over myself. One day, I'd pay those guards back for that. One day I'd pay the whole Taskforce back for everything they'd done.

Jake stepped forward with the key he'd 'borrowed' from the receptionist and unlocked the main gate.

"Almost there," Janine breathed, her voice tinged with hope.

I glanced at her, a half-smile twitching at my lips despite the gravity of our situation. "Don't jinx it."

And then, a soft click—the sweetest sound I'd heard in ages—as the lock disengaged. A collective shiver ran through us, the thrill of imminent victory.

"Let's move—"

"Going somewhere, are we?"

The stern voice cut through the silence, sharp as a razor and twice as cold. Warden Xavier Gray emerged from the shadows. His security team of at least ten strong fanned out behind him.

"Shit," Jake cursed under his breath, his earlier humor dying like a flame in a storm.

"Stay calm," Draven commanded, though the strain in his voice betrayed his own shock.

Our hearts, once buoyed by the prospect of escape, plummeted into our stomachs. I could see it in their faces. Their eyes wide, reflecting the harsh light that now flooded the area, painting us all in stark relief against the backdrop of our thwarted dreams.

"Did you really think you could just walk out?" Warden Gray asked, his tone devoid of any emotion except perhaps a hint of satisfaction. His dark eyes scanned our group, lingering on me with an intensity that felt like a punch to the gut.

"Thought it was worth a shot," I said, my voice carrying a bravado I didn't feel, as I stared down the man who'd made a career of caging people like me.

"Commendable. But foolish." He stepped forward, his boots crunching on the graveled dirt path.

We were caught—trapped by our longing for a life beyond these walls. At that moment, we were no longer predators or prey; we were simply prisoners of a fate we had tried so desperately to rewrite.

The illusion of freedom shattered, and chaos erupted around us. The cold steel grip of panic squeezed my chest as Warden Gray's security team descended like predators upon their prey.

"Run!" I screamed, but the word was a useless flutter in the roaring storm of bodies and commands.

Jake was beside me in an instant. "Not today," he growled, throwing himself between me and a guard's baton swing meant to cut my legs from under me. The impact thudded against Jake's shoulder, and he stumbled, but his grin never wavered. "Is that all you got?"

The scent of sweat and fear hung in the air, mixed with the metallic tang of blood as my Alphas clashed with the guards, a tangle of fury and desperation. But one by one, they were overpowered, the metallic click of cuffs punctuating the end of each struggle. Draven's face was a mask of silent rage as they forced him to his knees, his hands bound behind him.

"Draven!" I called out, reaching for him—until a booted foot slammed into my stomach, sending me sprawling. The breath whooshed from my lungs, and I curled instinctively, trying to protect myself from the next blow. It came, sharp and relentless, the kicks driving home the message: we were nothing but playthings for their cruelty.

"Stop it!" Janine yelled, her voice fierce with protective wrath, cutting through the haze of pain. She launched herself at my assailant, shrieking as he threw her aside.

Out of the corner of my eye, I caught a flash of movement—Nora, her blond curls a pale streak slicing through the dim light. Then the unthinkable happened. The scene was a blur of terror, a kaleidoscope of shadow and light, as a guard's hand lashed out with vicious force, a backhand that tore through the air with a heart-wrenching crack.

The taste of bile rose in my throat at the sickening sight of Nora's body being flung backwards as if she were made of paper, not flesh and bone. Time stretched into a cruel, endless moment as her head collided with the jagged edge of a rock, the impact reverberating with a sickening finality.

"NO!" I screamed, my voice tearing from my throat raw and broken.

"Please," Janine begged, dropping to her knees beside Nora, oblivious to the hands that yanked her up and slapped cuffs onto her wrists.

Blood pooled around Nora's head, a stark contrast against the stone. Her eyes were fluttering, eyes that dimmed, the sparkle in them waning. Her face was pale and confused, and her body was still, and as I reached her, tears streamed down my face. I cupped her cheek, looked into her eyes, and said, "You're free now, Nora. You're free."

A slight smile lifted her lips, and I watched as her chest rose one last time.

One guard pressed two fingers to her neck, searching for something we all knew wasn't there.

"Dead," he announced, his voice hollow, devoid of the triumph they had felt moments before.

"Janine!" I reached out to her, my heart splintering. Our gazes locked—a silent vow passing between us, a promise that this wouldn't be the end.

"Let's go," a guard barked, dragging Janine away. She fought against his hold, screaming my name.

"Get up," another commanded, hauling me to my feet. I stood, swaying, the world a blur through my tears. I couldn't look at Nora anymore—not yet. Not while there was still breath in my body and fight left in my soul.

Cuffs bit into my wrists, a cruel reminder of the price of rebellion. The guards yanked us forward, their grips unforgiving as steel traps. We were a procession of the defeated, our fight smothered under the weight of iron and despair. The night had turned against us, its shadows now witness to our capture.

The sound of metal zipping shut will forever remain etched into my soul as they encased Nora in a body bag, a macabre parcel discarded with indifference into the back of a van. I refused to look, to give them the satisfaction of seeing my pain. Instead, my gaze found the faces of my pack. The flickering torchlight painted our expressions with the same shade of hopelessness, eyes that screamed silent oaths of vengeance.

Chapter 25

Bound and gagged, we trudged on. Our steps were heavy, each one a promise of retribution. They'd killed our friend, our family. They'd taken our chance at escape. How did they know we were going to be there? Did removing our collars signal them?

Draven's jaw clenched; his eyes were ablaze with rage barely contained. Cole's silence was louder than any war cry, his stoic face a mask of resistance. They dragged Jake past me, his lip split, but his spirit unbroken, his glance told me this wasn't over—not by a long shot.

"Let's see how tough you are in solitary," one guard sneered, shoving the Alphas through a door that slammed shut with finality.

"Solitary?" I scoffed, the sound raw and grating. "That's your biggest threat? You clearly don't know us at all."

They ignored me, or maybe they didn't want to admit that cages only made us more determined to break free.

Janine's struggle was immense, her fiery hair a beacon of defiance as they forced her toward a separate van. She pounded on the window, her screams piercing the night. "Amy! AMY!"

"Fight, Janine!" I yelled back, my voice breaking. "I'm not done. We're not done!"

The van's engine roared to life, drowning out her cries, carrying away another member of my family and I knew, I knew where she was heading. The Birthing Grounds, never to be seen again. But I'd find her. We'd find her. Just like we'd find their sister Scarlett, and just like we'd set all Omegas free and burn the world to the ground doing it.

"Keep walking, Omega," the guard growled, mistaking my silence for submission.

"Sure thing," I muttered, the taste of blood and dark humor on my tongue. "One step at a time, straight into your nightmares."

As we stepped into the compact room, the incessant whirr of the machine seized my attention. The noise was sharp and relentless, a mechanical drone that seemed to drill into my consciousness with every rotation. In the middle of the room stood a steel chair, its metallic surface cold and uninviting. Thick leather straps dangled from the armrests and footrests, their worn edges suggesting a long history of use. The sight of it sent chills through me, evoking images of ancient dungeons and the grim implements of medieval torture.

I should be scared. Running away, clawing to get free. But considering how angry I felt, how much I wanted to rip everyone's balls off and feed them to their owner for dinner, I couldn't help but let a bitter chuckle slip out.

"Something funny, Miss Anderson?" The technician asked, narrowing his eyes.

"Absolutely," I spat back, tilting my head to meet his gaze. "You lot have a twisted sense of humor if you think this will break me."

The technician shook his head, tsking as if I was nothing more than a misbehaving child. "We only aim to correct your rebellious tendencies." The guard forced me into the chair and strapped me in, fitting a ball gag into my mouth so I didn't bite my tongue off.

'Correction' – that's what they called it. But every jolt that surged through me, every command they uttered, felt like an attempt to erase who I was. To dampen the fire inside.

Each session was a battle, the electric currents clashing against the iron will forged by years of oppression and the memory of Nora's lifeless eyes.

I held on to those memories, using them as fuel. Though my body might be confined and my movements restricted, my mind roamed free, untamed. I could feel the anger boiling within me, the rage at their audacity to mold me into another one of their docile Omegas. But as much as I wanted to scream, to lash out and fight, I knew I had to bide my time.

The technician removed the gag. "Is that all you've got?" I taunted through unsteady breaths.

"Your sarcasm won't save you," he warned, adjusting the dials. "But it might just earn you more sessions."

"Promises, promises," I whispered under my breath, a grim smile playing on my lips.

But it wasn't long before I passed out.

When I came to, I found I was still strapped to the goddamn metal chair. The straps bit into my wrists, shackles too snug, not an inch given for comfort. My heart thundered against my ribcage like it wanted out, but I slammed the door in panic's face. They had my body locked down, but my mind? That was a fortress they couldn't breach, no matter how many keys they jangled in front of it.

"Good morning, Amy," came the slick voice, greasy as an oil spill on pristine water. Andrew Calloway waltzed into the behavioral modification chamber like he owned it. The scent of rotting caviar followed him in.

I tilted my head up, eyes narrowed, and watched him strut his way toward me. His blue eyes were ocean-deep, but there was nothing serene about them. They were the kind that drowned you if you looked too long. His presence loomed over me, dark and heavy, like a storm cloud ready to break.

"Andrew," I said, the name leaving my mouth like I'd bitten into something sour. "Why are you here?"

His smile never reached those icy eyes. "I couldn't miss seeing the glorious Amy Anderson being strapped down now, could I." He stepped closer, running his fingers up and over my breast.

"Get the fuck off me!" I yelled.

He grabbed my mouth, squeezing it. "Now, what have I told you about using that language with me?" he growled, then pushed my chin away. I growled under my breath, my heart racing, fear gripping my backbone as I tugged at the restraints.

He laughed. "Oh, you're not getting out of those!" he said, circling me like a shark getting familiar with its next meal.

He bent over me and licked his tongue up and over my lips. "Mmm! I remember that taste from the woods."

I growled. "Don't you remember my taste, Omega?" I turned away from him, disgusted. "I know my two pack brothers remembered you, right until they were found poisoned by one of the herbs in the garden." He gripped my chin and made me look at him. "Now you wouldn't know how that happened, would you?"

I tried not to smirk, but the slight upturning of my lips gave me away.

"I thought so." He roared, then took a deep breath and straightened his shirt. "Oh, but don't worry, little Amy, as I have special permission from the Headmistress to teach you. She believes, as do I, that you can be taught to bow down to me, and be MY Omega."

My brow furrowed. "But, I'm scent matched!"

"On this occasion, your scent match will be overlooked and you will be placed with me and my pack when you leave. You need a man's hand, Amy. I will be that hand for you."

I growled under my breath, struggling against my restraints, resisting the urge to swear at him. Taking a deep breath, instead, I said. "Andrew darling..."

"Yes," he replied, smiling and coming closer to me.

"When I get out of these restraints, I'm going to hang you by your balls and watch you bleed to death."

His eyes widened, and he punched me, knocking me out cold. The fucker.

By the time I came to, Andrew was gone. Thank fuck.

Now where the hell were Draven, Cole, and Jake, and why weren't they saving my ass already? Because if that dickhead touches me again, I'm going to rip through this table like the damned Hulk and smash this whole place to bits using his skull.

The chill in the room clung to my skin, a physical manifestation of the Omega Taskforce's grip on us all. But here, in this stark box of horrors, with my defiance as my shield, I stood my ground—even if physically I remained bound to their damn chair.

I wouldn't mind so much, but I really needed to pee. How long had I been strapped to this thing? I looked around. There weren't any windows, so I had no clue if it was day or night.

My stomach grumbled. I'd missed dinner, but I wasn't overly hungry, so I'm guessing it was the middle of the night? I thought back to what happened. To Nora, my chest deflated, sorrow filling my mind, tears wrapping themselves over me. To Janine, being whisked away screaming in a van. I wondered if she wass there yet. At the Birthing Grounds. Wherever that was.

How was I going to get her out? Get any of us out? I bit my lower lip. There was no way I could spend the rest of my life answering to the likes of Andrew Calloway, son of the head of the Omega Taskforce. I just couldn't do it.

The door opened and Andrew waltzed in. "Oh good, you're awake."

"What time is it?" I asked him, coughing. My mouth was dry and I'm pretty sure I had a bloodied lip, thanks to that asshole. I shifted in my seat, wincing. Yep, a few broken ribs too.

Andrew unfurled a sheet of paper, his movements precise and calculated. "Today, I plan to teach you, considering that you have been hiding your Omega nature all your life. It is time you embraced it!"

"Huh?" Well, that wasn't what I'd expected to come out of his mouth!

"Your resistance," he continued, pacing before me like a general before his troops, "is not only futile but against the very fabric of our society. You will learn to yield, to bend to the natural order."

"Natural order," I echoed silently, the words sour on my tongue. Right, because there's nothing more 'natural' than a room that smells like bleach and despair.

As Andrew droned on about duty and compliance, I couldn't help but snicker internally. If he thought his pompous monologue could dismantle my will, he was sorely mistaken.

"Every Omega must serve their purpose," he said, eyeing me as if I were a disappointing science experiment.

"Serve my ass," I scoffed inwardly. The memories of us, huddled together, whispering plans of rebellion under the oppressive regime's nose, bubbled up within me. We wore our uniforms, those ridiculous symbols of subjugation, with sneers hidden behind polite smiles. It was our silent middle finger to the establishment.

"Your defiance," Andrew lectured, "is a defect we shall correct."

"Defect," I mused, a wicked grin playing on my lips in the sanctuary of my mind. "You keep using that word. I don't think it means what you think it means."

His condescending tone was meant to chip away at my resolve, to make me doubt myself. But every patronizing syllable only bolstered my determination. He didn't know it, but he was the best motivational speaker I'd ever had—the kind that fuelled my desire to shove his 'objectives' right back down his throat.

Andrew Calloway's shadow loomed larger as he leaned forward, his words slicing through the air with precision. "Let me paint you a picture, Amy," he began, voice dripping with a poisonous sweetness that made my skin crawl. "An Omega who refuses to bend will find themselves shattered. There are places far less accommodating than Stonehurst for such broken spirits."

I felt the chill in the room settle deeper into my bones, but I kept my gaze steady on him. The threat was obvious; it hung between us like a guillotine blade, gleaming and ready to fall.

Sounds like a real page-turner, I quipped silently, the sarcasm wrapping around my thoughts like armor. They could threaten all they wanted, but fear was a currency I had long since stopped dealing with.

Calloway's eyes narrowed. "Fine," Andrew said through gritted teeth. "We shall continue tomorrow."

As he exited, the door closing with an ominous click; I allowed myself a small, defiant smile. Tomorrow, then. Another day, another battle. But one thing was certain: I was no one's to tame.

Chapter 26

I awoke to Andrew's fingers lingering over my neck as he checked the fastening on my new electric collar. His face was close to my neck, his breath staining me with disdain, poisoning my skin with his touch. I shuddered.

As he pulled away, I saw the young technician sitting in a chair in front of a computer, my file open in front of him, and a remote in his hand.

"Let's see if discomfort can loosen that stubborn tongue of yours," Andrew drawled, his voice as smooth and cold as the stone walls enclosing us. He nodded to the technician.

I felt the prickle of electricity tease my skin before it sank its teeth in. A jolt shot through me, a white-hot wire of agony threading its way along my spine. I bolted against the restraints, back arched, gritting my teeth, refusing to let even a whimper escape. This was their game—a test of wills, theirs against mine.

"Is that all you've got?" I managed, the words were half-growl and half-challenge. Despite the tremors racking my body, I locked eyes with him, a snide grin plastered across his face.

"Mmm," he licked his lips, trailing his fingers over my body. "You do like pain, don't you?"

"Err Mr Calloway, I don't think you may touch the subject until the Initiation," the young spotty technician said, as he depressed the button. Relief flooded through me, and I fell back into the chair with tears beading in my eyes, threatening to spill.

Andrew growled at him, straightening his back, with his palms fisted, ready for a fight. "Do you not know who I am?" he boomed. "Do you not know who my father is?"

"Ye... Yes," he stammered.

"Get out!"

The technician fled from the room; the door banging closed behind him.

Andrew's lips twitched with the ghost of a sneer, but his eyes, those icy pools, betrayed more than just a flicker of irritation.

He turned back to me, looking over my body. "It's about time I had you all to myself, Omega," he grinned. His eyes were both devilish and dark. "Now, I want to see what I own."

His thick, grubby fingers started undoing my blouse one button at a time. My eyes widened, and I pulled against the restraints, kicking, moving, anything to force him away from me. It was no use. He enjoyed it. He was savoring the moment. Every inch of my skin that we unwrapped turned him on even more. He growled when he pulled my blouse open, revealing my white academy-issued lace bra.

"Mmm!"

"Get the fuck off of me, you asshole!"

His fist connected with my jaw. "What did I say about that vile language, Omega?"

I choked back a cry, trying my hardest not to let the tears flow. "Oh look, I made you cry," he said, grinning, licking my tears away.

I pulled my head as far away from him as I could.

"When my Alphas get here, they will kill you for this," I said, softly weeping, and hating how vulnerable I sounded.

He laughed, then grabbed my chin, narrowing his eyes. "Your Alphas?" He gripped harder. "I am your Alpha now. They no longer exist. Do you hear me?"

"No! They ARE my scent matches. Not you!"

He laughed, pushing my face away. "Why do you think I'm doing this Omega? It's the perfect revenge for what they did to me! Once the Initiation ceremony is complete, you will be matched to me and my pack. Your bond to them will be broken."

"It never will. Feelings won't ever go away!"

"Oh, I'll make sure they do!"

He grabbed the remote for my chair and laid it back. The straps tightened even more around my wrists. Then he yanked my skirt up and sniffed my underwear, making some kind of fucked up sexual noise I never wanted to hear again.

"Get off me!" I said, as he jumped onto the laid-down chair, pulled out his slimy cock and pulled off my panties and bra, not caring if he ripped everything.

I couldn't hear anything at that moment because of the screams. Screams that came from my mouth. Ones he seemed to enjoy, ones that made him harder as he impaled himself inside me and groaned. But before he could force himself deeper, he pulled himself out, took my collar's remote and pressed it again and again, watching me as searing pain drove through my body. My nerves were on fire. My body convulsed against the restraints. He thrust himself inside me again. He forced himself in and out, groaning against me, gripping my hair and yanking my head back, smashing his lips into my bloodied fat lip, kissing me hard.

I vomited at that moment, and I hoped he at least got some of it in his mouth. It didn't stop him though, as he pulled out and pressed the button again, delighting as my body convulsed in shock, electrocuted, screaming out in pain.

The next thing I knew, the door flung open so hard it flew off its hinges, and three fucked off Alphas stood there, their bodies shaking with anger. Behind them, a wide-eyed teacher, Miss Harlow, stood with the key still in her hand, jaw dropped, also shaking.

My eyes found Draven's, and he roared louder than I'd ever heard before. He leapt at Andrew, throwing him off of me in one fell swoop. Cole and Jake followed.

Amongst the chaos, all I could hear was Andrew's body being punched and kicked. His agonizing screams were music to my ears. I swallowed back the bile in my throat, but my hands shook in the straps uncontrollably, and my tears wouldn't stop flowing.

Miss Harlow unlatched my straps and held me tight while I sobbed. She placed her delicate hands on my face and looked into my swollen expression. "You'll be okay now, Amy," she said. "I am going to help you leave this place." Which, of course, made me cry even harder.

"Here," she said, taking Jake's shirt from him. Jake stood beside her, while Draven and Cole were still dealing with Andrew. "Let's get you cleaned up."

I nodded and carefully pulled off my blouse, my abdomen bruised from the guards kicking me when we'd tried to escape. I winced as I moved to place the T-shirt over my head.

Jake looked so sad, as he watched, trying to give me space at the same time. He fetched water from the sink and gently cleaned the vomit and blood from my face and arm.

Draven and Cole were soon by my side. Draven picked me up into his arms and his chest vibrated, soothing my tears away. As we left, I turned to see a wide-eyed Andrew whose neck had been snapped, after they had ripped his cock off and made him eat it.

"Amy?" Draven said, "he won't hurt you ever again." Miss Harlow looked over to Andrews' body and winced.

"We need to get you all out of here," Miss Harlow said.

"W... why are you helping us?" I asked her.

"Because no Omega deserves to die so young," she said, her words like steel wrapped in velvet. "Because what they did to Nora. What they do to all of you—it's monstrous."

My eyes brimmed with tears at the thought of my best friend Nora's glassy eyes as she lay dead on the cold, hard dirt.

A pin-drop silence fell between us, filled with the ghosts of Omegas who weren't as lucky as I hoped to be. Miss Harlow's gaze held mine, steadfast and brimming with conviction.

"Years ago," Elena began, her voice dipping into a lower octave, "my sister was like you, marked by birth, to serve their design. But when my sister—a spark of life snuffed out too early—fell victim to their cruelty, I vowed to fight back." A shadow of sorrow crossed her features, but the hard glint of resistance quickly replaced it. "So here I am, standing with those who dare to defy the chains we're born into. For my sister, for Nora, and for every Omega that dreams of freedom."

"Thank you," I managed, the words clumsy in my mouth, an odd blend of gratitude and determination. "For risking everything."

"Hope is a dangerous thing to kill," Miss Harlow said, her lips curling into a wry smile that didn't quite reach her eyes. "It has a way of rising from the ashes, fiercer than before. Now, let's get you the hell out of here!"

Draven looked down at me in his arms. "Hey Amy," he said, kissing my forehead. "Everything will be alright once we're on the other side of that gate."

I nodded. My anxiety was acute at the thought of the warden catching us again. What would he do to my boys if they were caught? They had killed the son of the leader of the Omega Taskforce. There was no coming back from that.

"So, what's the plan?" Cole asked.

Miss Harlow smiled. "I already have someone on that."

"Huh?" I said. "There is someone else helping us, too?"

She nodded. "Yes, we plan to blow the gates and give every student a fighting chance."

I smiled, my lip cracked, but I didn't care. This was worth the pain. Then I tugged on my collar.

"Don't worry, Ava has passed a device to every apartment block in the Omega Complex. All Omegas know to use them in..." She looked at her watch. "Fifteen minutes."

"That doesn't give us much time!" Cole said.

"I have bagged up food and water for you, and a change of clothes for each of you. The bags are hidden in the van."

My brows furrowed. "There's a van?"

She nodded. "Yes, I'm afraid after this..." she pointed to Andrew's body. "They will hunt you. I have given you access to the van to give you a head start. In the backpack, there's a rough guide to where Eden is."

"You know where it is?" Draven asked, pulling me tighter to his chest.

She smiled.

"Are you part of the resistance?" Jake asked. She smiled once more. "Since when were there teachers in the resistance?"

"Who do you think started it?" Elena replied.

His mouth dropped.

Elena Harlow looked at her watch again. "We need to get going to make it to the gate on time."

"But... but what about you?" I asked. "Won't you come with us?"

She smiled. "No honey, I need to stay here and play the shy teacher role to save any more Omegas that get trapped in this place."

I nodded, smiling faintly, remembering the threat of being a traitor, and being hung on the wall. "Please be careful," I said.

She nodded. "Always am!" With that, she opened the door, waved us out, and ran down the corridor.

Chapter 27

We slipped through the Omega Complex's back passageway.

"Wait," Elena muttered as she reached a corner, waiting for a guard to pass by. My eyes flicked to the antique clock hanging precariously on the wall. It was ten to six in the morning.

"Cutting it close," Draven said, his voice reverberating against me, as I lay snuggled in his chest.

"Life's no fun without a little risk," Jake countered, his grin unseen but palpable in the darkness.

The door to the outside swung open, and a guard passed by.

"Move," she whispered, stepping into the abyss beyond. We darted across the open space, shadows hugging our forms, cloaking our escape.

When we came to a stop by a collective of different vehicles, Elena reached into her pocket and pulled out the keys for the van at the far end.

"This is as far as I go," she said. "Once you're in the van, keep your head down, and make sure you reach the gate just after the explosion at six."

Draven nodded, and Cole got the keys. "I'll drive," he said.

"Drive straight until you reach the main road. From there, travel approximately thirty miles and take the third turn off. It's all on the map."

Draven placed me down, kissed my forehead, and snatched the keys from Cole. "I'll drive!"

Cole huffed. "Fine! At least it means I get more time with our girl."

I smirked.

"Thank you," I said to Miss Elena Harlow. "You may have very well saved our lives."

She nodded and pulled me into a hug. "I hope so."

"What about the other Omegas?"

"Some have families, some know of your Safehouses," she smiled.

I grinned. "So, it still exists. They're all okay there?"

"Yeah, we've been taking care of them."

"Oh, thank fuck!"

She laughed.

"You did a good job all these years. But you don't have to do it on your own anymore."

I took a deep breath and felt like crying again. Damn Omega hormones!

"Anyway go! You've got five minutes until the explosion!"

And with that, we ran, waving goodbye to Miss Harlow, hoping I would one day see her again.

Draven reached the van first, unlocked the side and we all jumped in, grabbing the backpacks and pulling out the map ready. He got in the front and started the van.

"Oh look," Jake said, leaning over Draven. "They even filled the tank up for you!"

I laughed and Draven pushed him back, just as the first of three explosions sounded.

In the backpack, I pulled out the device, checked the watch in there, six in the morning, and zapped myself until the collar clicked and dropped off. Cole grabbed it and tossed it out of the window, just in time for Draven to reverse over it, releasing a satisfying crunching sound.

A sudden shout fractured the silence, as both Omegas and Alphas alike were running for the gates.

A distant figure, a guard, perhaps even the Warden himself, raised an alarm, his voice a harbinger of chaos.

"Drive!" I screamed, primal instinct overtaking strategy as we sped toward the fiery inferno. Pieces of electric fence and gates were hanging off of their hinges.

I could see Ava running for her life from a guard with a taser in his hand.

"STOP!" I screamed.

Draven slammed on his brakes, realized what I was pointing at and jumped out, smacking the guard in the head as hard as he could. Ava was gasping for breath.

"Get in!" I yelled to her, opening the side door.

"I can't! My Alphas! I need to find my Alphas!" she yelled.

Damn it!. "Where are you meeting them?"

"Just past the gates."

"Then get in. We will see them on the way!"

Draven started the van up again and Ava grabbed my hand, jumping in the back with us.

She stood forward, looking out of the front window.

"Thank you for all your help, Ava," I said. She turned to me and smiled.

"Girl, I've always got your back."

I smiled and nodded.

"There! They're there!"

"Tell them to get in," I said to her.

"No, it's okay. We're going to Dillon's cabin. He's got a car stashed out there." I nodded in understanding. "You go," she said, hugging me as we pulled up. "We'll be fine."

"I'll miss you!" I said.

She laughed. "Well, don't get into any more trouble, will you?"

I smirked, and Cole laughed. "We'll try to keep her out of it."

She jumped out of the van and as we left, she waved and said, "Fat chance there."

The forest was a blur of shadow, and sunrise as we drove through it. Considering I had been brought here with a hood over my head, I had no clue where we were, so I took out the map.

"Looks like we can drive for part of the journey, but then the rest will be on foot."

Draven growled.

I took a moment to rummage around in the backpack, pulling out pants and a t-shirt, which I immediately changed into. Anything to get rid of that disgusting uniform Andrew had touched.

The forest gave way to a clearing, bathed in the sterile glow of technology. It was like stepping into another world—a world where Warden Xavier and the Omega Taskforce reigned with cold precision. The road we were on became larger, just as Miss Harlow had said it would. I followed the map, drawing a line with my finger.

"Okay, so from here, she said it would be about thirty miles."

"Then the third turn," Cole reminded me.

I nodded. "After that, we need to ditch the van."

Jake groaned. "How far do we have to walk?"

"It doesn't say. It just has an arrow pointing in the direction to walk. So, I'm presuming we go that way until we find it."

I shivered, my arms spurting goose pimples in protest. Pulling on a hooded jacket, I warmed up a little, then climbed over and sat in the front passenger seat with Draven.

He glanced at me, and then his eyes were back on the road. "Even though I love being near you, Amy, do you think it's the best idea to be upfront with all these windows?"

I smirked. He was always so protective. "I could say the same about you."

Draven grinned. "Well, someone's got to drive!"

I sat in silence for a moment, taking in the awe of the sunrise. Yellow ochre bled into cadmium red, arching across with white fluffy clouds that blessed the sky as the sun rose to greet us. Feeling the warmth of the sun's rays caress my body, captivating my breath, I let out a sigh of relief. We were free. I smiled.

I pulled over one backpack from behind the seat. "Do you fancy a bite to eat?" I asked, pulling out an energy bar.

He nodded. I unwrapped it for him and placed it in his mouth so he could take a bite. "Mmm! I could get used to you feeding me."

"Well, it's best you keep your eyes on the road, Mr."

He laughed, and I shoved the bar in again.

He laughed again. "Hey not so hard, or I'll have no teeth left!"

Grinning, I unwrapped the last of it and placed it in between my teeth, then leant over and kissed him, passing him the rest of the bar.

"Damn Amy, if you keep doing that, we'll be pulling over!"

I laughed, took out the map, and studied it to check where we were. "Hey, was that the second turnoff?"

"Yeah."

"Okay, then you want this one."

He nodded and turned off the main road, heading down a road that turned into a thinner back-end country lane. "Right, when we reach the Statue of Justice, we pull over."

I looked around as Draven kept driving. A small brown sign signaled a left turn into a car park to view the Statue of Justice.

"There!"

"I see it," he said, chuckling.

We pulled up before a giant, overwhelming golden statue of a lady with a blindfold, carrying a set of weighing scales. Behind her lay a dark, uninviting forest. I checked the map; the arrow pointed to behind the statue. Shit. Even with it being morning now, the daylight barely reached the floor in that creepy forest. I shuddered.

"So where are we going, Sweet Girl?" Cole said, as he pulled open the side door and jumped out, kicking Jake awake.

I pointed to the deep, dank forest.

"Oh, that looks fun!"

I rolled my eyes.

"Are you sure you're up for the journey?" Draven asked me, as he opened my door and helped me out. I nodded. I had to be.

After a while, my lungs burned, every breath a stolen gasp against the viscous air, thick with the scent of pine and the undercurrent of fear. Even the trees were fighting for their lives in here, strangled by the vines that encapsulated them, as their piercing thorns serrated their bark.

Every snapped twig underfoot was a gunshot in the silence, every rustle of leaves a whispered threat. It smelt like death in that place, a dank, rotting, painful death.

Panting heavily, we crouched together in the dim recess of a small hollow, our chests heaving as we tried to steady our breaths. The dense foliage around us rustled softly, a stark contrast to the chaos we had just escaped. Each member of my pack, faces smeared with dirt and sweat, had eyes that blazed with an intense mix of emotions. The fear was palpable, a sharp edge that pushed us through the tangled underbrush. Anger simmered beneath the surface, fuelled by the relentless pursuit we had endured. Despite the exhaustion weighing down our limbs, there was a silent promise among us. A vow to keep running until our legs could carry us no more, or until freedom wrapped its gentle arms around us.

"East or west?" Jake panted, his chest heaving as he peered through the trees, searching for signs of pursuit.

"Neither," I said, my mind racing faster than our frantic escape. "Straight ahead. It's what the arrow showed." But straight ahead seemed full of more twisted vines, sharp spear-cut bushes and a darkness that screeched out a warning of the fear of the unknown.

The fierce independence that had always been my compass now warred with my bond with my Alphas. I had the map, and they looked to me for direction, and damn it, I wouldn't lead them astray.

"Trust me," I said, softer this time, meeting each pair of eyes.

As we moved, a new challenge loomed before us; a ravine, its jagged maw gaping wide enough to swallow any hope of a straightforward path to salvation. A collective curse rose from the group, but I was already assessing and calculating.

"Cole, can you have a look for the narrowest point? We'll make our way across there," I asked.

Cole sprang into action, a well-oiled machine fuelled by necessity and trust. Draven pulled me into his chest, rubbing my back. "How are you holding up?"

"I'm okay," I said. "Tired, but okay."

"Here!" Cole called out.

I exhaled a breath I hadn't realized I'd been holding.

Draven, Jake and I made our way to Cole, who had found a dilapidated bridge.

"Listen up!" Cole said. "We're crossing here. One at a time. I'll go first to check that it's safe on the other side."

Cole made his way across the rickety bridge with ease. I however, held my breath and winced whenever the bridge creaked or groaned.

"Come on, Amy, your turn," Cole beckoned from the far side, his hand outstretched.

Taking a deep breath, I focused on Cole, who stood firmly on the other side of the swaying rope bridge. The wooden planks creaked underfoot as Draven held my arm, guiding my shaky steps onto the first plank. "You can do it," Jake encouraged from behind, his voice steady but edged with concern. "Just don't look down!" His words made me clench my fists in frustration. I hadn't wanted to look down, but now the urge was irresistible.

My gaze drifted downward, and my stomach lurched. The chasm below seemed endless, a dizzying abyss that yawned open beneath me. Shadows danced over the jagged rocks that lined the base, their sharp edges glinting in the sparse light. Falling would mean certain death, the thought of those menacing spikes causing my heart to race.

"I can't," I said, looking at Draven. His face softened, and he looked over at Cole. Taking a deep breath, he took my hand.

"I'll come across with you."

"Will it hold us both?" I asked.

"It'd better do," he said and smiled. My eyes widened, and he pulled me in for a hug, kissed my lips and I lost myself in him for a moment.

"Ready?"

I nodded.

Exhaling slowly to steady my nerves, I tightened my grip on Draven's arm. The bridge seemed to groan under our collective weight, a haunting sound that did little for my fraying confidence. My eyes locked onto Draven again, and taking a deep breath, I stepped forward.

With each hesitant step, the old rope fibers that held the wooden planks groaned and twisted beneath our feet. Dust motes swirled around as if agitated by our audacity to cross this rickety bridge. Soon enough, I found a slow rhythm in braving one plank at a time. Placing my left foot forward, I steadied myself; then, my right foot followed. The repetitive, mechanical mantra helped keep me focused on what lay ahead.

As we crept closer towards safety, towards Cole, the planks grew more dilapidated; their edges rotten and worn out by weather or perhaps despair itself. My heart thumped wildly and suddenly, a plank right before me gave way just as I stepped forward. It cracked underfoot like thunder ripping through clouds on a stormy night! A terror unlike anything else seized me; adrenaline surged through my body as I felt myself fall. My heart pulsed at an extreme level. Danger, so visceral you could almost touch it.

Draven grabbed me around the waist before I could fall through. His grip was iron, unyielding as he pulled me back, our bodies colliding with a jolt that pushed the air from my lungs. The bridge swung violently under the sudden shift of weight, its moans a grim soundtrack to the heart-stopping moment. From across the expanse, Cole watched with wide eyes, his stance wide as if he could somehow brace us through sheer will.

"Careful!" Cole shouted over the wind that whipped around us, carrying with it a cold bite and the faint scent of rain. His voice was tense, laced with concern not only for our safety but for the integrity of the bridge itself.

Jake's chuckling broke through the tension. Strangely enough, his laughter rang clear even amidst our precarious situation. "Never a dull moment with you lot," he called out, sounding as if he was half amused and half exasperated by another brush with disaster.

Gritting my teeth, I focused on Draven's steady presence beside me. "Thank you," I gasped, still feeling his arms solid and protective around me.

"No need to thank me," Draven murmured close to my ear, his breath warm against my chilled skin. "I've got you."

Shaking from my near fall, but bolstered by his reassurance, I nodded and tightened my hold on his arm once again. Looking down through the hole, I could see my certain death. My body would have shattered into a thousand bloodied pieces at the body of the chasm if I were alone on that bridge.

We resumed our treacherous walk painfully slow. Each step was an exercise in trust and focus, trusting that the ropes would keep us from plummeting into the abyss below and focusing solely on reaching Cole safely.

As we moved forward, each creak of the worn planks under our combined weight was a stark reminder of how fragile this crossing was.

Finally reaching the other side after what seemed like an eternity on a swaying death trap, Cole immediately reached out to help pull us onto solid ground. His hands were firm and warm as they steadied me, and I couldn't help but notice the muscles play beneath his skin—a quiet strength that had always drawn me to him.

"You made it," Cole said simply, his relief clear in his furrowed brow, which was now easing somewhat.

"Yeah," I responded breathlessly, allowing myself a weak laugh of relief as I glanced back at the perilous bridge now behind us. "Thanks to you guys."

"I would never let anything happen to you," Draven added.

I turned to see Cole yell out, "Weeeeeee," as he ran at full pelt across the bridge. I watched in pure horror, expecting the thing to collapse at any second. He jumped over the last few gaps of the bridge and clapped me on the back. I staggered back, even now that we were on stable ground. "Made it!" he said.

"You're fucking nuts!" I cried out, wide-eyed.

He grinned. "All the best people are!" He grabbed my face, kissed me hard, and slapped my bottom. "Come on, let's find Eden, shall we?"

Chapter 28

A sudden crackle of distant voices sliced through the muted symphony of the woods, halting us mid-stride. My instincts spiked, adrenaline flooding my veins. Someone was coming!

"Voices," I whispered, the word hanging heavy in the air. We ducked behind a thick copse of trees, hearts pounding a frantic rhythm against the stillness. Peering through the underbrush.

Jake chuckled at me, holding out his hand. "Baby, there's no one there. It's the wind."

The stillness of the forest broke with a collective exhale, as if the trees themselves were holding their breath along with me.

I huffed, standing up.

The further we trekked, the more the landscape seemed to turn against us. The forest soon gave way to rolling hills and an expanse of desolation, the government's scarred fingerprints on every inch of soil. Dilapidated buildings loomed with darkened windows, a stark reminder of what happened when you crossed the Omega Taskforce. A shiver snaked down my spine as we crept through the deserted streets. Every creaking sign, every rustle of wind-blown debris, sounded like imminent destruction.

"There used to be a town here," I thought aloud, the dark humor a lifeline in the oppressive gloom. I wrapped my arms around myself. "Now it's just a graveyard with a view."

Every so often, we'd pass the remnants of propaganda posters peeling from the walls, their bold letters once proclaiming Omegas as society's saviors, now nothing but a cruel joke. We saw surveillance cameras hanging from corners, their lenses blind and broken, yet the threat of being watched remained ingrained within us. It was a world stripped bare by tyranny, where even the air felt like the warden's breath on your neck.

"Feels like the whole place could collapse on our heads," muttered Jake, his voice barely loud enough to stir the heavy air.

"Then let's get moving," Draven shot back. My nerves were as taut as bowstrings as we found our way through the silent town. The stillness was oppressive, thick enough to choke on, yet beneath it all, something stirred within me. A need to fight, to succeed, and shove every member of the Taskforce into an early grave.

We'd been on the move for hours, muscles aching and nerves frayed like the hem of my old academy blazer. I was bone tired and couldn't take the screaming of my muscles any longer.

"Can we stop, just for a while?"

"Do you need to rest, sweet girl?" Cole asked, turning back and running his fingers along my cheekbone. I nodded, dropping the backpack.

"Here," Jake said, pointing to what appeared to be someone's home from the late eighties. I could tell the date because of the newspaper that was still laid on their enclosed porch.

Cole took my bag, and checked the house was safe to enter, then whistled for us to join him. Draven picked me up and carried me in. The relief was instantaneous.

My muscular Alpha crossed the threshold and carried me all the way up the stairs and into the main bedroom, placing me gently on the bed. "Get some rest. We will call you when dinner's ready."

He didn't need to tell me twice. Within minutes, I was out like a light.

"Amy," Cole whispered, trying to shake me awake. "AMY!" he yelled.

I jumped up, startled. "What?"

"We've got to move. There are guards outside!"

"Shit!" I said, trying to walk but banging into the wall. My balances were still fucked after being punched in the head countless times.

Draven ran in, picked me up and told me to hold on tight!

Jake was still trying to finish a bowl of soup while grabbing his pack and mine, and legging it out of the back door.

"I hope you saved some of that for me!" I whispered.

Jake smirked, patting a flask that he'd hooked onto the side of my bag.

"Where are we going?" I asked.

"As far away from the patrols as possible!" Draven whispered through rushed breaths. "They must be tracking down survivors."

My brow furrowed. "But how did they find us?"

Silence. Then Draven growled, and placed me on the floor by the window, the night sky enveloping the room. He started inspecting my skin.

"What the hell Draven?"

"You've been chipped!"

"Cole, check Jake, make sure we haven't either."

"Damn it!" I almost yelled, forgetting about the soldiers outside. Draven clamped his hand over my mouth.

"When you got here, what did they do to you?"

"Er... I don't know. I had been injected at the clinic and whatever it was knocked me out."

"Anything else?" he asked, checking my arms.

"No, except my neck hurt before they put the collar on."

Narrowing his eyes, he traced the bruise where the collar had been and found a small five-millimeter scar. "Found it."

I nodded, relieved. I gave him my father's penknife. "Get it out of me!" I demanded.

He took a deep breath. "This might hurt a bit!"

"I know."

Opening the first-aid kit Miss Harlow had placed in my backpack, he used the alcohol to sterilize the blade, then proceeded to make a small incision. I gritted my teeth as he pushed a small silver shiny device out of me.

"Are you okay?" he asked, as he cleaned me up and placed a butterfly strip over the minor wound.

I nodded. "Yeah, I'm just worried about the other girls. What if they don't realize?"

He sighed. "Let's hope they do."

"Nothing," Cole said after they had both checked each other's necks and arms. "It looks like they were only bothered about the Omegas escaping."

"Come on, let's get the hell out of this place," I said, standing up.

Packed tight against the rough brick of the abandoned house, we entered a passageway between the streets. Draven's breath was steady beside me, a contrast to my own ragged inhales.

A guard hovered beside the entrance to the passageway, his searchlight spilling over the debris-strewn street, inching closer to our hiding spot. My heart thudded so hard I feared it would give us away.

I dared a breath, shallow and silent, tasting the metallic tang of fear. This was the hide-and-seek where getting found meant losing everything. As the torch's light receded, I allowed myself the tiniest sigh of relief.

With a cautious glance to ensure the coast was clear, we slipped back into the embrace of the town's deserted streets. Bypassing two more guards, we made our way through. My heart was pounding like a runaway train by this point. Palms clammy, eyes wide and alert. When we reached the other side of the town, I almost jumped for joy!

The guards were still looking around the area where I last had the chip in my neck. So, we took our chances and ran across the open field where the wilderness welcomed us back with open arms.

Branches snatched at my hair, and undergrowth tugged at my boots, but I kept moving. My thoughts raced faster than my feet, darting between Eden's whispered promises and the revolution that pulsed in my blood.

"Still think we can make it to this promised land of yours?" Draven's voice cut through the silence, his question laced with skepticism.

"Damn right," I shot back without missing a beat. "And when we get there, we're going to light a fire they can't stamp out."

He smirked, grabbed my hand and pulled me into him, pressing his lips on mine, deepening the kiss, our tongues exploring each other's. I moaned, my legs buckling. He chuckled as he pulled away, holding me up.

"Soon," he said, kissing my forehead. "We can play together soon."

Cole and Jake stopped and turned around. "Are you two coming?" Cole hollered. I smirked, and Draven took my hand as we ran over to them.

"I was just entertaining our Omega," he said.

"Mmm hmm!" Cole said. "And where was our invite?"

I laughed. "Soon," I said. "Soon."

Chapter 29

The terrain grew rougher, and the sky lightened with the first brush strokes of dawn. But with each step, my resolve hardened. The warden and his goons would be scratching their heads by now, scouring empty maps and questioning their infallibility. And we, the elusive prey, would ghost through the woods, defying their every move. A laugh bubbled up from my chest, humor as dark as the soil beneath our feet.

The first rays of sunlight filtered through the canopy, dappling the forest floor when we heard the rustle of leaves. My heart thumped a warning against my ribcage. Draven stopped and pulled me behind him. Cole and Jake stood beside him, poised and ready to do battle.

"Who's there?" A young female voice sliced through the haze, cautious but not fearful.

Emerging from the shadows, a trio of Omegas looked around, then set their sights on us. They paused, regarding us warily, their eyes alight with a mixture of hope and desperation. They were a rare sight—free Omegas, unmarked by the oppressive uniforms that clung to my past like a second skin.

I stepped around Draven. Even though he tried to stop me.

"Are you okay?" I asked them.

The one with deep brown hair stepped forward. "Are you heading to Eden too?" It was more of a statement than a question. Their gaze flickered over our ragtag group with an understanding that only comes from shared struggle.

"Trying to," I admitted, keeping my voice steady despite the drumbeat of anticipation in my chest. "Do you know where it is?"

She nodded. "We came from there. But be careful. There are a lot of uniforms in the area."

"Yeah, we came across a few."

"Are you from the academy?"

"Yes."

She stepped forward, and Draven growled. I smirked at him. "It's fine Draven."

"Let me see your neck."

"I removed her chip, if that's what you're questioning," Draven said. His face was still firm.

She nodded when I showed her. "Good. Then, all you need to do is head down to the river. Follow it north until you see the twin pines," she said, her tone laced with urgency. "There's a cave beneath the roots—one of the few places still blind to the Taskforce's eyes."

"Eden is a cave?"

She laughed. "No, that's just the way in."

"Ohhh, okay! Thank you," I breathed out the words, the information sparking a fire of determination within me.

"Be careful," the blond Omega behind her warned. "They've been hunting down escapees. Taking them back, changing them."

"Reprogramming?" The word tasted like bile on my tongue, a sour twist to our newfound hope.

"Exactly." The Omega's eyes held a haunted depth that sent a shiver down my spine. "They come back different—hollowed out, obedient. Like puppets with their strings pulled tight."

"Damn them," I muttered. They must be using a new form of behavioral modification.

As they slipped back into the shadows, I squared my shoulders, refusing to let the threat smother the embers of the revolt that burned within me.

"Listen, Amy," Jake said, placing his arm around my shoulder. "Maybe we should lie low for a while," his gaze darting like a caged animal.

"Jake's right," Cole chimed in, his usually stoic demeanor giving way to visible tension. "We can't risk you getting snatched up and twisted into whatever those Taskforce bastards call 'reprogramming.'"

I halted, feeling their eyes on me. "Hide? And then what?" I shot back, my voice slicing through the murmurs of uncertainty. "Wait for the Taskforce to crumble by wishful thinking? We know that won't happen."

Their faces were a mosaic of concern and resolve, each one etched with the scars of battles fought, both internally and against the system we all despised.

"Guys," I began, softening my tone, "I get it, okay? The risks are towering over us like those damn walls back at the academy. But so is our chance at something real—freedom."

"Freedom or death, you mean," muttered Draven darkly. "I can't lose you Amy."

"I would rather take death than be forced to watch you three be executed for killing Calloway," I said, looking at them one by one. Draven took a deep breath.

"We have a chance. A chance at a real life, together," I said, letting hope flare in my chest.

Draven took a deep breath and pulled me tight into his chest. Cole held me from behind.

Jake, being the usual Jake, gripped us all and shouted, "GROUP HUG!"

"Together," Jake said. "Or not at all."

Their hands on me were electrifying, sending jolts of life coursing through my veins. I turned into their embrace, my lips finding theirs in kisses that spoke of passion and protest. Our breaths mingled, and our bodies pressed close, seeking solace in the heat of our combined resolve.

I groaned, wanting, needing more... but knowing now wasn't the time. We had to reach safety first. I pushed them off of me and sighed.

"Come on, let's make those assholes regret ever messing with us!"

The day rolled by quickly as we made our way through the thick of the forest, taking brief breaks to catch our breath. Eventually, as the sun dipped below the horizon, and a glorious magnitude of crimson and magenta bled across the sky, we were met by the shimmering waters of the river.

“It can’t be far now,” I said, taking a rest against a rock, watching the water flow by.

Jake sat beside me, pulling me onto his lap. “Mmm! That’s better!”

I rolled my eyes.

Looking back, the darkness of the tree line seemed eerily quiet. I stretched out my fingers, took a deep breath, and narrowed my eyes. Something didn’t feel right. It’s that feeling you get when you know someone’s watching you, but you can’t make out where they are. That sixth sense clawing at my gut.

“Something's not right,” I whispered to Jake. He stopped and turned toward the tree line, eyes darting to catch any hint of movement.

“Voices,” Draven hissed, pulling me down to the ground. “Get behind the rock!”

My heart was pounding against the dirt floor as I strained to listen. They were distant, yet carried with clarity in the still evening air. An eerie chorus of orders being barked, the Warden's hounds on our trail.

"Keep it together," Jake breathed in my ear. He could hear my panicked breathing at the thought of being caught and sent back there. He rubbed his hand up and down my back, his chest vibrating to soothe me.

A rustle to our left had us tensing, but it was only a rabbit darting from its hiding spot.

"Move!" Draven ordered; the urgency clear in his command. We were up and running again, the sunset's beauty now a mocking backdrop to our flight.

As we ran, my mind couldn't help but play out the scenarios. Would we stumble into a trap laid by our pursuers? Or would we finally glimpse the beauty of Eden?

We reached a clearing, the sight before us halting our hurried escape. Another cliff drop. A chasm, wide and deep, sliced through the land—a monstrous scar left by the regime's relentless mining of resources. On the other side, nestled between the arms of two imposing mountains, were the twin pines, and the outline of what could only be... Eden.

"Son of a—" I caught myself, words swallowed by awe and frustration.

"Great! A giant ditch. Does anybody have a ladder?" Jake's sarcasm was a welcome distraction from the sinking realization that our journey had taken a shitty turn.

The billowing sound of booming voices shattered the calm, the sound jolting us to attention.

"Looks like we're about to get some company," Draven growled.

"Let them come," I cried, standing tall as defiance surged hot in my blood. "We'll show them exactly what happens when they corner us." My body was taught with adrenaline, on fire with vengeance, but quaking internally at the reality of what was to come.

We readied ourselves with our backs to the chasm, facing the oncoming threat. Our fate teetered on the edge of survival and capture.

"Get ready for the fight of your lives," Cole declared, his voice steel wrapped in velvet, the moment of truth upon us. My three Alphas stood in front of me, ready to die before they let them take me again.

And then, suddenly, a glint of metal from the other side of the divide, a signal flashing in coded urgency. Help? A trap?

"Looks like the game's just begun," I said, my heart hammering with anticipation.

Chapter 30

Within minutes, the forest erupted. The Warden's forces bled into the moonlit clearing like a flood of nightmares come to life. The soldiers fanned out, encircling us with grim precision, their numbers easily doubling our own. My pulse hammered in my ears, a frantic drumbeat urging me to flee or fight. But as the stone-cold reality of our situation settled in, a simmering defiance took hold.

Draven stepped forward. "Amy, stay close, and look for a way over." Draven's directive was sharp, each word etched in Alpha mode.

I barely suppressed a snort. Close? Did he really think I'd cower while the world went to shit around us? Still, I nodded, more to acknowledge his protective instincts than any actual intention of playing the damsel in distress. This Omega had teeth, and I wasn't afraid to bear them.

I looked behind me at the drop. We needed to find a path over, quickly. One false move and we'd be pushed off of the edge.

"Are you ready for this?" Draven asked, looking back at me. I nodded, knowing full well that the Warden and his soldiers were likely to take us down. But I damned well wouldn't go down without a fight.

We were so close, though. I could see it there. The cave. The entrance. I almost cried at the thought of how far we'd come, how much we'd survived. We were more than just Alphas with their Omega; we were a pack. A family.

"Charge on my mark," Draven called out, stance wide and unyielding as the tide of uniforms surged towards us.

"Charge?" I echoed; my voice laced with dark amusement. "How positively medieval of you."

But when Draven shot me a look that could melt steel, I knew it was not time to mess with him. He was scared. Not for himself. He was scared for me.

The forest itself seemed to hold its breath as my alphas charged forward. Cole's strategy was a deadly dance choreographed in the shadows, slicing and dicing soldiers like a ninja assassin. Despite my pounding heart and the acrid taste of fear, there was an undeniable thread of admiration for the Alpha who could wage war with such unshaken composure.

Meanwhile, Jake darted toward them. His laughter rang out, a jarring note of mirth amidst the snarls and roars. I caught glimpses of him as he darted between the trees, teasing them in the regimented darkness.

"Hey, soldiers! Bet you can't catch me!" His voice carried, lilting and mocking. A group of Beta enforcers, momentarily distracted, peeled away from their formation, lured by the challenge. It was classic Jake: turn the fight into a game, and play it better than anyone else.

He zipped past a burly Beta, close enough to ruffle the man's uniform before leaping over a low bush, his booted feet barely touching the ground. "Oops, too slow!" he taunted, ducking a clumsy swipe.

I couldn't help the grin that spread across my face, even as my muscles coiled, ready for the next move. In this grim tableau, Jake was the wildcard, the unpredictable spark that could ignite victory or disaster. But as he wove his way through the enemy, drawing more attention to himself and away from the rest of us, it was clear which outcome he was gunning for.

"Keep them off balance," I muttered, eyes tracking the ripple of confusion spreading through the Warden's forces. Draven and Cole were carving a path through this nightmare, not saving any of them for me. Maybe, just maybe, we had a shot at turning the tables on Warden Gray and his army of control freaks.

The forest floor blurred beneath my sprinting feet as I ran alongside the cliff edge, looking for a way across. Pine needles and soil kicked up in our desperate wake. I could hear the thrum of our pursuers' boots pounding a death march behind us.

Then, without warning, we were cornered. Soldiers were on all sides and a gaping chasm behind us. Every fiber in my body screamed, "Stop!" My legs locked, and I skidded to a halt at the clearing's edge. Draven, Cole, and Jake snapped into position around me, a bristling shield of love and adoration. Their defensive perimeter was instinctual, drilled into every Alpha's bones, but it wouldn't hold for long against the tide about to crash down on us.

Warden Xavier's forces poured into the clearing like a flood of nightmares, their numbers a suffocating blanket of malice.

"Stand your ground!" Draven roared, "Protect Amy!"

"No!" I said, trying to push out from behind them. "I won't let you die for me!"

"Tough luck, beautiful," Draven said, turning around and kissing my lips. "We love you." He smiled and pulled back. "We could never live in a world without you."

My lower lip quivered. "I... I love you too, Draven." Looking at Cole and Jake, I said, "I love all of you."

The salty taste of tears caressed my lips. Cole wiped them away. "You're ours, sweet girl."

"Always and forever," Jake said, taking my hand and kissing it.

I took a deep breath. "If you die today, I'm going to be really pissed at you."

They laughed. "Noted."

"Boo hoo," the Warden said. "Have you quite finished with your goodbyes?" I glared at him with such anger that if it were to manifest, it would rip him to shreds in an instant.

"CHARGE!" the Warden yelled. "Kill the Alphas and bring me the Omega!"

"Sir, yes, sir!"

The soldiers ran forward, and I braced myself on the edge of the chasm, looking behind me at the abyss below. If it came to it, I knew what I'd do. I wouldn't let them take me again. Never again. Goddess only knew what the head of the Omega Taskforce would do to me now that his son had been murdered.

The forest air crackled with a tension that could snap bones. The Warden's soldiers encircled us, their sneers as sharp as the teeth they flashed in the dappled sunlight. My heart hammered against my ribs like a caged bird desperate for escape. But when you're cornered, with nowhere to run, you don't cower—you fight.

"Is this your idea of a fair fight, Xavier?" I taunted, stepping forward, my voice dripping with dark humor despite the pounding threat. "Or did you forget how to count?"

The Warden's eyes, cold and calculating, narrowed at my challenge. He was about to retort when a sudden, distant rumble rolled through the clearing. Heads turned; even the trees seemed to hold their breath. Then, like an unexpected storm, reinforcements thundered in, breaking the heavy silence.

And there she was—Miss Elena Harlow. Her stern figure sliced through the chaos; her brown hair pulled back so tight it could command respect on its own. The Betas at her heels fell into formation with military precision, their presence a jolt of electricity to our frazzled nerves.

"Form up!" Miss Harlow yelled, pulling us back from the brink of panic. Her hazel eyes swept over us, assessing, calculating. There was no mistaking that look—it meant business.

I blinked, surprised but ready, feeling a surge of something fierce and unyielding bubble within me. Miss Harlow was here. Since when did she know the first thing about fighting in a battle? Let alone commanding her own army of rebels? She really had been the perfect actress back at the academy!

"Let's give them hell," she yelled, catching my eye. I nodded; a silent agreement passed between us.

We surged forward, a force reborn from the ashes of our fears and doubts. Jake charged forward like an alpha on steroids. "YOU WANNA MESS WITH ME?" he yelled at a soldier. The soldier dropped his sword and ran off. Jake laughed, picked up his weapon, and bowed. Then ran in with his sword raised high.

Cole had already disappeared into the thick of the fight, dancing from body to body, and each enemy he came across fell in mere seconds.

Draven stayed near me, but used one of the soldier's shields to crush his skull open. Which was rather disgusting, but satisfying all the same.

I got a few hits in here and there. But I wasn't as strong as I used to be. I planned on rectifying that soon! Back to training, just like I had with my brothers!

The Warden's troops, once an unbreakable wall of iron resolve, now faltered with the sound of steel against steel. The clearing that had once seemed like a death sentence was now our arena, and we were claiming it inch by hard-fought inch. I could taste the change in the air—the tang of victory just out of reach but drawing ever closer. It fuelled me and filled my lungs with the kind of fire that burned all doubt away.

The Warden, with that cold emblem of oppression, moved through his forces, desperately attempting to reclaim control. But when his eyes met mine, he found only the glint of challenge. No more fear. No more submission. Just the unwavering resolve of an Omega who refused to be broken.

"Is that all you've got?" I sneered, the words slicing through the tension. "Because we're just getting started."

In those last moments, the Warden, exhausted from battle, roared and ran at me with nothing more than his fists. Draven threw me a knife, which I caught and pierced into his bitter heart. The balance shifted irreversibly in our favor. The regime's grip loosened, and in that fracturing, we found our strength, our hope, and our victory.

The remnants of the battle clung to the air, the scent of pine and sweat mingling with the copper tang of blood. I stood in the center of the clearing, my alphas flanking me, our chests heaving in unison.

"Would you look at that," I managed between breaths, nodding toward the horizon where the first blush of dawn was painting the sky in shades of rebellion. "Almost pretty enough to make you forget the hell we just went through."

Cole offered a rare, approving nod, his gaze scanning the perimeter as if the shadows might betray us again. Draven's hand came to rest on my shoulder, a grounding weight that spoke of solidarity more than any words could. And Jake? He kicked at the dirt, a lopsided grin spreading across his face.

"Damn if this doesn't feel good," Jake said.

"Feels like freedom is what it does," Draven replied, his voice still carrying the command of the battlefield, even in this moment of reprieve.

We all knew the cost of what we'd done—bruises would bloom, bones would ache, and memories would haunt us. But standing there, with Eden calling to us, those wounds seemed a small price to pay.

"Alright, enough gawking," I said, shaking off the fatigue that threatened to bow my shoulders. "Eden isn't getting any closer on its own."

With a collective nod, we began moving, following Miss Harlow and her band of rebels further along the chasm and across a sturdy wooden bridge about a mile down.

The forest floor yielded beneath our boots, each step taking us away from the oppressive grip of the Omega Taskforce and towards something that felt like hope.

Chapter 31

We stumbled out of the forest's embrace. My lungs heaved, drinking in the open air like it was spiked with liberation. My Alphas walked beside me, each step away from the tangled darkness, a dance between relief and disbelief.

Eden drew closer, a hidden valley unfurling like the first page of a story you hoped won't end in tragedy. Sunlight trickled through the canopy, casting a kaleidoscope of shadows that danced over our bruised bodies. Nature had a twisted sense of humor, painting beauty on the canvas of our pain.

"Would you look at that," I said, voice as dry as the leaves crunching beneath our boots. "They've got more tech than the Omega Taskforce's wet dreams." Sensors dotted along the tree line, winking at us like nosy neighbors. It was a fortress disguised as Eden; a concept so foreign that I almost laughed.

"Alright," Draven said, shifting to a tone that meant business, no matter how much my insides squirmed. "Let's find out if this haven is all it's cracked up to be, or if we've just swapped one cage for another."

I nodded, gulping at the thought of more bars.

We walked past the twin pines and through a labyrinth of caves, following Miss Harlow and her rebellious band of soldiers.

On the other side, the gates parted with a silent grace that belied their monstrous size, and the steely gaze of Eden's guards met us. They were an odd mix of muscle and tech, with eyes that flickered over us like we were puzzle pieces they couldn't quite place. I straightened my spine, feeling every bruise shout in protest.

"Welcome," one of them said. "We've awaited your arrival."

"Hope you weren't holding your breath," I muttered under mine, the words slipping out before I could cage them. Jake smirked, and Cole rolled his eyes.

"Your reputation precedes you," another guard said, stepping forward, her gaze lingering on my face just a second too long.

"Great, we're infamous," I replied, my lips pulling up into a smirk that felt more like a barred-tooth warning. "Just what every girl dreams of."

But beneath the surface, my heart hammered with a cocktail of fear and anticipation. These guards—they looked at us not as threats, but as, what? Equals? Saviors?

"Please, follow us," the first guard beckoned, pivoting on his heel with military precision. We fell into step behind them, trudging onward.

As soon as I stepped foot into Eden, I was greeted with a kaleidoscope of colors. Lush forest greens surrounded me, with bursts of vibrant flowers scattered throughout. In the center of it all sat a sparkling lake, adorned with its majestic fountain. On one side, there was a cozy picnic area, inviting visitors to relax and enjoy the serene atmosphere. This place exuded an aura of ethereal beauty, a harmonious blend of nature and modern technology that ensured its survival.

As I explored further, I noticed the people living here were just as delightful as their surroundings. There were no cruel electric collars or forced smiles here, just genuine warmth radiating from their cheerful faces as they worked together to maintain the self-sufficiency of this wondrous place.

“Amy Anderson,” a leader called out. I jumped, turning toward the voice.

All eyes were on me. “Sorry, I was taking it all in!”

He smiled. “Yes. It’s a lot when you first arrive, isn’t it?”

I nodded.

“You and your Alphas have become symbols of the resistance.” I narrowed my gaze and pursed my lips. What was he on about? All we did was save our own asses. It was Miss Harlow that blew up the gates.

Draven placed his hand on the small of my back, the heat from his touch sending welcome shivers down my spine.

“Your actions at the academy have meant the freedom of several Omegas.”

“Only several?” I said, saddened.

He nodded. “Yes. But that is several more that now have their freedom, thanks to you four.”

“Freedom's a strong word,” I retorted, my gaze sweeping over the gathered faces. “Let's see if it has the same meaning here.”

He smiled, accepting the challenge. "You will find everything you need here. We hope it becomes your home. And in time, that you will join our army and take down the Taskforce once and for all."

"Now you're talking!" Jake said, and I grinned at him.

"For now," I said to Jake. "Let's not make promises we can't keep," I added, softer this time. A promise to myself as much as to them.

"Then let us show you," the leader urged, gesturing expansively. "Let us be the proof that freedom is more than a word here. It's our way of life."

"Lead the way," I said, and as we followed, I allowed myself a sliver of hope that maybe, just maybe, they were right. The promise of Eden was real.

It unfolded before us, like a vision from a world that shouldn't have existed. Alphas, Betas, and Omegas mingled without the usual tension that marked our previous lives. No sneers of superiority or heads bowed in submission. They walked shoulder to shoulder, laughter blending with conversation in a symphony of what could only be called equality. My eyes narrowed as I took in the scene; disbelief gnawing at me.

"Looks too good to be true," I murmured.

"Or maybe we've just been dealt a shitty hand for far too long." Cole's voice came from beside me.

As we moved through the throng, I saw it, the casual touch between an Alpha and an Omega that didn't reek of possession, the Beta speaking with authority to a group that listened intently. Every interaction was a slap in the face of everything I knew. The suppressants I'd taken all my life felt like a chain around my neck, a reminder of the facade I'd had to live under. But here, those chains seemed to dissolve.

"Could be an act," I said. But even to my ears, I sounded unconvinced.

Later, after we'd had time to settle in, shower and change, we found seclusion in a quiet corner of Eden beside an old oak tree. Draven sat on a picnic bench and pulled me onto his lap. Cole paced in front of us and Jake twiddled with daisies, making a necklace for me.

"Eden is one thing, but we can't forget who we are," Cole said.

"Who we were, you mean," Jake corrected, looking up from his creation. "Here, we don't have to be just another Alpha pack, flexing muscle and asserting dominance."

"Then what?" Draven challenged, his hot breath tickling my neck as his hands pulled me closer to him. "What do we become when the fight's stripped away?"

"More than that," Jake said. "We become leaders by example. Protectors, equals."

"Equals," I tasted the word, unfamiliar and round on my tongue. "That's something I'm not used to!"

"We'll all have to learn," Jake stated. "But we have time. For now. I think we've earned ourselves a break, and time to ravish our gorgeous Omega here." He grinned up at me, closed the daisy chain, and carefully placed it over my head.

I pulled him to me, kissing him hard in thanks. He groaned, edging closer.

"Mmm... we could make use of that bed right now!"

I laughed, batting him back. "Soon," I said. "Soon."

Cole watched with lust in his eyes.

I licked my lips, looking at him. "First we play, then we tear down the old world," I declared, my voice a whisper that held the roar of revolution, "and build a better one right here."

The sun dipped low, staining the sky in shades of rebellion, fiery oranges, and defiant purples, as I saw other Omegas watching us and grinning. My Alphas remained close, their presence a tangible warmth against the chill of the evening air.

"Alright," I murmured, my voice rough with emotion, "let's not get too hot and flustered out here... we're being watched."

Jake, broad-shouldered and ever-watchful, offered me a knowing grin. "Maybe they enjoy being a voyeur?"

"Maybe I don't like to be on display!" I shot back, panting, as Draven started teasing me through the fabric of my pants.

Draven threw me over his shoulder and ran with me bouncing up and down, laughing, as I batted at his back to put me down. Which is precisely what he did as he ran into our newly acquired nest. A room of luxurious cushions, soft blankets, and satin sheets. I laughed as he growled at me, my slick dampening my panties as I ached for him.

He growled, smacking my bottom and tossing me onto the bed. "You are feisty," he purred, watching as he pulled off his top.

Cole and Jake ran in, scenting the air. "She's ready," Cole said.

"I'm what?" I asked, just as the air shifted with a crackling energy that sent my senses into overdrive. Full heat slammed into me like a tidal wave, snatching my breath away. Sharp, searing pain ripped through me, and I cried out.

The world narrowed, honed to the vital presence of my Alphas. Their scents enveloped me, earthy and potent. I gasped, pulling at my clothes.

"Are you going to strip for us, baby?" Jake purred.

I pulled at the surrounding blankets, moaning, writhing on the bed. My back arched as a tingling pleasure warmed through my body, driving the heat between my legs. My heart pounded, my body shivering from desire. Jake growled, standing over me. A sudden flush of heat spread between my legs and I shuddered, bearing down. "I need..."

"What do you need?" Draven asked, crawling over the top of me.

"I need you." I gripped his hair and pulled him down. His lips crashed into mine. Sweet flutters of excitement soothed the ache between my legs. As Draven pulled back, I gasped, my body alight with a fire I'd long suppressed. They were there, instantly, hands steadying me, eyes darkening with desire and concern.

"Easy, sweet girl," Cole whispered, his thumb tracing the line of my jaw. "We've got you."

"Take off those clothes, Amy," Draven demanded, pulling his clothes off and helping me with mine. Cole and Jake watched, licking their lips. Every touch ignited my body with heat, as raw earthen pleasure pulsated deep within my core.

Cool air wrapped over my naked body, and I writhed on the bed, groaning at the sensation and pulling at the surrounding blankets.

Draven yanked me to the end of the bed, giving him access to my clit as he traced his tongue up and over my slit. My hips bucked up towards him, wanting, needing more, as he continued, making me cry out in ecstasy. "Damn, you taste fucking good!"

Jake pulled off his clothes and crawled up next to me, placing butterfly kisses up my neck, before nibbling and sucking my earlobe as I inhaled his masculine scent. He paid extra attention to where I needed his bite to be. I wanted him there now, needed his touch, his taste.

"Jake, I think our girl could do with something to suck on." Cole said. I bit my lower lip, watching as he moved up the bed, sitting on his heels, stroking my hair as his cock teased my lips. Hungrily I grabbed at it.

Jake chuckled and pulled back. "Play nicely, baby, or you won't have it."

I nodded, biting my lower lip and stroking it, urging him forward. Wanting his cock in my mouth, deep down my throat. Wanting to taste him, just like I had tasted Draven. I needed him.

His hooded eyes looked down at me as he slowly eased into my mouth. I moaned in approval, taking him in further, relaxing my jaw as he pumped back and forth, gripping the back of my head, forcing himself in deeper. Gagging, I coughed as he pushed harder and faster, my fingernails embedded into his buttocks. I held tighter, wanting more of him. Needing him all the way back. The salty taste of his pre-cum soothed the raging cramps within me as spit dribbled down my chin.

"Do you want my cum, baby?" Jake asked. I looked up at him and moaned for more. "It's coming baby..." He sped up, gripping my hair tighter, and I dug my nails in more. I needed him. Needed him desperately!

The sensation of slickness pooling between my legs was so strong that I couldn't ignore it. My body trembled with pleasure as Draven intensified his attention on my clit, and my body exploded into the throes of an orgasm. Flecks of shimmering lights dance before me as I arched up, my heart racing, clit pulsating, leaving me with a euphoric wave of warmth surging through me.

Draven pulled away, and I whimpered, needing his touch. But it was soon replaced as he moved up my body and pushed his cock deep inside. While at the same time, Jake forced himself to the back of my throat, making me gag. He exploded inside of my mouth. His head falling back as he held me onto his cock, deep in my throat, cum spilling out the side. I tried to lap up as much as I could when he pulled away.

Draven flipped me over so I settled on top, while Cole stroked his thick length, watching us. Cole inched closer as I continued riding Draven's cock for everything it was worth. I needed Draven to come. I needed his knot and his pleasure. Had to feel his cum as it exploded out, wetting my insides and pooling out of me.

"Cole, I need you too!" I cried out, watching Cole eagerly.

Cole moaned, pushing me down, using my slick to lubricate my back hole as I continued grinding on Draven's cock like there was no tomorrow. Draven was captivated by me, pulling me down to him, and kissing me hard.

Then, as he kissed me, Cole pushed his finger into my back hole. When he breached the tight ring, I gasped in pleasure.

Cole chuckled. "Sweet girl, do you like having your ass played with?" I moaned some more, then he pushed another finger in. "I wonder what sounds you'll make as I slide my thick cock through that tight hole of yours."

"More!" I cried out.

Draven laughed, pushing harder and faster. Jake remained next to me, teasing my lips with his cock.

Cole pushed my body down, my chest lying flat on Draven's. His thick length teased the opening, pushing into me as I stretched around his cock. I could feel the fullness easing the aches from the heat. Two thick cocks were buried deep inside me, their movements igniting waves of pleasure through my body.

"Jake, you too," I almost begged.

Without hesitation, he pushed his thick length inside, filling me, thrusting as his cock took the sounds of my pleasure.

"Are you ready for me, beautiful?" Draven asked, his breath hot and rapid.

I moaned, swallowing back Jake's salty cum as he exploded into my mouth again.

Cole tensed. "So, fucking tight!" he yelled. "Can't hold on much longer!"

Draven squeezed me harder, his groin rubbing my clit as he moved. I was almost there. Had almost reached the top, when Draven exploded with a cry, setting Cole off behind him. Cum filled me, pooling out of me.

"KNOT!" I screamed, a raw, desperate sound, as Draven's shaking intensified, his roar echoing in my ears as he dropped his face to my neck, his teeth sinking into my skin with a sharp, searing pain. The sensation of the bite was both exhilarating and overwhelming, causing me to climax instantly.

Draven's touch was gentle yet powerful, as he turned us onto our sides, and we lay there knotted, basking in the afterglow, entwined on the bed, coated in slick, sweat, and desire, thoroughly exhausted, and I fell softly and soundly to sleep.

Chapter 32

When I woke, my alphas were nowhere to be found. I groaned, heat surging through my body still. My temperature soaring highier. The shower was running, and the scent of champagne flooded my nostrils. Cole.

Whimpering, I moved to the edge of the bed. His scent calling to me like the Pied Piper luring me in.

It was nighttime now, and besides the light from the moon blissfully coating my hot rampaging body, there was no way to guide my path to our en-suite. But I could find him with my eyes closed. All sensations were on overdrive, and Cole's scent overpowered me, promising release from the aches, and an end to the searing cramps that had me doubling over as I made my way to the bathroom door.

Pushing it open, I must have looked like a mess, covered in sweat, slick, cum and goddess only knew what else. But I wouldn't have had it any other way. I wanted them all over me. Needed their scent ravishing my body, coiling over my skin, embracing me when they could not.

The shower turned off and Cole walked out butt naked.

"Amy!" he exclaimed. He closed the distance between us in a few quick strides, and before I could react, he had me pinned against the wall, his body pressing into mine. Heat radiated off him as the hard length of his cock pressed against my thigh.

"I need you!" I said, crying out as the pain took me again.

"Oh, sweet girl! I thought you'd sleep longer than that!" he said, helping me back to my nest.

"It hurts Cole. Make it go away, please!"

I hated begging, but I hated the pain more, and I needed him more than the air I breathed right now.

As he laid me down, I gripped his shoulders and pulled him on top of me, moaning out his name.

He growled, licking his lips, crashing them down onto mine, kissing me hard, and fast, his tongue searching, needing just as much as I was. He was dripping with a raw, primal need that made my knees weak. My hole clenched around nothing, already slick with the kind of wetness that only an

Omega in heat could produce. I was a goddamn mess, and he knew it.

Hitching up my up my legs, he spread them wide apart. His fingers teased, exploring, rubbing my clit with an urgency that made my body shiver and my toes curl.

His fingers brushed against my slick hole, and I moaned, my body trembling with need. He pushed a finger inside me, and I cried out, my hole clenching around him. He added a second finger, stretching me open, and I could feel my body opening up for him, ready and willing to take whatever he gave me.

"Please," I begged, my voice trembling.

I could feel the slick leaking out of me, dripping down my thighs, and I knew he could smell it. He growled, low and deep. My body was screaming for him, begging for him to take me, to claim me, to make me his.

"Fuck, you're so ready, sweet girl!" he groaned. "Now, give it to me!"

His huge warm cock pressed at my entrance and he pushed in, slowly, deeply. Filling me up and sending more shivers through me.

He was so big, so tight. I moaned into his touch as it felt like every inch of him was stretching me and claiming me for his own. He didn't stop though, grinding his hips and thrusting hard, deep into my pussy.

"Oh, yeah?" he panted. "This is what you wanted?"

I nodded frantically, biting my lip at the feeling. It burned, but it also felt so good to be taken by him.

He smiled down at me before burying his face in my neck and once more resuming the long languorous fucking that had me squirming underneath him. It felt like heaven as he filled me up and emptied himself into me again and again.

"You're mine," he growled, his breath hot against my ear.

My breath hitched as his cock slid deeper, stretching me, filling me. My body trembled like a leaf in a storm as wave after wave of desire rippled throughout.

"Knot," I whimpered. "I need... I need..."

He laughed, pushing himself in harder, deeper. "I'll give you my knot, sweet girl. But first, you're gonna take every inch of me."

My pussy clamped down around him like a vice, hot and wet and so tight as I cried out for more. My walls were pulsing, milking his cock, needing every drop of cum inside of me. "MORE!" I screamed out, digging my nails into his back, leaving angry red marks.

I was dripping everywhere, my slick and sweat soaking the sheets. It smelled like sex and sin in here, and I wanted to drown in it.

He slammed into me harder and I screamed out in pure joy. Shivers of primal lust filled every part of me. I never want this to end. This feeling, this pure ecstasy. I want to feel him inside of me for days. His ass was rock solid and ramming me, thrusting harder as the sound of skin slapping against skin echoed through the room like a drumbeat.

"You gonna come for me, Amy?" he growled, his voice rough. "You gonna cream all over my cock and let me mark you?"

"Yes, Cole, yes! I'm so close!"

He grabbed my hips, pulling himself back onto me with every thrust, his cock bottoming out inside me every time. My pussy was so wet he could barely keep his grip on me, but he wasn't letting go. Not until... until...

I screamed when it hit me, my whole body shaking. My pussy clamped down, squeezing him so tight he could barely move. But he wasn't stopping. He wasn't done yet.

My breasts bounced as he slammed into me again, my pussy still throbbing from my last orgasm. I was so fucking tight, so fucking wet, I thought I might lose my goddamn mind.

"Mine," he growled.

He grinned, that wicked curve of his lips that spoke volumes. He leaned down, kissing me hard once more, his movements becoming even more urgent, his thrusts deep and relentless.

"More!" I cried, needing another release.

"Good," he murmured against my lips. "Because I'm nowhere near done with you."

His hands moved to my waist, gripping tightly, controlling the rhythm, each movement designed to bring us both closer to the edge. I could feel the building pressure, the knot that was beginning to swell, locking us together in the most intimate of embraces.

The room was heavy with the scent of our arousal, thick and intoxicating. His pace quickened, and I met every one of his thrusts with an eagerness that matched his own. Our bodies were slick with sweat, sliding against each other with every move.

I wrapped my legs tighter around him, pulling him deeper into me. The sensation of being so full, so stretched, was overwhelming. My senses were overloaded with each stroke; it was pure bliss.

"Cole," I gasped, struggling to keep up with the relentless pace he set. "Please..."

He knew what I needed before I even finished speaking. With a final powerful thrust, he let go, his body stiffening, back arching, groans of pure joy released from his lips, and he buried himself deep inside me as his knot locked us together completely. The sensation was exquisite torture.

His breath was hot against my neck as he stilled, allowing us to savor this closeness for a moment longer before he moved again. Small, shallow thrusts that had me moaning from deep within my throat.

"You're locked now," he whispered huskily in my ear. "No running away from me."

As if I would run from this.

The waves of pleasure crashed through me again, as if they were trying to escape my body and fill the surrounding room. My fingers clawed at his back as another orgasm shattered through me, larger than the last.

Cole's movements became less rhythmic but more intense as he chased his own climax with a singular focus that made my head spin. His grip tightened on my hips almost painfully as he delivered one final deep thrust.

With a growl that seemed to shake the very air between us, Cole reached his climax alongside mine. His recent release filled me completely; and as it did, he cried out and bit down, marking me, intensifying the orgasm to a point where I could no longer cope, screaming out. The door burst open and Jake ran in, grinning.

"Room for one more?" he said, stripping off. I watched him, panting, as his muscular abs stretched against the fabric of his shirt.

"Need you!" I cried out to Jake as Cole planted soft kisses along my collarbone and up my jawline.

Cole's knot slowly eased, and he kissed me softly. "I love you, Amy Anderson," he said, kissing the tip of my nose and pulling away.

I smiled, "I love you too, Cole Hawthorne." He grinned and walked out of the room to take another shower.

Chapter 33

"But, but..." I said to Jake as he lit candles around the room.

"But what baby?"

"I need you now, Jake! I don't need candles!"

He chuckled. "Oh, but candles make things even more romantic."

"I don't care, Jake. I need your knot NOW!"

"Whoa, you are a feisty one, aren't you?"

By now, he had stripped off and placed a tray of food on the bed in front of me. "Here, eat something first."

"No. KNOT FIRST."

He laughed. "No... the apple. Then knot."

I growled at him.

He continued laughing and lifted the apple to my lips. "Come on. The quicker you eat this, the quicker you get my knot."

"Damn you, Jake."

"Oh, I love it when you talk dirty!"

I grabbed the apple and stuffed it in my mouth, chewing as fast as I could. This is not what I wanted in my mouth right now!

"There, finished."

"And..." he pointed to the bottle of water.

I narrowed my eyes at him, grabbed the bottle and chugged down half of it, not caring if it split all over me.

He licked his lips. "You know," he said, moving the tray and taking the water from me, as he climbed over me, forcing me back onto the bed. "You even make messy eating look sexy."

I was neck-deep in heat, my body slick with sweat and slicker still between my thighs. My skin was on fire, every nerve ending screaming for release. I gripped him, pulling him down to kiss me. He obliged, growling into my mouth, his thick cock pressing up against my clit, pulsating against it, causing moans to escape me as I widened my legs, urging him to rub up against it more.

He chuckled darkly and gently kissed up my neck, breathing heavily, making my heart race.

"You ready for my knot, baby?"

My hips bucked against the air, my pussy throbbing, dripping, aching for him to fill me up.

I pushed myself against him faster, wanton and desperate. "Jake. Now!"

The scent of my need was thick in the air, a cloying mix of maple and musk.

He groaned, his hand finding my wet entrance. "Fuck, you're still so tight."

I arched into him as he pinned me down, pushing more of his cock into me, thrusting deeper and deeper with each groan. He lifted his hips and slammed into me with force, causing me to cry out as the head of his cock hit that perfect spot inside me. My walls clenched around him as he filled me and I cried out in pleasure. "Jake!"

He grinned devilishly down at me, pulling out slowly before slamming back in with a growl, hitting the same spot again and again. His muscles flexed as he pounded into me, moaning in pleasure at the tightness I offered him.

The smell of sex and sweat grew stronger by the second. "Fuck, yes!"

He growled again as he fondled my breasts and kissed me hard, his tongue pushing deep inside.

I needed to feel his teeth in my neck, claiming me as his, his knot locking us together as he pumped an entire load of his seed inside of me. I needed to be filled and owned.

Slick was pouring out of me now, soaking the sheets as he fucked me harder. My thighs trembled, my ass clenched, and I could feel the edge of my orgasm teasing me. My breath came in ragged gasps, my breasts bouncing with every thrust of his cock.

"Fuck," I moaned, my voice shaky and wrecked.

Jake's eyes were dark with hunger as he took me in. His hands gripped my hips hard enough to bruise as he shoved his cock into my soaked pussy again and again. I screamed, my back arching as he filled me to the hilt, his knot already swelling at the base of his dick as he pounded into me with animalistic fury.

I could only whimper in response, my pussy clenching around him as he fucked me deeper, harder. His hips slammed into mine with enough force to make the bed creak under us. My orgasm hit me like a freight train, my pussy spasming around his cock as I came hard, my slick gushing out around him. But he didn't stop—he kept fucking me through it, his knot swelling until it locked us together, his cum flooding me as he growled in satisfaction.

"Mine," he snarled, his teeth sinking into my neck as he claimed me completely. The most ecstatic pleasure rippled through my body, sinking me deep into another orgasm, just from his bite.

By the time I eased into his body, his arms wrapped around me, holding me close, I was exhausted, but the pain had gone. The heat diminished.

His weight pressed me further into the bed, and for a moment, we lay together in the throes of spent passion, our bodies melded into one.

As his grip relaxed, Jake lifted his head, his eyes locking onto mine with that fierce yet tender gaze that only he could deliver. His voice, hoarse with lust and effort, was soft but firm as he whispered against the sensitive skin of my ear.

"I'm always going to be here, to protect you... to love you."

The words sank deep; they stirred the simmering turmoil beneath my fierce exterior. At Stonehurst Academy, where Omegas were often seen as mere pawns in a larger game dictated by the Omega Taskforce, his vow felt like an act of rebellion—a deliciously dark promise that bucked against all norms.

I traced my fingers along Jake's jawline, feeling the stubble that prickled beneath my touch. "And I'm yours," I murmured back, feeling the swelling pride within me as his knot slowly relaxed, yet our connection remained unbreakably strong.

We knew we should move—uncouple—but neither of us made to shift from our intimate embrace.

The shower turned off in the en-suite and Cole walked out in a towel, scenting the air. "It's finished." He said.

Draven walked in. "What's finished?"

"Oh, speak of the Devil," Cole said, pulling me up to sit on his lap, and covering me in a blanket.

"What?" he asked.

"Amy's heat has finished," Jake said. Draven smiled, walking over and kissing me on the forehead.

"Where did you go?" I asked him.

He grinned. "I, beautiful, went to bring you these."

He pulled a bag from behind his back.

"Ooh, a present?"

He laughed. "Not quite. But I thought it would be perfect for you."

Opening the bag, I looked inside, and there, staring back up at me, were two shining daggers. I looked at him and grinned. "How did you know?"

"You'd said your brothers had been training you. I guessed it was with knives, considering you can't throw a punch to save your life."

I narrowed my gaze and swatted him on the shoulder. He laughed.

"Well, you guessed right. Where did you get them?"

"Miss Harlow showed me around and found them in the armoury for me. They're yours if you want them."

My eyes widened. "Heck, yeah!"

I'd missed training! I jumped up, wielding the knives, and my Alphas laughed.

"Well boys, looks like we're ready to take on the world now," I said.

"How about we start with the Birthing Grounds?" Draven responded.

I pursed my lips and nodded.

"Too damn right. Let's go find your sister!"

The End.

Find out what happens at the Breeding Grounds in the next book, Omega Scarlett.

Click here.

BELLA DONNA
Omega Scarlett
A Dark Reverse
Harem Omegaverse

Omega Scarlett Blurb

Captured and thrown into the Breeding Grounds, hiding from the Alphas; can she survive?

Since the pandemic, Omegas were the only ones that can breed. We are rare, studied, captured and auctioned off. They execute those who try to save us, calling them traitors. My parents chose to save my siblings, giving me up to the Academy for re-conditioning.

I didn't stay long.

Strapped down like a laboratory test subject, forced into heat, studied and pulled apart is any Omegas nightmare.

I'm biding my time here, hiding in the shadows, hoping not to be chosen. If I am, I'd be meat for the next Alpha pack that walks these halls.

Except for that scent, it's like sunshine and apple blossom drifting my way... It couldn't be. Could it?

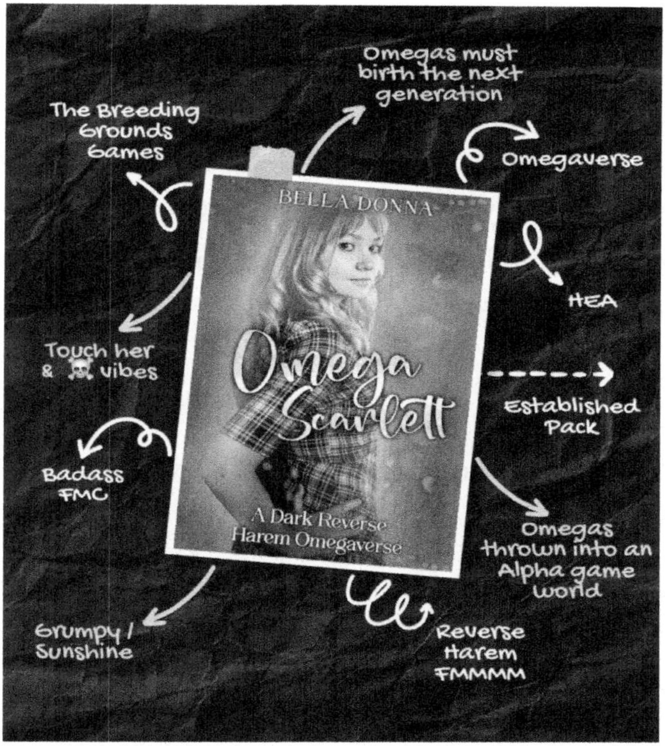
Omegas must birth the next generation
The Breeding Grounds Games
Omegaverse
BELLA DONNA
HEA
Touch her & vibes
Omega Scarlett
Established Pack
Badass FMC
A Dark Reverse Harem Omegaverse
Omegas thrown into an Alpha game world
Grumpy / Sunshine
Reverse Harem FMMMM

Author's Note

Thank you for reading Omega Amy, I hope you enjoyed the story! I always appreciate your feedback and would be grateful if you could leave me a review on Amazon– just a few words make all the difference!

As with all authors, reviews mean the world to me. It keeps me going, helps me strengthen my writing style and helps this story become a success.

Connect with Bella Donna

Join Bella Donna on social media. She is regularly posting videos and updates for her next books on TikTok and Facebook in her group:

Bella Donna's Omegaverse Academy

TikTok: @author.belladonna

Email: BellaDonnaTheAuthor@gmail.com

About Bella Donna

Bella Donna is a dark Omegaverse author, and lover of animals, southern comfort, beach life, and sleep!

She was born in Ashby de la Zouch, England, and lives with her husband, two fabulous children, little dog Milo, and cat Luna. She loves long walks on the beach, strong cups of tea, and reading a good book.

Printed in Dunstable, United Kingdom

69101553R00211